MILL CREEK MYSTIQUE SERIES

A collection of stand alone, small town, romantic suspense novels.
Each book can be read independently but features characters from the
Mill Creek town.

Suggested Reading Order
Trent's Redemption
Hidden Identities
Breaking Point
Kane's Reckoning - Coming Soon
Legally Bound - Coming Soon

BAILEY THOMAS

Breaking Point

MILL CREEK MYSTIQUE
BOOK 3

BTA PUBLISHING

Published by BTA Publishing

Cover Design: Melody Pond

melodyypond.weebly.com

Interior Design: A Fabulous Production

(@afabulousproduction on Instagram)

PAPERBACK ISBN: 978-1-967156-06-1

Second Edition: March 2025

Contents

Dedication	VII
One	1
Two	22
Three	37
Four	51
Five	67
Six	86
Seven	102
Eight	120
Nine	134
Ten	149
Eleven	162
Twelve	173
Thirteen	188
Fourteen	202
Fifteen	217
Sixteen	234

Trent's Redemption   253

Hidden Identities   269

More by Bailey Thomas   293

Acknowledgements   296

To my wonderful husband: You are
my inspiration, support system, and
happily ever after.

In loving memory of my dad—
a humble miner.

One

Jasmine West flipped through her interview notes for the umpteenth time at the small desk in her London, England, hotel. The anonymous email she'd received a few weeks ago intrigued her. She'd never seen anything so cryptic. Her source had mentioned that they were a friend of the prominent Dubin family and wanted the truth to come out. That alone made this adventure exciting because she didn't know where it would end up. She'd even titled her article *"Senator Thomas Dubin and Secrets of the Mangled Family Tree."* A burst of giddiness flooded her system due to all the potential story outcomes.

She'd spent the first part of this week in Washington, DC, interviewing some of the senator's past and present colleagues and his late wife's best friend. Her source had suggested she meet the woman, which turned out to be rather informative.

The senator and his wife seemed to have a turbulent marriage, and her trouble with conceiving hadn't helped matters. His wife had been adored by everyone, but no one would talk to Jasmine about the events surrounding her death.

After Washington, Jasmine had hopped a flight from Dulles International Airport to Heathrow to investigate the small town of Holmberry Hill. There were definite concerns of infidelity and a cover-up. This town seemed to be the link.

She finger-combed her hair, now dry enough to sweep up into a messy bun, as she looked out her window at the big red double-decker buses passing. The streets were filled with people dressed for work and play on this early Friday morning.

She tapped her pen against her forehead as she thought. This anonymous source mentioned that Jasmine's photography, her primary source of income, which allowed her the freedom to travel and research, had caught their eye. They'd learned about her journalistic endeavors from her website.

A part of her wanted this exposé to be the story of a lifetime—Pulitzer-Prize worthy. That would irritate her dad because he couldn't downplay that honor. Oh, she knew she'd already succeeded with her photography, but her father would never give her credit for those accomplishments. All Dad saw was that she wasn't married and had strayed from his plan for her life. It was the same for all his daughters—who lived close to him and Mom and raised their grandchildren.

She liked adventure, traveling, and, most importantly, choosing what to work on because it intrigued and excited her. She sipped her coffee, hoping to wipe the fog from her brain. At least she'd gotten a good five hours of sleep, but hopping into another time zone had zapped her energy.

Thirty minutes later, she packed up the last of her belongings and headed toward the car she'd hired to take her to Holmberry Hill. She planned to stay the night at the local bed and breakfast before returning to the States the following day.

When she approached the man waiting at the curb alongside his vehicle, she confirmed his name, then slid across the back seat while he stowed her luggage in the trunk. The steering wheel on the opposite side of the car made her smile. It was those differences that made her adventures memorable.

The overcast day matched her mood. The wipers screeched across the windshield as the car merged into traffic. The driver caught her gaze in the rearview mirror. "Miss West, shall I drive straight to Holmberry, or do you have additional stops along the way?"

"No, please head straight to St. Paul's Church."

She planned to take pictures of the private hospital that closed a little over a year ago, as it was down the road from the church. When that institution closed, various documents, including adoption records, were sent to the church for safekeeping.

Her source had noted that the senator had made several visits to the area. Could the truth be that easy to uncover? Something told her no, but her curiosity had been piqued. The drive into the countryside was beautiful, and the history of the place left her speechless. The brick homes with multiple fireplaces surrounded by lush greenery were truly picturesque. They looked like a Thomas Kinkade painting.

Two hours later, they arrived at Holmberry. The chauffeur drove up the cobblestone drive toward the top of the hill, where the episcopal church stood, peering down over the small town.

Jasmine tapped the driver's shoulder. "Pull over here, please. I want to take some hospital pictures."

She lowered her window and used her phone, deciding to leave her camera in her backpack for now. Once her window closed, the car ambled forward toward the circular drive of the church.

A vehicle was parked in front of the entrance, so her driver opted for the other side to leave the doorway clear. The rental car barcode sticker on the back window of the other car caught her eye. She'd noticed similar ones on cars she'd rented in the past as she bent to grab her backpack from behind the driver's seat.

When she sat up, a large, brawny man exited the church when she sat up. He stopped to survey the area momentarily before descending the steps to head to his vehicle. She had a fleeting thought that he seemed out of place. Nothing gave her a foundation for that revelation other than an instinct shouting at her.

"Please wait here. I won't be long," she said, halting the driver's exit to open her door.

The structure of the old church and its stained-glass windows charmed her. She could only imagine how many events had happened right here over the years. When she glanced to the right, she saw the town nestled below. It created a picturesque view that had a place on postcards, she imagined.

The concrete steps were steep, but when she opened the door to enter the structure, she couldn't help but smile. The exposed wooden beams, ornate carvings, and statues dominated the space, but the decorative windows softened the room with different hues of color. It was breathtaking.

"Welcome to St. Paul; how may I help you?" asked an elderly lady with a duster.

"Hi, I'm Jasmine. I'm looking for Father Duncan."

The woman nodded and guided Jasmine toward a door on the opposite side of the church. Their footsteps echoed as they walked farther into the empty space.

"It must've been hard on the town when the hospital closed," Jasmine said as her gaze took in the church's beauty.

The woman slowed and turned back to address her question. "The residents use the medical facilities in the next town over. The hospital was private and catered to people from around the world who had the means to take care of delicate matters."

That comment swirled around in Jasmine's thoughts, intriguing her with all the situations that the hospital must have handled. Then, one particular question snapped to the forefront. "Do you get many visitors here and for the hospital?"

The woman stopped so she could face her. "No, not really. I wouldn't call this area a big tourist spot. Our busiest days are Wednesday and Sunday." Then she continued her way down the hallway. When they reached the closed door, she cracked it open briefly to converse with someone on the inside before swinging it wide.

Father Duncan stood and extended his hand. "Hello, how many I help you?"

She couldn't help but notice how soft and smooth his hand was. "Hi, I'm here for a birth certificate and an adoption record. I'm hoping you can help me. The father's name is Thomas Dubin."

Father Duncan folded his arms in front of him. "Please, have a seat. I'll go check. I can't remember the last time we had two people on the same day searching for records."

That admission had her sitting up straighter. The image of the man leaving the church flashed again in her head. Never one to ignore her gut, she glanced down at his desk and scanned the surface. There was a basket on the corner of the desk with a file folder and a log of some sort on top. Only a matter of minutes extended between that guy's visit and hers, so that log interested her.

Twisting her head left and then right to ensure she was alone, she removed her phone from an exterior pocket on her bag. Her heart hammered against her chest as she aimed the device at the document. She snapped two pictures, then shoved the phone back into the backpack as she heard the father coming back down the hallway.

"I'm sorry," he said as he reentered the room. "I don't have any records with that name listed. If you have the birth mother's name or the child or adoptive parents' information, I could look again."

"I don't, but could I contact you by telephone?"

"That would be fine," the man said and found a pen. "Here's the number. Can I have your last name for my tracker, Jasmine?

"Yes, it's West. Thank you. I really appreciate your help."

She smiled and exited the office, hurrying toward the car. An insane thought drove her next action, but every fiber of her being told her to do it. This was what made a story. Having the courage to chase the unknown, even if it might be the stupidest idea. That very idea was why she found herself at odds with her parents, especially her father.

He'd prefer she was married and raising her children like her sisters. Instead, she followed the man who'd exited the church right after she arrived. If luck were on her side, and the fact she'd only been inside for a short time, the one-lane country road would slow him so they could catch up to him. It was a long shot but worth the try.

She slid into the back seat. "Remember that car that left right after we arrived?"

The driver turned around to look at her and nodded, his expression guarded.

"Good. I need you to find that car and follow it. I'll pay you double the rate agreed upon, but in cash. And if we do, don't let the man know we're following him."

The driver uttered his confirmation before he returned his focus to the road. He must have understood the urgency because they arrived back to town in half the time. They might not find the vehicle, or this might not lead to anything, but sometimes there was only a fine line between luck, gumption, and hunches.

The driver made a left on the main street that bisected the town and found the car leaving the bed and breakfast where she was going to stay. Her driver followed the car, and it wasn't long until they were back on the roadway that would eventually lead them to London. Her stomach fluttered with both excitement and concern as they tailed the man.

She called the inn to cancel her reservation for the night. Then she sent a text to her big sister to say she was fine and having fun. Her family didn't know the real reason behind her trip, and according to her father, Jasmine had ruined Thanksgiving by booking a trip to the UK rather than celebrating with her family. Once her story was published, she would share all the details about how she'd accomplished it.

The driver cleared his throat. "Miss, it appears he's heading toward Heathrow. Do you want to continue following him?"

She finished sending her text and responded, "Yes, but when he pulls into the rental facility, drop me off outside their office. I need to ride the shuttle, or I'll lose him."

"Forgive me for overstepping, but are you sure you want to do this?"

She gathered her belongings and took out her wallet. "Yes, thank you."

When the car stopped just outside the agency, she handed him the cash they'd agreed upon and exited. The balance would be billed to her credit card. She waited for him to retrieve her bag from the trunk and thanked him for helping her.

As she walked farther onto the property, one of the workers approached her. "Miss, can I help you?"

She'd learned long ago that if you acted like you belonged, most people would let you pass with minimal interference. "I'm heading inside to pick up a bag I accidentally left behind earlier today. I'm so thankful you had it."

"Oh, that's great. Have a good afternoon."

She wheeled her bag through the line of vehicles and toward the crowd of people waiting for the shuttle after completing their returns. She caught a glimpse of the man toward the back of the group, so she turned to the female next to her to start a conversation. This way, she could keep an eye on him while it looked like she was conversing with a friend.

When the shuttle arrived, he boarded toward the rear and stood in front of the door, holding on to the overhead bar. Jasmine opted for a seat in the back of the bus. After all, she was one in a thousand people flying out of an airport to some destination. Why would he think anything different? He didn't seem to be paying her any attention, or he was just good at hiding it.

When he jumped off at the terminal, she followed him and got into the same line. She watched him approach the counter, then was waved forward to the open station next to him. That was when she heard the ticketing agent say Mexico City, so now she knew where he was headed. She bent to retrieve her wallet from her backpack as he passed by heading toward the security.

Jasmine told the ticketing agent. "I need to purchase a ticket on the next flight to Mexico City, please."

The agent asked for her identification, then proceeded to click a ton of keys on her keyboard before coming back with an answer. "First, business, or coach?"

"Coach is fine. I'd prefer an aisle seat, if available."

"It'll be $843.00 dollars, and I'll need your credit card."

She handed over her plastic and stood there while the agent's fingers danced on the keyboard. Finally, she gave Jasmine a receipt and boarding pass.

"The gates are to the left; have a safe flight," the ticket agent said.

Holy crap, what am I doing?

Jasmine's stomach rumbled, reminding her that she had skipped lunch and needed dinner. Once she cleared security and located her gate, she would eat, do a little work on the plane, and then sleep for the rest of the flight.

A pub across from her gate caught her eye. A burger, fries, and cold beer sounded delicious. She had just over an hour to kill before she boarded her flight. When the time came, she paid her bill and moved toward the boarding area, pleased to see that her male companion had boarded with the business-class travelers. At least she knew for certain he was on the flight.

After her group was announced, she forced her eyes toward the rear of the plane and walked right past him. The moment she was clear, she let out a deep breath and found her seat.

The flight was uneventful and quiet, which made her happy. She slept for most of it and had just finished her breakfast when the pilot announced they were preparing to land. Deciding it was best to use the facilities now so she wouldn't risk missing him, she made her way to the rear of the plane. She brought along her small toiletry kit to freshen up and brush her teeth, that way she'd be ready to go when the aircraft door opened.

After the plane arrived at the gate, and she cleared the jetway, she picked up her pace until she had him in her line of sight. She weaved her way through people until she closed the gap, but careful to keep some distance between them. He walked at a decent pace with his long stride, so she had to walk faster than usual to keep up with him.

He exited the airport and climbed right into the back of a waiting Range Rover complete with tinted windows. *Crap!* Her stomach tightened because she was going to lose him. Seeing the taxi line, she dashed over and cut in front of everyone. Since she only knew a small amount of Spanish, she hoped this would work instead of making a big scene.

"*Lo siento, tengo la emergencia con mi familia. Por favor,*" she said to the people in line.

The family in the front of the line relented and motioned for her to take their cab.

"Gracias," she said, then jumped into the waiting vehicle. "*Sigue a ese Range Rover negro. ¡Rápido!*"

The man turned, pointed forward into traffic, and said in perfect English, "That one way up there?"

She saw his line of sight when she leaned forward. "Yes, and please don't make it obvious."

He smiled and steered away from the curb, her back molding to the seat when he stomped on the accelerator. The knot in her stomach increased with every mile they covered. She glanced at her watch and noted they've been driving for close to forty-five minutes.

Her body listed right when the taxi merged lanes and exited the highway. After passing a series of traffic lights and making several turns, the cab came to a stop at an open market. Across the street, the black SUV they'd been trailing stopped behind two identical rovers.

"I'm going to leave you here," the driver announced while he printed the receipt for her ride.

She took the slip of paper and looked it over. "Where are we?"

"Bonita Verde."

The driver accepted the wad of cash she handed him. "This includes your tip, thanks."

After she retrieved her suitcase from the trunk, she moved away from the cab. Glancing over her shoulder, she saw movement across the street. Since her phone was already in her hand she used it to snap a few pictures before removing her camera from her bag and shoving her phone inside.

The weight of the camera felt good in her hands as she moved between the groups assembling in front of the restaurant. She adjusted her lens and snapped a few of the surrounding area and open market.

When she tried to turn back around to focus on the group across the street, a strong hand grabbed her arm and jerked her backward. Shock and fear snaked down her spine. The man snatched her camera from her neck and demanded her phone. Panic flooded her system as a black hood came down over her head. She kicked and screamed, trying to break free or get someone to help her.

The grip on her arm tightened to the point of pain. "This is your only warning," a deep voice said into her ear. "Be quiet and I won't drug you. Do you understand?"

Tears pooled in her eyes and threatened to spill down her cheeks. She nodded. "Are you going to hurt me?"

"I won't, but I can't answer for the others. Why are you taking pictures of my boss? He values his privacy and has found your actions reprehensible."

"I'm sorry, I didn't mean to upset your boss." Her voice wobbled. "I'm visiting the area. If you give me my camera, I'll delete the photos."

There was a loud, grinding sound, and she was shoved into a vehicle. No more words were spoken to her, and forceful hands pushed her to the floor. Her legs were cramped in the small space. At first, the roads were smooth, but the terrain changed and became rough and bumpy like they were on a mountain path. She figured they'd been moving for at least thirty to forty minutes.

Abruptly, the wheels skidded to a stop, and before she could catch her breath, the door behind her opened. Hands slid underneath her armpits, and she was dragged backward and onto her feet. It wasn't long before a tingling sensation slammed her extremities as blood rushed back into them.

The hood she wore was snatched from her head, temporarily blinding her from the bright sun. She caught a glimpse of the man who had taken her camera back at the market before he hopped back into the running rover and disappeared.

A man with a gun in his hand spoke rapid Spanish and motioned for her to walk forward. When she passed him, he prodded her toward a hut and shackled her ankle to a giant cement block inside. The moment he turned back to face her, he holstered his weapon and assessed her from head to toe. Then, his gaze swept over the small space.

Dread filled her, and her stomach churned with anxiety. All she could hear in her head was her father telling her over and over again that she shouldn't travel alone.

"*Quiero tus zapatos,*" the man said, pointing at her feet.

A split-second decision had her acting like she didn't understand his words or intent. Having shoes would be better than being barefoot. Seconds felt like hours as he repeated the command and glared at her.

Finally, he squatted in front of her to remove her shoes. His grimace worried her. The moment he stood, something hit the back of her head, and her world went dark.

T HE CLACKING OF POKER chips and male laughter echoed down the hallway toward the kitchen in Noah Parker's new house. He'd officially been a resident of Mill Creek for over three weeks, and he loved it.

The quaint old styling, especially on Main Street, reminded him of an old western mining town. The decorative storefronts, hitching posts, and wooden-planked sidewalks added to the allure. The small-town atmosphere appealed to him. So far, he'd spent his time getting to know many of the residents and eating at all the local restaurants. The area was a foodie's paradise.

Mill Creek was totally different from Washington, DC, and that was a cathartic release. The small town had politics, but those were centric to its residents. Some might say people were nosy, but the residents protected their own. He preferred the different vibe to constantly having to watch his back. Maybe that was harsh, but it was his perspective.

Being closer to his friends and his recent promotion made him happier than he'd ever thought possible. His new role allowed him the freedom to work on special assignments that leveraged his cyber and analytic skills. He loved working for the Federal Bureau of Investigation because he knew his contributions helped to make the world a safer place. There would always be threats, but he could sleep a little easier knowing he did his best to eliminate a few.

Noah turned from the cabinet where he stored paper napkins and plates and asked his friend, Trent Jacobs, a question that had been on his mind. "Do you miss working with our team back at the Bureau?"

Trent opened a package of plastic cutlery. "Yes, but after Dalton's death, everything changed for me. I miss being an agent, but I don't regret becoming the sheriff of Mill Creek. I needed that change for me, even if I had trouble seeing it so clearly at the time."

Noah snorted. "Yeah, that whole hindsight thing's a bitch."

Trent turned to face Noah. "What's gnawing at you? Do you regret moving here?"

"No, not at all, I couldn't be happier. It's just...my father called and pissed me off. He tried to hold the *son card* over my head. He even tried to act like my decision to move here without telling him had hurt him."

Trent's forehead crinkled in confusion. "Why? It's not like you two are close or even communicate regularly."

Noah ran his hand through his hair and sighed. "I know, right? Something about there being a target on his back, and he needs his son to stand by his side. But here's the kicker, he says it's complicated. Blah, blah, blah."

Trent's eyes widened. "What does that mean?"

"Don't know. What I do know is that he only cares about being a senator and getting reelected. Looking back, he was self-absorbed and really lacked the ability to demonstrate empathy. He disappeared from my life altogether after the death of my mom and baby sister," Noah said, shaking his head.

"Sorry, man, his actions were cruel, and there's no excuse. How'd you end the call?" Trent asked in a low voice.

Noah shrugged. "I suggested he use his vast network of resources to save his ass."

Trent's face showed his concern. "You may never get to witness this, but I do believe at some point your father will realize how badly he fucked up."

Noah appreciated his friend's support, but he didn't want to waste any more time or thought on his father this evening. He'd rather focus on what mattered—his chosen family. He grabbed the supplies, then the parmesan cheese from the refrigerator. "Maybe, but right now I have a house full of friends with wallets that need to be emptied. Let's join the others."

"Pizza and beer have arrived," Clarke Dragoon said, his booming voice filtering into the living room from the front door.

"Bring it in here. I have a separate table for food and a cooler," Noah said as he sat and shuffled the playing cards.

Clarke entered the room with two boxes of pizza stacked up in one hand and headed toward the space with all the food displayed. "Hey, what the hell is that green shit?"

Micah, Trent, and Noah all snickered at Clarke, who pressed a case of beer to Kane's chest and pointed at the cooler.

Kane Miller tore into the packaging and buried each bottle in the ice. "Annika wants us to have a healthy choice. It doesn't mean you have to eat it."

Trent clapped his college buddy on his shoulder. "Yeah, go easy on the poor bastard. Annika loves greenery and does push the benefits of eating a salad at every meal. I witnessed it this past summer when they stayed with me."

"Seriously, dude?" Clarke asked and closed the lid on the ice chest after Kane added the last beer. "Well, Aimee made us brownies for dessert. Also, she insisted I bring a plate of leftovers from our Thanksgiving dinner. She's apparently worried you may starve."

Noah started to deal the cards around the table. "It's doubtful that would happen with all the restaurants in this town, but I appreciate her concern because she's a great cook."

Micah Parker raised his hand drawing attention his direction. "Uh, I'd like to point out that I'm the town's veterinarian, and my animals don't know how to cook, so where is my plate of goodies?"

Clarke barked out a laugh. "Good point, I'll let Aimee know she hurt your tender feelings."

Trent folded his pizza slice, ready to take a bite, then stopped. "What about me? Maggie has a lot of talents, but cooking is not one of them. Aimee is aware of that fact because she tried to teach Maggie the basics. Good God, I love my wife, but she could burn water. Both Noah and I suffered on Thursday. I'm pretty sure she overcooked the bird by two hours."

Noah burst out laughing. "It wasn't that bad. I mean, who doesn't love turkey jerky? I keep forgetting that you two are married now. It's weird."

"It's not bad, Noah. You may want to keep an open mind," Trent said.

Noah clapped his friend on the back. "Nah, the whole family thing isn't for me. My childhood zapped that desire. Man, at times, it seems like only yesterday that we were working side by side, chasing Falcon to Mill Creek."

Trent chewed on his food, then swallowed. "Yeah, I know what you mean."

"What are you doing for the FBI now, Noah?" Micah asked.

"I'm working directly with Special Agent in Charge Tim Guzman on a wide range of assignments. The best part is that I have full autonomy while in the field."

Clarke laughed and raised his beer to toast Noah. "That's *special*, but I'm glad you're a permanent resident now. Having Cyber God practically next door is a game changer for sure."

The clanking of beer bottles echoed, and everyone took a drink.

"All right, enough chatter; ante up," Noah said, tossing his chips into the middle of the table.

The next hour flew past as everyone played, ate, and ribbed each other. Noah's pile of chips had grown mostly from Trent and Clarke, along with their incessant whining. "You two want to go another round, or should you drop out so Micah, Kane, and I can get serious?"

Trent leaned back and interlaced his fingers, cradling the back of his head. "Shut up and deal. There's still time to win my money back."

Clarke's beer hissed as he twisted off the cap. "Everyone's entitled to a lucky streak."

"Nah, I think you two just suck." Micah flipped his money onto the table.

Kane removed two twenties from his wallet, then slid one toward Clarke and the other to Trent. "Put your money where your mouth is. You can pay me back later."

Noah added his money into the pot. When his cards were dealt, he arranged them in his hand before increasing his bet. He answered his cellphone on the first ring, not bothering to check his caller ID.

"Hello," he said, holding his money in his hand.

"How's the shoulder healing?"

Noah's eyes widened at that question. He tried to match the voice to a name but came up empty. "Who the hell is this?"

"The one who squeezed the trigger that night in the forest."

Noah's heart thudded against his chest while his mind raced with the implications of that statement. He'd taken a round on the right side of his chest that had collapsed his lung and required surgery to remove the bullet.

The night his team went after Talon, the leader of Falcon––the crime syndicate the FBI had invested numerous time and resources, investigating–– he'd come across mercenary soldiers fleeing the scene when he'd been shot.

"Waltzer?" he asked, his tone cautious yet direct.

"Ah, you'd be correct. I'm sorry about our last encounter. Hazards of the job, right? I have something for you, but you need to hightail it to Mexico City. A female has been kidnapped, and the window to help her will close soon. I'm assuming she's an agent, but I'm not entirely sure. She'll only be at this camp for maybe seventy-two hours before she's moved."

"Excuse me for not jumping at your suggestion. Why are you telling me this and not doing something about it yourself?"

"It's simple. I can't. But I trust you to get the job done like you did for Dalton's sister, Maggie. Your new role will allow you to move quickly while avoiding all the normal red tape the Bureau requires."

"How the hell do you know about my new position? I want some answers that make sense."

"We don't always get what we want," Waltzer snapped. "We're not that different, Noah. We protect those who need it, whether they realize it or not. The only difference is how we engage to get our desired results. All you need to know is that I'm on the right side of the fight. Don't overthink it. Have Guzman inquire about Orion, but watch your six for blowback."

"Who the hell is that?" Noah bit out the question a little harsher than he wanted. "Never mind, I'd rather know what's in this for you."

"You're wasting precious time with needing to be coddled. I only wanted to know why the woman was following me. It's a win-win. You save the girl, and I get my answers. When you arrive, drive to the city of Bonita Verde, and at the resort, the front desk will have an envelope for you that contains the coordinates of her location."

Noah looked up to see Trent glaring at him, but he returned his focus to the call. "How do I reach you?"

"You don't. I'll make contact if it's necessary."

The deafening silence on the line told him Waltzer had terminated the call. Maybe it was the adrenaline coursing through Noah's body now, but his scar burned. He continued rubbing the spot while he processed what he'd just heard. Holy shit, that was one call he'd never expected to get.

"What. The. Hell?" Trent asked in a tight, clipped voice. "Why is Waltzer contacting you?"

Clarke grabbed his seat and turned it around so he could straddle it and rest his arms across the back. Micah and Kane sat watching.

Noah dropped his hand. "The whereabouts of a kidnapped American woman in Mexico."

Clarke's deep voice penetrated the silence. "Do you trust him? How do you know this isn't a setup?"

"My wife will not handle this news well." Trent's irritation was evident by his sharp tone. "Do you think he's looking to tie up loose ends?"

Kane leaned forward. His face was tight. "Waltzer's the guy who shot Noah, right? He worked for the leader of Falcon, who trafficked weapons and drugs?"

Noah nodded while he continued to rub his chest. Waltzer had revealed a key piece of information on the call that Noah needed to research before he shared anything further. After a minute, he responded. "Yes, but I don't sense an ulterior motive. The night he shot me, he had the advantage, but he chose to wound rather than take the kill shot. He's also known about Mill Creek this entire time, so I don't get the sense he's after retribution."

Kane pointed at Noah. "You're actually considering his request to fly to Mexico City?"

"All I've got is animal tranquilizers," Micah added. "They would work on humans with minimal risk."

Noah stood. "Thanks, buddy, but I'll be able to have my gun since I'll be flying on the FBI's jet. There's a woman whose life depends on me finding her. My gut is telling me that this information is solid. So, yes, I need to go, but not until I update Guzman. I'll also do some research during the flight."

Trent stood and gripped Noah's shoulder. "I get why you're going, but be careful. We'll increase our security measures here while you're gone."

"Stay in contact, and let us know what you find," Clarke said.

"Will do." Noah stood and shook every man's hand. "Thanks, guys. I'll talk to you soon."

He headed toward his office to call his boss. He'd see if an FBI agent had been assigned to Waltzer or the region and also try and find out what the hell Orion meant. Afterward, Noah would clean up the mess from tonight before he left.

If the woman in question was not one of theirs, it would take Guzman time to find out if another agency had deployed an asset, assuming they would share that data. If neither was true, could she just be a citizen who happened to be following Waltzer? The clock was ticking if Noah wanted to get to that location to do a little reconnaissance before he attempted rescue.

He planned to take a chopper to the airport in Boise and then fly on a chartered flight. Since his window was tight, he would fly direct and with his equipment. The part he had to figure out while in flight was his exit strategy. His preliminary plan was to get to the coast and take a boat, assuming he could get in, rescue the woman, and get them both out alive.

Two

A RUCKUS AWAKENED JASMINE. She sat up cursing her light-headedness as she strained to hear what all the chaos was about. There were male voices shouting and the sound of gunfire. She also heard grunting and what sounded like flesh being pounded by a fist.

Her stomach knotted tighter as fear wormed its way down her spine. It didn't help matters that her head hurt from where she'd been struck, and a headache of mass portions had formed. Still missing her shoes made trying to escape even more difficult, which frustrated her. Not that she thought she could, but if the possibility presented itself, she would take her chances.

Something scraped the ground outside, and she could hear two men conversing. They seemed to be getting closer to her position, and she forced herself to lie back and pretend to be asleep. The earthy smell and tiny particles of dirt tickled her nose. Maybe they were only checking on her to see if she had awakened.

Her heart pounded against her ribcage, making it hard to control her breathing. The last thing she needed to do was sneeze. The lack of sunlight told her it was still night, so maybe they were just checking on her.

When the makeshift door to the hut opened, she forced her eyes shut. There was a big thud like a sack of potatoes being dropped. Then, another few whacks and a low moan that sounded male. The men laughed, and when the door closed, she popped her eyes open to see what the hell had just happened.

The space was dark, but as her eyes adjusted, she could see a man's body. She scooted as close as her chain would allow and nudged him with her foot. She didn't want to hurt him, but she tried a little harder to see if he would respond. *Please wake up. I don't like being alone in here.*

"Hey, you okay?" she whispered. Only silence answered her, which made her heart sink.

He could be dying right there, and she couldn't do a damn thing. This person might be her lifeline. Keeping him alive meant she wouldn't be alone. She rotated and stretched out her body so she could use her hands. The metal cuff dug into her ankle, but she didn't care. She barely reached his foot but had enough to tug him toward her a bit. Okay, dead weight was difficult to move.

She repeated the process a few more times, gaining precious inches. Her breath sawed in and out of her chest from the exertion. Once she had him close enough, she moved again, fighting her restraint until she could slide her arms under his armpits and heave him backward. Satisfied with his proximity to her, she sat in the dirt. Next, she arranged his body, so he was supine with his head in her lap.

Not sure how to kill time, she sang old television show theme songs in a quiet voice. It didn't matter if they were comedies or cartoons as she went through the list she knew. Her only comfort was his shallow breathing, but at least he was alive.

She closed her eyes, letting her mind drift to better times. Like Saturday mornings when she fought with her sisters about what cartoons they should watch as they ate their cereal in front of the TV. How many times she'd borrowed her sisters' clothes or makeup. Or how they would stay up late at night talking about their dreams. Her body protested from sitting in one place for so long, and when she shifted, he stirred. His eyes opened.

"Ruh-roh," he mumbled and gazed up at her. "I love that cartoon and all the mysteries they solved. Thanks for the entertainment."

She laughed at his comment. That wasn't the first thing she'd thought he'd say. "Me too, but anything with a dog will hook me. How do you feel? It sounded like you were their punching bag earlier, before you ended up here with me."

"Perceptive and kindhearted. I have to admit, I've been better. However, this is nothing I can't handle, so no need to worry. How long have I've been out?"

She shifted to the side, letting his head rest on the ground. "I can't judge that for myself until the sun rises. All I can tell you is that it seemed like a long time."

"Got it. Well, I'm Noah Parker. What's your name?"

"Jasmine West, and it's nice to meet you. I don't suppose you have superhero skills and can break us out of here? Or a team of people coming to rescue you? If not, I'm pretty sure this isn't going to end well for us."

"Shh, we don't want to be overheard, even if the camp is quiet." His voice was low and scratchy as he spoke. "Not exactly, but I do plan on getting us out of here. How'd you end up in here?"

"It's a long story, but the shortened version is that I took some pictures of a group of people, and that apparently upset someone. A black hood and rough handling later, I ended up here."

"Who's your target, and which alphabet agency do you work for?" Noah asked.

She snorted. "Did you hit your head? You're not making any sense. What's an alphabet agency?"

He tried to sit up and grunted. "Damn, that hurt. My ribs are sore. Are you an agent or citizen? I think at this point, honesty and transparency would be best."

Her mind raced with what he implied. She agreed with his comment about transparency, but she decided to proceed with caution until she knew more about him and why he was sitting next to her. How did he even know she was there? "I only arrived this morning. It was more of an impulsive trip, you could say, and I don't have a target."

"So, you're gonna stick with your cover story? I can appreciate your dedication, but I'll put my cards on the table. I'm here for you. The more I know, the better it will be for the two of us."

"How'd you know I was here?" Jasmine's voice was clipped and tense. "No one knows I'm here. I mean, I didn't even know I was coming to Mexico City. You are making it sound like I'm what...CIA? Is that what you meant by alphabet?"

She was thankful the darkness helped mask her reaction, but it also made it difficult to gauge his sincerity.

"Fair enough. I have no evidence to support my latest theory, but I'd stake my life on it. What that means is that I'm putting my trust in you. I'm with the FBI."

What the hell had she gotten herself into? Who were those people she photographed? Who had reported her situation to the FBI? Her stomach roiled with fear. All of a sudden, nothing made any sense, and all she wanted to do was get the hell out of there.

He inched backward until his back touched the wall and continued. "Yes, that's slang for the various agency acronyms. The person who reported your situation thought you might be an agent, so I'm asking. Right now, I'm getting the distinct impression that you are not. So my theory is that you captured something you shouldn't have since you're now being held in a makeshift prison. Am I right?"

She felt compelled to clarify any misconceptions. After all, he was sitting next to her because of her decisions. If he would extend some faith in her, she'd reciprocate. At this point, what did she have to lose? "Yes. I'm a photographer and freelance journalist. The first pays my bills, and I love it, but I enjoy writing articles on topics that interest me. About a month ago, someone contacted me about a story about infidelity and adoption records that would expose an important man's family secret. I've been researching leads to develop the story. I don't understand how I got you involved. Who's the person who contacted you?"

His prolonged pause irritated her because maybe she'd been wrong about his intentions. She didn't like that he was thinking about what to say. The truth should rattle off a person's tongue. It wasn't a trick question.

She blurted out, "You're the one who wanted transparency, so don't lie to me. If you don't want to answer, say so."

"I promise that's not the case. I'm an analyst with the Bureau, so I tend to dissect everything before proceeding—occupational hazard. The other part is I'm trying to figure out how to explain why I'm here, because that's a little sketchy. There are parts of my job I can't divulge, and what we do discuss must remain between us. We can't share any of this with our captors or others along the way. Do you understand?"

Jasmine scooted as close to him as her chain would allow. "Yes, I do, but promise me you're being truthful."

He leaned toward her so he could whisper in her ear. "You have my word. I'll start by providing some background information. A few months ago, a long-term assignment I'd been working on ended with me being shot. The man who shot me called me last night to tell me that a female had been kidnapped. He wasn't sure if you were an agent. As you can see, I'm a little confused about the whole thing. Why did he call me? What's his motive? And, are you working for an agency?"

The dropping temperatures sent a chill down her spine, making her body tremble. "Did you purposely get caught because someone is coming to rescue us?"

"No, but I'd like to lie about that because it hurts my pride. I triggered a pressure mat covered in dirt in front of your door. I did some surveillance before entering the camp, but my plan went out the window when I triggered the alarm. The silver lining is that my boss is aware of my location. Pull your knees to your chest and wrap your arms around them. It'll help to keep you warm."

She moved her body and rested her cheek on top of her knees. The moon must have climbed higher because a silvery light streamed through the cracks in the roof. Her first glimpse of Noah revealed that he was an attractive man even with the beginnings of a black eye.

She'd never known anyone who'd been shot. The fact that those types of injuries were a part of his job stunned her. She'd thought about what he'd told her and knew she had to tell him about the man she'd followed from London. It had to be the same person. The timeline fit. He had to be the one who called Noah.

"Noah," she whispered, remembering his earlier warning. "There's a chance that the man who called you is the same one I tracked from London to Mexico City. He must have known I was tailing him, and one of those men ordered my abduction. After I arrived in Bonita Verde, I took a picture of him with some other people. Unfortunately, my camera and phone were taken after making it clear that I'd upset the boss."

"Did the guy look military? You get his name?"

Jasmine closed her eyes, trying to remember details. "Uh, he was a big guy, but wasn't dressed in fatigues. There wasn't any use of rank when they spoke. I didn't hear the name used, but I think he is Darren Rosen. It's a long story, but I took a photo of the log the church keeps of people requesting adoption records, and that was the name of the man who visited the church just before me."

"The church was in London or here? Is that the man you're researching?" Noah asked.

The rapid pace of his questions combined with what he asked sent a chill down her spine. What the hell had she gotten herself into? "Yes. Well, no, I--"

"What? You're not making sense. Rewind some and go easy. My head is pounding, so I'm processing slower than usual," Noah urged, rubbing his brow.

She stretched her head from side to side, trying to get her thoughts together. "Sorry, in England, Holmberry Hill, and he was there too. He'd just exited the building when I arrived. The father I met with at the church had made the comment that he hasn't had this many people interested in adoption records in a very long time. That piqued my interest, so I decided to see where he went. At the time, I thought, what were the odds that two of us were at the same church at the same time?"

"How did you manage to do that without him knowing?" Noah asked using an incredulous tone.

"The private driver I hired followed his rental back to Heathrow. I shadowed him to the ticket counter, discovered his destination, and bought a ticket. Then, after we landed, I hired a taxi to pursue his Range Rover to Bonita Verde," she retorted.

"Holy shit, I'm impressed. That man, if he's the same one, is highly trained. We can talk more later. Now, we need to rest. Who knows what tomorrow will bring, so we have to be ready. I'm going to move back to where they dumped me. I don't want them to think we've bonded."

She watched Noah's darkened form inch over into his original position. Once he was settled, she rolled over onto her side facing him with her arm tucked under her head. A hot shower and some dinner would be wonderful.

She disliked being cold, but these were the cards dealt to her. Recharging her body was what would help her the most right now. Creature comforts would have to wait. At least she had Noah to keep her company, and they had a better chance at escaping together. He seemed like a good man, but only time would tell.

PAIN STABBED AT NOAH'S side when he tried to rotate off his stiff back. Sleeping on the cold, hard ground sucked in general, but it was tortuous with bruised ribs. The camp remained quiet, so he figured most were still sleeping, and not paying them any attention.

He hadn't sensed any dishonesty from her and was beyond impressed with how she had held herself together considering the circumstances. He could still hear her sweet voice in his head singing those theme songs.

If she had tailed Waltzer, that was an impressive feat all on its own. The bigger question was, why did their paths cross? What was Waltzer doing in Holmberry in the first place? Noah had already discussed with his boss the possibility of his involvement with the cartel now that Falcon was dismantled.

But why was Waltzer digging for adoption records? Noah's mind had worked over what he'd learned from their conversation until he'd finally drifted into a fitful sleep. A hard kick to his foot had him jolting upright, which he immediately regretted. His ribs didn't like the abrupt movements, spreading fire down his sides. Two men stood inside the hut speaking Spanish to someone who stood outside the door.

Jasmine shouted as the two men removed her restraints and dragged her toward the door. "Stop it, you're hurting me. I can walk."

The door swung shut, blocking his view of her as they took her away. He rolled to his side, using his hands to thrust himself upward. Every ache and pain from the punches he'd taken last night screamed in protest. Noah inched toward the door and listened, trying to figure out what was happening. All he heard were fading voices.

Well, screw that. He wasn't letting her out of his sight if he could help it. Noah was surprised the door opened when he shoved it forward. Today, he'd used the pressure mat to his advantage and stomped until the alarm sounded. He leaned inside the doorframe and listened to the chaos. Thirty-seconds later, a man arrived with his gun drawn and pointed at him.

"Bathroom," Noah said, thankful the man didn't have a twitchy trigger finger.

A slew of Spanish poured from his mouth in short bursts. No doubt, Noah had pissed him off. Two additional men appeared, also carrying guns, and motioned for him to walk, so he did. No need to be difficult and give them a reason to react.

They escorted him to an area to relieve himself, then took him into another hut. Noah's eyes adjusted to the darker interior, and relief washed over him when he saw Jasmine sitting in a chair. It was the first time he'd seen her in daylight, but he'd recognize that beautiful face anywhere.

"Missing your cellmate?" the man who stood in front of Jasmine said to him instead of a greeting.

"Actually, I had to pee. A little breakfast would be nice—eggs, bacon, and sourdough toast," Noah said.

One of the men standing behind him kicked the back of Noah's knees, making him fall to the ground.

The man in front, who seemed to be in charge, returned his attention back to Jasmine. "Why were you taking pictures of Mr. Garcia and his company?"

"I've already told you my answer. I was taking pictures of the area because I'm on vacation. I don't know who that man is, and if he jumped into my photo, that's his fault."

The man backhanded her, causing her head to jerk to the right. "Don't think to play with me. Who's the man who came for you last night? Who does he work for? I'm not a stupid or patient man. You best remember that when you answer me."

Noah hadn't realized that her hands were tied to the back of the chair. Her head lowered for a moment, and when she answered, her voice quavered. "I've never seen that man before in my life. I just don't know who Garcia is. If you'd give me access to that computer, I'll show you my website for my photography business. I was taking pictures like any tourist on vacation."

Noah glanced at the table littered with folders and paperwork. In the corner sat a laptop and a satellite phone. These are interesting items to have in the middle of nowhere. These men were probably part of the Garcia cartel or at least on his payroll. Now this whole situation started to make a little sense. Jasmine had taken pictures of the cartel's leader, which was why they kidnapped her. She'd managed to worm her way into some serious danger.

"All right, then this won't bother you since you don't know him." The man jerked her chair to the side so she could see the back of the room.

Two men flanked Noah on his right and left. Rough hands hauled him upward until his feet hit the ground. Next, his hands were secured to handcuffs that hung from a ceiling beam he hadn't noticed. *This is going to hurt.*

Boss man uttered one word, "Proceed."

The first punch landed lightning fast, giving Noah no time to tighten his core. Air whooshed from his lungs. Then, the two took turns punching him in the stomach and side. The taller one of the two landed a right hook to his cheek. His body burned with searing pain that continued for a few more rounds until Jasmine shrieked at them to stop.

The leader raised his hand. He pivoted to face her. "I thought you didn't know that guy."

"I don't, but you're hurting him for no reason. Who does that to a person?" she spat, her cheeks flaming red from anger.

He whipped out a wicked blade from a sheath on his belt, causing her to flinch. "Want to fill in some gaps?"

"My answers are still the same," she said. Tears streamed down her cheeks. "If you want me to lie to stop this insanity, just tell me what you want me to say."

He bent to cut the bindings from her wrists.

"Show me." He gestured to a chair at his desk. "If you don't have a website, my men will kill him." The barrel of a gun was pressed into Noah's temple at his command.

Jasmine's eyes widened when she glanced at him, which made him nervous. He hoped she hadn't lied about her website. She rubbed her wrists as she approached the desk. She tripped, knocking off some paperwork, which caused a scene.

"Sorry," she said, scrambling to pick up everything she had displaced.

He noticed she wore shoes as she crawled on the floor. Why had they given her back her shoes? Was she leaving after this little show? She handed the ringleader the pile when she finished gathering everything, and he pointed at the chair.

Once she sat, he placed the stack on the desk and slid the workstation toward her. He leaned over and pressed his finger into the biometric scanner, which allowed him access. He clicked his mouse a few times, typed something on the keyboard, probably a password, and then gave her a stern look. Her hands vibrated as they hovered over the keyboard.

A few seconds later, she sat back and tapped the screen. "See, I told you the truth."

Relief washed over Noah. God, now he hoped he'd keep his promise of nothing having him shot. Noah's gaze now glued to the leader to see what he'd do next. After an exaggerated pause, the man's head rose, and he barked a series of commands out in Spanish. More of his men entered the hut before rough hands released Noah's restraints, dropping him to the ground with a thump. Next, he and Jasmine were escorted back to their holding cell. This time, to his dismay, they shackled them both to the cement block. *Shit!*

Once they were secured, another man entered with a tray containing two beers, flour tortillas, and a bowl of beans and placed it between them. Noah's stomach rumbled, but his brain worried the food might not be safe. The moment they were alone, Noah shook his head and flattened his lips, hoping she'd understand that now wasn't the time to talk.

He sniffed the bowl and used his finger to check the contents, satisfied when he didn't find any foreign objects or smell anything out of place. Cold beans weren't very appealing, and the tortillas were hard around the edges, but both were edible. At this point, he needed something in his stomach.

He motioned for her to eat and waited until she passed the bowl in his direction. The swollen lip she sported irritated him, and he'd like to return the favor with an added lesson on how to treat a woman. He loved watching how the slender column of her neck flexed as she swallowed. Such a contrast to the feisty and strong woman who lurked under all that beauty.

The way she had handled herself during that interrogation had earned his respect. He could trust her. Not many people would have kept their cool, so he appreciated her that much more. He'd also learned that it didn't appear that Waltzer had caused her harm. It was the pictures she'd taken of the cartel that had gotten her in hot water.

So Waltzer's call had been legitimate, but he wouldn't be pleased to know a civilian had managed to tail him. The next thing Noah had to figure out was if Waltzer had landed a new contract or was operating under the remnants of Falcon's organization. Was that what Orion was?

When they finished eating, Noah leaned forward and whispered, "Get some rest now. We'll talk later."

He'd kill for a pain reliever at this point. The good news was he was confident that nothing was broken. Everything just hurt. His brain worked double time on an escape plan because he wasn't sure they'd be there or alive much longer. The biggest obstacle was the damn restraints.

The afternoon passed at a snail's pace while they rested. Guards poked their heads inside periodically to check on them. When the interior darkened, he rolled his head toward her and whispered, "You awake?"

"Yes. Are you okay?" she asked, her concern written across her face as she turned to look at him with those wide hazel eyes. "I'm so sorry you're being hurt for my actions."

He cupped her cheek, loving how soft the skin felt beneath his fingertips. "It's not your fault. These men are not good people, which is why we need to get out of here."

She reached into her pants pocket and produced two paper clips. "Would these help? I was kind of hoping you had some skill with picking locks."

His laugh caused his ribs to hurt. "You're my hero, Jazy. Are you sure you're not a spy? That move may have saved our bacon."

"I've learned some things from watching all those movies and television shows," she said with a big wink.

He snatched the paper clips from her hand and went to work. He uncoiled the clip, keeping one bent while he straightened the other. After a few attempts, his lock finally clicked. After he had removed his cuff, he went to work on hers until she was free. He liked her resourcefulness.

"That stunt you pulled earlier was sheer genius. When we get out of here, I'll buy you dinner. Okay, Jazy, this is what I'm planning. Tell me what you think," he said, using his finger to draw a rudimentary outline of the camp in the dirt.

He added the buildings he could remember and the location of their hut. The lighting was low but enough to continue. She said her two cents, and over the next several minutes, they modified the plan and route they'd take once they left the hut. The goal was to cover as much ground as possible during the night if they could find a car to take, even better.

He wanted to head to the coast and find a boat to take them up the Gulf of Mexico to Brownsville, Texas. Now, they had to wait until the right time to slip away. So many things could go wrong, but dying there was not an option.

Three

W AITING FOR THE CAMP to go completely silent was torture. Jasmine's thoughts vacillated between them kicking ass and getting caught or worse. As the time ticked by, the base noise faded along with the guards checking on them. Nervous energy had her twirling her thumbs while she waited for Noah's signal that it was time.

Staying held no appeal, but the idea that they could be shot at or recaptured scared her. This line of thinking had to stop. It was a waste of energy. A long time ago, she'd learned that you had to make the most out of every opportunity, or they would pass you by. This was no different—maybe a little more dire—but in the end, she would fight for what she wanted.

Noah's presence comforted her. They were in this together. She'd appreciated his sense of humor and that he'd included her in the planning. The sheer fact that he'd treated her like an equal, asking for input and ideas as they strategized, blew her mind. It also made her happy.

When his fingers had brushed across her palm to take the paper clips, tingles of energy had flowed through her body. Even the bruising under his eye didn't diminish his appeal. His eyes reminded her of the deep blue Caribbean Ocean.

"You ready?" he asked, interrupting her thoughts and causing her cheeks to warm. Thankfully, the darkened interior would hide her reaction. "The moon is high enough now to provide some light.

"Let's do it," she replied.

Her legs wobbled a bit as she stood, a result of a mix of nerves and being forced to sit on the hard, cold ground for hours. She closed her eyes and took a deep breath to center her courage. She would not let these horrible men win.

He moved toward the door, and looked back at her and smiled. "Our captors didn't lock the door, probably because they thought we were shackled."

He waited a few seconds before inched it open and peering outside.

He motioned for her to come toward the door and murmured into her ear, "Look at the outline of the mat. They didn't bother covering it back up with dirt, so when you exit, you have to clear it."

When she nodded, he held the door wide open for her. She took two steps backward to give herself a little extra room to propel herself forward, clearing the object. When she landed, she headed to the side of the building and crouched. The longer she waited for him, the harder the butterflies fought deep in her stomach. *Where the hell is he? What was he doing?*

A minute later, he stood at her back. She whirled around to look at him and saw the flashlight he held up and couldn't help but notice the Cheshire cat grin that covered his face. He placed his hand on her shoulder while they stood silent. Not a sound was coming from the camp, signaling that everyone still slept or was consumed in something else.

His warm breath tickled the outer shell of her ear as he whispered, "Okay, that's the cluster of trees. You ready to run as fast as possible for as long as we can?"

She rotated her head so only he'd hear, "Lead the way."

He gripped her hand. Then they sprinted out into the clearing. Her heart pounded against her chest, not from the exertion, but from the threat of being caught. When they made it, she sucked down a deep breath, more to settle her nerves than anything else. As they climbed and worked their way through the dense foliage, the sounds of nature surrounded them. A loud, ominous chorus of howls scared the crap out of her.

She yanked on his hand, bringing him to an abrupt stop. "What's that noise? What animals are out here? I'm not a fan of wild creatures, spiders, or snakes. Just so you know."

"I'm not either. Those are howler monkeys, and they're just communicating. They tend to like the rainforest. They aren't known for hurting humans unless provoked. You okay?"

"Got it. Don't make them angry. Yes, sorry. I just wanted to know what made that horrible sound. I guess I should be happy that it's not an alien creature or something worse."

"The first time I heard them, it worried me too. I'm going to ask you to hold my belt so I can use the flashlight. That way, I'll know you're still behind me."

She wrapped her hand around the leather and stayed as close as possible. They traveled in silence and walked for a long time. Her feet were killing her, and her calves burned from all the hiking.

When the sun started to peak over the horizon, he turned to face her. "We need to find a place for the day to rest and hide."

She was about to acknowledge that when her gaze darted over his head to the top of the tree line. "Look, smoke. Maybe it's a house. We can hide there or see if they can help us?"

"It's hard to know who's loyal to whom here, but let's check it out. At worst, maybe we can find some food and something to drink."

They watched the gray plume for about twenty minutes and then squatted down behind a bunch of bushes to check out the place. An engine started in the distance, and after a few minutes, a truck rumbled past them, leaving a wake of dust until it disappeared.

He motioned for her to stay put and continued to monitor the area. The plume appeared to be subsiding, giving the appearance that the house might be empty now. "I need to take a closer look. If it's empty, I'll motion for you to come forward. If it's not, I don't want you to present yourself for any reason. When it's clear, follow this road until you find the town and find help. Just continue being cautious because we don't know who to trust."

"I'm not leaving you," she said, shaking her head with vigor.

"You have to if you want to survive and help me. Once you do, call the FBI Headquarters in DC and tell them it's Falcon calling for Guzman from Mexico City."

An overwhelming need to hold him overrode her. To anchor herself to someone solid and safe who could calm the fear threatening to explode from the unknown, she threw her arms around his body and hugged him. His strong heartbeat against her chest.

After a few seconds, she inhaled and mumbled against his chest. "I'll do it, but I don't like this at all."

"Noted," he said, his hand trailing down the back of her head to hold her tight.

He let her go and crept forward. Jasmine's heart hammered against her chest with every step he took. The path he carved out took him behind trees and shrubbery until he reached the house. She watched him approach several different windows to peer inside before moving to the next. At the front door, he paused before easing it open to slip inside the house.

The next several minutes were excruciating as she waited, straining to hear or see something. When the door opened again, she sucked down a deep breath when he waved her forward. Forgetting to use any form of sneakiness, she ran in a straight line toward him.

"That guy seems to live out here alone. I found some dry food and jerky we can take along with these water bottles. Drink this one now."

She caught the bottle he tossed to her and twisted off the lid as he headed down the hallway. The moment the cool liquid hit her throat, she moaned her appreciation. She almost downed the entire bottle in one swig. When he returned with a bag, he held it open, and she stuffed the supplies he'd found inside.

"Okay, let's head out and find our resting spot for the day. When they search for us, I'm confident it'll be in the daylight hours unless they pinpoint our trail," he said.

She trailed behind him, which gave her time to study him. His lean body was fit and toned in all the best places. He had to be close to six feet tall, and she itched to run her fingers through his wavy brown hair. It was just long enough to dust his collar.

They had hiked away from the cabin and down the hill. She had zero doubt he'd find the perfect spot. Forward progress came to a sudden stop, almost causing her to plow into him. He scanned left and right, picked up a big branch, and dragged it toward an overgrown cluster.

"This is the perfect spot for our lean-to. Find loose branches like this one so we can pile them up on the open side so we'll be concealed inside. Unless they have search dogs, we'll be safe," he said.

It wasn't long before he had them tucked inside their shelter for the day. He handed her a bottle of water and gave her the bag so she could pick what she wanted to eat. After she had made her selections, she looked up and smiled.

It didn't go unnoticed that he'd allowed her the first pick. Another example to add to her growing list of how different he was from the men she'd known. She took the granola bar, split the top of the wrapper, then peeled back the sides.

She patted his leg after swallowing a small bite. "I like this hotel, especially the spectacular views. I thought Mexico was all deserts and ocean. The lush greenery is beautiful."

His smile transformed his face, and his deep laughter made her heart flutter. "Jazy, you're something special, do you know that? You could be complaining or worse, but here you are joking and making the best of the situation."

His words touched her as much as his nickname for her. She didn't think, only reacted, and hugged him. She held on tightly and mumbled against his shoulder. "No matter how this ends, thank you for coming to my rescue and for believing in me."

"Anyone who doesn't is a fool. I'm pretty sure I just slowed you down," he said.

She retreated, missing his touch. "You'd be surprised. My father thinks I'm crazy for wanting to travel and take photographs. He also thinks journalism is a waste of time unless it's for the news networks. My mother is more supportive, but changing my dad's mind would be like winning the big prize in the lottery."

"I'm sorry. It's hard when your family is against you. It just further proves my point that you're determined," he said, grabbing the bag of food and removing a stick of meat and a granola bar.

"He loves me, but he's very old-fashioned in his beliefs. In his mind, a woman should stay home and raise the children. My two sisters followed his vision, but I wanted a career. He and I have this argument at least twice a year. Don't get me wrong, I think it's great that my sisters are dedicated to being strong homemakers and having children.

It's what makes them happy. I only wish he supported my need for a different path."

"There's nothing wrong with not wanting to marry and have children. You have a right to put your career first," he said, tearing into the wrapper. "I understand completely because I've got zero interest in getting married. The ones who get crushed when things go south are the children."

Those words carried a heavier meaning and intrigued her curiosity. Something she'd file away and circle back to later.

"You misunderstand. I want marriage and children, but I want to do it on my terms. I need a husband who's willing to be my partner in life. Someone who'll continue having adventures with me. Someone who'll support my dreams. Not someone who wants to put me in a box for my safety. When my father hears this story, his head will explode."

Not knowing what else to say, she finished the rest of her water and closed her eyes. Her feet throbbed, and her legs felt like she was still trekking up and down the mountainside. In the distance, she heard the whir of a motor.

Her eyes popped open. "What is that noise...a helicopter?"

"Yup, that's a scout looking for us, which means there are people searching on the ground. I would say it's somewhere between four to five miles away," he said.

"Should we get moving?" she asked, her body stiffening as she sat up straighter.

"No, we're covered from top to bottom and need our rest. We are in a great spot. That bird is searching away from where we're located. If that changes, I'll wake you up, and we'll move."

Her stomach felt a little queasy at the thought that they were being hunted. She trusted Noah's knowledge, and logic told her to rest. This would be a great adventure to tell people, if she survived. That was what she'd focus on now.

Forcing her eyes closed, she tried to relax and concentrate on anything that didn't involve running for her life. This tiny space they shared put them on intimate terms, which calmed her nerves. It was the same feeling as when she had a nightmare as a child, and her parents came to chase away the monster. If she were being honest with herself, Noah's presence made all the difference.

NOAH DOZED INTERMITTENTLY, TRYING to balance resting his body and keeping his focus on his surroundings. The helo concentrated on a search grid to the north and northwest of their position. It seemed the assumption was they had headed toward the city rather than the coast. Pleased that his gut instinct was right, he hoped by the time they figured out their mistake, he and Jasmine would be on a boat headed to Texas. Her soft snores and even breathing told him she was still sound asleep.

At some point, she'd repositioned herself so her body leaned against his side with her head on his shoulder. This woman exuded sexiness, even with her hair falling free from her bun and not a drop of makeup on her face. Like an automatic reaction, he wrapped his arm around her shoulder, anchoring her to his side. His ribs screaming in pain protested the movement, but he'd deal with the discomfort.

Jazy, with her feisty attitude and audacious spirit, fascinated him. He still couldn't believe she'd had the forethought and sheer gumption to get those paper clips. He'd never met anyone quite like her. At the end of this rescue, he hoped they would stay in touch.

He mulled over the events of the last two days and realized he still didn't know who the subject of her story was. Between trying to escape and his fixation on Waltzer, Noah hadn't circled back to her reason for going to London in the first place. He intended to ask if she stored her work in the cloud. If luck were on their side, some might still exist since her camera and phone were destroyed. What had Waltzer been doing in that church?

The sound of a gunshot snapped Noah out of his contemplation. He lifted his elbow to nudge Jasmine, who yawned and stretched. He placed his finger at his lips and made the hand sign for gun. Her eyes widened, but she remained calm, which he appreciated.

A tug on a branch gave him enough room to peek outside of their shelter. There were no signs of people, and everything had calmed back down. Even the birds had returned to their perches.

He turned back to face her. "Sorry for that startle. I wanted to make sure we weren't in immediate danger. A handgun fired, and the sound can travel one mile, give or take. Can you be ready to leave in about five minutes?"

"Sure, I'll just take a quick shower and be ready in a jiffy," she said, finger-combing her hair and pulling it back into a ponytail. "Hey, I do need to use the bathroom. Don't suppose you have any toilet paper in that bag?"

A big smile tugged at his lips, but he shook his head. "See that tall, leafy plant? It's called mullein, and the leaves are super soft. It's safe on those delicate areas."

Her lips pursed, and her eyes narrowed. "Wow, never thought I'd have this conversation in my life. Okay, I'll let you know how it rates against the big brands."

While she took care of business, he went to work to deconstruct their shelter. The moment she returned, he tossed her a granola bar and bottle of water. While she ate, he shared his plan for the day, soliciting her views and opinions before they left.

The sun had almost dipped halfway below the horizon, leaving them with a beautiful view of an orange sky. They probably had twenty minutes of light before the sun disappeared and the stars brightened the sky.

They had hiked for close to two hours when the lights of a small town became visible. With haste, and Jasmine keeping pace at his side, they headed in that direction. Once at the town's edge, he crouched, taking her down with him. The bar was closed, judging by the neon signs being off and a lack of activity. The good news was that there were two cars left in the small parking lot.

He leaned toward her and whispered, "We're going to hurry over to that bar and see about borrowing a car. The odds that any workers are—"

"I got it. Let's just get to the doing." She nodded, then yanked him upward.

He gripped her hand and ushered them across the road. As he passed the front of the bar, he checked for cameras and was relieved when he didn't see any. Scanning the parking lot, he chose the old hatchback that seemed to be in better shape.

When he lifted the handle to the driver's door, he smiled. Once inside, he leaned across to unlock the passenger's side. Not holding out much hope that the owner had left the keys behind, he still checked the interior and the glove box—no key or tools. The lever to the trunk was on the floor, and when he popped the release, he hustled to the rear of the vehicle.

Bingo. The tire well contained a variety of tools he could use. He used a wrench like a hammer to pound a flathead screwdriver into the ignition, then turned it like a key.

When the car purred to life, he pumped his fist in the air. "Hot damn, it has a full tank of gas to boot. Buckle up, Jazy. Our next stop is the coast. Keep your eyes peeled for mileage signs."

She pulled the belt across her body and clicked it into place. "I can't believe that worked. Did you attend a school that teaches unscrupulous activities one must know to be an agent?"

"Totally, and I got an A-plus," he said, turning onto the main road and away from the town.

"Imagine that, and I bet you over-examined everything. Now, put the pedal to the metal, Super-Agent Man. I'm dying for a shower."

A flutter of excitement buzzed around in his stomach for the first time since he'd triggered that alarm. They might just make it out of Mexico unscathed, for the most part. He forced himself to concentrate on the drive ahead of them.

He hoped there were mileage signs to confirm, but he figured they had close to a three-hour drive. He hadn't expected what had transpired, but he knew the odds of something going south were high. The longer they stayed in the area, the greater the risk of them being found.

The urge to share that probability with her and to prepare for various contingencies fell silent on his lips. Sometimes, it was just as good to revel in the victory, even if the outcome wasn't guaranteed. He'd cross that bridge later if necessary.

"Are you going to tell your father all of this or just select parts?" Noah asked.

"It's a pretty incredible story, and it'll blow his mind." She paused, rubbing her brow. "No, he should know what I endured and that I survived. They raised a strong and capable woman. It's not like every adventure will end in me being kidnapped. In this case, we survived because we worked together."

Noah squeezed her hand, suddenly needing to touch her to reinforce his message. "You are indeed, but it's hard to change a person's perception. It sounds like your father will always view you as his little girl. My two cents? Do what makes you happy. It's your life and legacy."

"True, but I'd love nothing more than to know that he brags about my accomplishments to his friends, that he's proud of me. My mother worries but understands that I have different goals. I only wish she'd stand up for me with Dad, but she doesn't."

He returned his hand to the steering wheel. "Why did you go to London in the first place? You know, before you decided to follow Mr. Doom and Gloom?"

She rolled her head against the headrest to face him. "When I agreed to take on this story, my source wired me ten thousand dollars to help with expenses. They mentioned a concern around infidelity and a possible baby that might tie to St. Paul Hospital in Holmberry Hill. So, I started in DC with in-person interviews to reach those who refused to talk to me on the phone. I figured the surprise-I'm-here approach might work best with them. Plus, you can gauge body language in person."

"How do you know any of it is legit and isn't a wild goose chase?"

"The fact they sent me money is a pretty strong indicator. The other is the fact they want someone outside of DC's inner circle with an independent voice. The more we've corresponded, the more I've realized this is personal. So far, this friend of the family has shown they're invested in being a part of the discovery process. The better question, is there even a story? At this point, I have a strong feeling that this story does have potential."

"Gut intuition works for me. I can't argue that logic. I've trusted it many times in my career. So how did this person hook you?" he asked, glancing in the rearview mirror.

She removed the band from her hair and slipped it onto her wrist. Slender fingers massaged the base of her head before ruffling her hair. "The subject of the email read: 'Secrets of the Mangled Family Tree'. "

"Whose family tree?" he asked.

"Senior Senator Thomas Dubin. He's also the chairman of the appropriations committee. Isn't that wild? This person is adamant that the senator must be held accountable for his mistakes. There are quite a few people who have mixed opinions about him. I also picked up a few more interesting tidbits to dig into from my interviews. So far, this story is compelling."

Noah gripped the steering wheel so hard he thought he might crush it. Hearing his father's name was akin to a sucker punch in the gut. *What the fuck?* "Well, mine aren't mixed. I dislike the man."

She jerked her head to look at him. "Why? Have you met him?"

His chest constricted as a burst of memories overwhelmed him. Rapid thoughts, like rays of light, seared his brain. "What we discuss is off the record—everything." His voice deepened, sounding hoarse to his ears. "I'm serious. You do not want to cross me on this."

"I promise," she said, her eyes were wide like saucers.

"He's my father."

"What? His son's name is Michael Dubin. How do you fit into his life--?"

"Estranged," he mumbled as he glanced at her momentarily before returning his eyes to the road. "Michael Noah Dubin, I changed my name when I turned eighteen to Noah Parker. I dropped my given name and took my mom's maiden name."

"Holy smokes. You've blown my mind," she said, placing her hand on his forearm. "I can't believe we live in such a small world."

Speaking about his childhood wasn't something he did often. Only Trent and Dalton knew some of the sordid details. It had sucked, and Noah wanted to forget he even had one. He'd analyzed his life over the years before concluding that he'd never get the answers he sought. He'd made peace with that fact, so he buried his hurt and anger to survive.

He'd learned that his parents' marriage had been a façade. A tool used for gain, and when one's life ended, the surviving parent could turn his back on his child. Leaving his son to fight for survival.

Four

Jasmine squeezed her eyes closed at Noah's explanation. Never in a million years had she expected that admission. Good grief, she was in the same car with the senator's son. So many questions came to mind. Questions like how had he navigated all his grief? He'd been shipped off to boarding school the year after his mom had murdered his sister before taking her own life.

The news cycle had been heavy with broadcasting his family tragedy from the personal angle and political. She couldn't imagine the pain and torment he had been forced to endure with a murder-suicide story tied to his family. Kids could be cruel, so she wondered if he'd had a hard time in school, too.

"This is uncharted territory, Noah. I'll honor my promise to you because you've earned that much from me, but I'm going to move forward with my story. I wanted you to know my intent upfront. Do you want to be a part of this or be the FBI man who helped me escape?" she asked in a soft tone.

"I don't know...what do I say? My go-to is to process scenarios and overthink everything before committing. On the other hand, I don't know if I have that much energy left in my tanks to cut open those scars."

"You? Analyze something?" She giggled. "I had no clue, but what I can tell you is that this story is now connected to someone I know and respect."

The car went silent. Her response hung heavy between them. Blurred images zipped by the windows as they headed down the road. The scenery hadn't changed, but on the horizon, a light line started to bisect the darkness. The lack of conversation inside the tin box seemed to make every bump in the road more pronounced and the grind of the motor louder.

The last thing she wanted to do was rush him. Depending on how this story unfolded, he had to assess what this could mean to him and his father. She straightened and looked out the passenger window. The sun had started to rise, casting the first rays of light across the sky, illuminating the foliage and trees that lined the pavement they were traveling on.

In any other circumstance, the view would be breathtaking, but now, it only cast light upon the distance growing between them. She had meant what she said, but he had to choose. She dozed for a while, letting him have his space.

A yellowish ball on the horizon traveled upward when she opened her eyes again. Excitement fluttered in her belly that they were getting closer to the coast because the road was flattening out, and the land-scape had slowly shifted. All she could do was hope the rest of their escape would be smooth. The constant threat of being recaptured sat like a boulder on her chest.

Finally, Noah inhaled and spoke. "You seem to have a strong moral compass, but I'm not sure I'm worth that loyalty. My family isn't, but you've accepted an assignment and must see it through. I want to be involved since you're still in the discovery phase. I haven't decided how much I want my name associated, but I can help you sift through everything. My offer is also selfish. I want all the information you have on Waltzer. We have some unfinished business."

She contemplated his offer. "I can handle that, but as of now, all information with the barest of exceptions is on the record."

"I understand, and there's a good amount of discomfort with my consent," he said. Noah checked the rearview mirror. "Do you back up your phone and camera to any type of storage on the cloud?"

"It's automatic as long as I have a signal. The picture of the adoption record will be there for sure. The pictures I took at the market in Bonita Verde are questionable. The problem is my camera's upload is manual."

"Did you take any pictures of the man you saw at either the church or airport?"

"I wish, but when we get access to a computer, I'll show you everything I have so far. I might have a picture of him from the market on my phone, though."

"Good, I'm looking forward to seeing who's in those pictures," Noah said.

Jasmine took a deep breath. She wanted to start the conversation because she had so many questions. "The volume of news coverage on your mother and sister and all the conspiracy theories that followed must be overwhelming."

"It was relentless. Since the bodies were never recovered, it'll never truly end. The reasons behind the suicide debate every political angle from marriage to cover-up. Some think the Potomac River's strong currents swept the bodies away. Others have strong opinions that it was murder or an assassination. I'm sure that somewhere, a handful of people think aliens beamed them up to a spaceship. It's mesmerized the public for years, even though it's not a leading story. Every so often, someone resurrects a piece of it," he said, his voice raw with emotion.

He rubbed his temple, then turned to glance at her. "It's a scab ripped from my skin over and over again. It's not something I would wish on anyone. All that thirst for answers makes people forget that at the center stands a human being whose life is being destroyed again."

Her stomach tightened from the picture his words painted. She couldn't imagine what he'd been through, not to mention the sheer fact that he has unanswered questions too. "I can see why you changed your name. You were so young. It must've been hard to escape the shock of it all."

His head snapped toward her. "You've misunderstood my reason. It's simple. When I turned eighteen, I changed my name because I wanted nothing to do with my father."

"Why?" she asked.

"He was self-centered, with no honor. Everything in his life was staged for his benefit."

Jasmine's thoughts drifted toward her interviews. "When I spoke to several of his colleagues on Capitol Hill, there wasn't a lot of admiration or kind words uttered about him. Listen, Noah, I can't imagine how difficult this has been or will be for you, but this could be your chance to bring all of the speculation to a close. The difference this time is you're leading."

His gaze moved toward the rearview mirror. "We have company. The vehicle behind us is closing the gap quickly. Get down."

Her heart thudded hard against her chest. She scrunched her legs further into the floor and curled up on the seat. She watched him checking both the rearview and side mirrors. "What are we going to do?"

"Drive for now. Listen, we just passed a mileage sign that we're only five miles from Veracruz. I say jump, you're out of the car, and you keep heading toward town. Don't stop or look back––"

"What about you? I can't just leave you," she squeaked out, finding the words stuck between the pounding of her heart.

"You help me by running. Head toward the marina and find a phone. I want you to call Trent Jacobs. He's the sheriff of Mill Creek. You can trust him; we used to work together at the FBI. Then, stay in public places where the tourists are hanging out. Blend in as much as possible and stay alert. If I can, I'll meet you there."

"That's the plan? Are you freaking kidding me? That's not a plan...I call bullshit," she sputtered, forcing herself upward to argue her point until a hand cupped the top of her head, holding her down.

"Stay down. The car with two men is right behind us. I'm sorry you don't like the plan, but it's the best I have now. I don't like it, but the odds are stacked against us if we've been located. We have zero weapons."

Well, that's a good point, but I wish all of this would end so we could go home.

She decided to let Noah concentrate. She did the next best thing and said a quick prayer. She figured it couldn't hurt, and hopefully, the lack of consistent church visits over the years wouldn't be held against her. The car lurched right and then left, the undulations from the road making her stomach churn. Seconds turned into minutes before the motion evened out.

"Hang on, they're making a move," he directed. His grip on the steering wheel tightened.

She heard the engine whine and saw the sun's glint reflecting off the metal roof as it passed the driver's side window. She sucked in a deep breath, preparing for the following words Noah would speak.

"I think we're okay; that vehicle passed without even a sideways look. Stay down, though, for a bit longer until that vehicle is further ahead. When we get to town, I want to take a few precautions to ensure they aren't interested in us."

"Uh, did they pose some risk you didn't tell me about?"

Noah flashed her a brief smile. "No, but I would be remiss if I didn't ensure it was a random occurrence. When we get to the marina in Veracruz, we'll scout for boat options that will take us to Brownsville. Here's the creative part of the plan, but first, do you trust me?"

"Really, that's your question?" she asked, breaking the last granola bar in half and handing him one section. "Yes, I think we've proven we have each other's back."

"I've processed a few scenarios, and the best option is to act like we're a couple as opposed to two people on the run."

She gave him the hand signal for okay, popped half of the bar into her mouth, and chewed. That worked for her, but now she wished she had a toothbrush and paste. What if he wanted to kiss her? Butterflies fluttered in her belly when he parked the car in the alley across the street from the marina. *It's showtime.*

When they exited the car, humid, brine-stained air surrounded her. He reached for her hand and guided her across the street toward the boat dock. They set a casual pace as they strolled, stopping to look at the scenery and point out areas of interest. She knew he was scanning the area, so she played along and noted things that stood out to her.

She mimicked the action when he wrapped his arm around her and looked right and left. Their interactions were easy and natural, which was odd since they had just met.

In the distance was a yacht with the words *American Dream* painted on the stern and the state flag of Texas hanging from the flagpole. She ran her hand up his chest and patted the spot between his pectoral muscles to get his attention. The strong beat of his heart pulsed against her palm.

When he leaned down, she whispered in his ear, "Look left toward the back. Do you see that boat with red, white, and blue?"

He pressed a kiss to her temple and nodded. "That's a good option. We'll head that way."

They continued toward the vessel, and as they approached, she saw a woman and two kids on the deck. She waved and almost jumped for joy when the woman reciprocated with a perfect Texan drawl of greeting.

Looking up toward Noah, Jasmine winked. "I think we found our ride. You follow my lead. I've got this."

His hand fell from her back with each step she took toward the gangway. A moment later, a man appeared from below on the deck. She assumed he was the woman's husband because one of the kids launched herself into his arms. Jasmine glanced right and left and didn't see anyone approaching, so she made her move.

"Hi," she said, walking over halfway up the plank. "Oh my gosh, we are having a bit of bad luck on our honeymoon and need some help. I promise we're not asking for money. I saw your flag and hoped we might be able to sail back with you to Texas, if that's where you're heading. My husband and I are desperate for a little kindness."

The man beamed and put down the child in his arms, directing the girl toward the woman. "That's my wife and our two children. Come aboard to talk and see if we can find a solution."

Noah came up behind her and tugged the back of her pants, his voice low but urgent. "Do not board the boat. Stay on the edge of the passageway. If you sense anything is off, decline, and we're out."

She walked toward the boat but remained on the walkway. "I don't want to intrude if you're unable to help. Our car broke down, and to make a long story short, we were robbed at gunpoint, and everything we brought was taken. Thankfully, we were left on the side of the road unharmed, but everything we had in the car, the gunman took. We have nothing but the clothes on our backs. We must get to the US to call our family and get home."

The wife rushed past her husband and embraced her on the gangway. "Oh, honey, that's horrible. Of course we'll help. Won't we, dear? We're headed back to Brownsville, so it's not a bother. Y'all hungry?"

"Yes, famished," she said, feeling some of her tension lessening. She followed the woman onto the vessel, glancing over her shoulder to ensure Noah followed.

"I'll make sandwiches for lunch," the woman said. She gathered the kids and went below deck.

Noah approached the man with his hand outstretched. They got down to business after the niceties were out of the way. She heard the man ask Noah if they wanted to report the robbery. "No, they took our identification and threatened to kill us if we reported anything to the police. My wife has had enough excitement for one trip."

The man agreed and gripped Noah's shoulder. "I can't imagine how frightening that must have been. Not an ideal honeymoon, but maybe one day it'll be one hell of a story to tell. Let's bring a happy ending to your trip. Come down to the galley with me. I have a sat phone in the cockpit. You can call your family now, and I'll get us moving. Here's the hull number of our boat. You'll want your family to contact the port authority because I assume you have no other identification. There might be a little delay on your end until you can clear customs. It'll take us about fifteen hours. After you call your family, we can scrounge up some spare clothing if you'd like to shower."

Noah took Jasmine's hand and went with the man. "That would be amazing. Besides, she kind of smells."

Jasmine punched his arm, rolling her eyes at him. "I'm pretty sure we both smell. Thanks for helping us out."

The man held the phone out to Noah. He dialed a familiar number, ready to relay his information without tipping his hand. "Hey, Dad, we ran into some trouble in Mexico. We're both okay, a little rattled from being robbed, but Jazy found a nice family taking us to Brownsville. Yup, we have no paperwork. Okay, I have the number of the boat we're on. Appreciate it."

When the call ended, Noah handed the phone back to the man. "Thanks, my father is working on everything."

"That's got to be a relief. Okay, give me a few minutes to grab some clothing for each of you, and then you can shower while I get us moving. Afterward, we'll eat."

Noah turned and climbed the ladder. The moment Jasmine cleared the opening behind him, he tugged her into his arms. His lips hovered over her ear, and the warmth from his breath tickled her neck as he spoke.

"I called my boss. He'll have a car waiting for us at the marina and a plane to fly us to Mill Creek, Idaho, where I live. He'll arrange our customs clearance through Homeland Security, so we're set."

"What about my identification?" she asked, hugging him back a bit tighter, enjoying the comfort of his firm body.

"You're in luck. He's working on getting your license and passport replaced. He's got friends in all the right places."

They stood like that for several more seconds before he stepped back and pressed his lips to her mouth. She liked that kiss—it was the perfect balance of sweet and tender, melting away the world around them for a few precious seconds. His touch tingled her lips, and warmth traveled across her body to all the right places.

Oh, this man was trouble, but only the very best kind. Finally, they would leave Mexico, but now the work would begin. Together, they had to find the meaning behind the cryptic message she'd received. *Senator Dubin's Mangled Family Tree.*

N OAH COULDN'T BELIEVE IT was only a day shy of a week since he'd received that call from Waltzer. He and Jazy had been through a lot but made it out by working together. Yesterday had been a long day. They'd crossed the Gulf of Mexico, then travelled northward by plane to land in Boise. The FBI's helicopter had been unavailable due to routine maintenance, so he'd opted to be driven to Mill Creek instead of calling in a favor from one of his friends.

Upon their arrival, he'd grabbed his car to take Jasmine to Rayna's Outpost to buy some clothing, then to the drugstore for the rest of the stuff she needed. They were dead on their feet from the strain and stress of the last several days and had just enough energy to return to his house and crash with no want for dinner.

Noah had awakened somewhat refreshed on Friday morning, but his belly rumbled from hunger, and he figured hers had to be rumbling, too. Since moving to Mill Creek, he usually met the guys for a quick breakfast before work on Friday mornings. It served as a good way to introduce Jazy and fill the group in on what had happened south of the border. He headed her direction to share his idea and to his delight, she agreed. In short order, they had both showered and dressed and were ready to leave.

He held the door open for her to enter the Knotty Pine Tree. The chimes above the door jingled, prompting an automatic greeting from Sally, who buzzed around inside the restaurant. "Morning, Noah, and pretty lady who I'll meet in just a second. Coffees?"

"Double, yes, Sally," he said.

Jazy grinned and looked back at him with a quizzical look on her face, so he filled in the gaps. "Sally and her husband, Peter, own this diner. She's also a huge gossip and busybody, but in the best possible way. Bottom line, she's like the headquarters of Mill Creek."

"Noah Parker, I heard that, and now you owe me details so I can live up to my notorious reputation," Sally hollered over her shoulder while she headed back toward the kitchen window.

He ushered Jazy to the long table toward the back and slid a menu in her direction. "You can't go wrong. It's all delicious."

Sally appeared at the table seconds later with two mugs of fresh brew. She winked at Jasmine and then moved her gaze back to Noah, raising one eyebrow in his direction. He didn't even pretend not to understand her meaning.

He'd been in town long enough to know that evading Sally was futile. "Sally, Jasmine—"

"Hold your horses, don't let Noah skip the part that explains his black eye," Irene said as she took the open seat next to Jasmine. "I'm Irene, by the way. I've lived in Mill Creek for far too long, but I always love to meet new faces."

Jasmine extended her hand to Irene, then to Sally. "It's nice to meet you both."

Noah continued his introduction. "Jasmine's a journalist and photographer, and we're working together on a story. I upset one of her interviewees and took a fist, but you should see the other guy."

Jazy laughed at his comment, and Irene patted Noah's hand. "Poor baby."

"Oh, that sounds like fun. What's the story about?" Sally asked, waving to another diner who'd entered the restaurant.

"That's the part we can't share, but once it's published, I'll send you both copies," Jasmine said.

"How cool. Well, welcome to Mill Creek, Jasmine. Do you two know what you'd like, or do you need a few minutes?"

Jasmine nodded. "I'm starving. I'll have eggs in a basket with crispy bacon, hash browns, and fresh fruit."

He handed Sally the menus. "I'll take my usual."

She turned to Irene. "You want your usual?"

"No, today I'll have an orange pineapple smoothie and blueberry muffin to go," Irene said and turned to face Jasmine. "It's nice to meet you, dear. Where are you from?"

"Chicago," Jasmine said. "I was born and raised there."

"Oh, I love that city. There are so many things to see and do, and Lake Michigan is so beautiful. A tad cold in the winter, but still spectacular. If you have any spare time while you're here, I run the library and host an after-school youth group for the younger children to help the town's working parents. I'd love for you to be a guest speaker and talk to them about photography and journalism. I think it's important for the younger generation to hear about the different careers available worldwide."

"Thanks, Irene. I'd love to come if there's time," Jasmine said, giving the sweet woman a big smile.

Irene patted her hand and stood. "Wonderful, I look forward to it. Learn something new today."

"She's great. Is everyone in this town so welcoming?" Jasmine asked after Irene left.

"Yes, and you can't go anywhere without a social visit or six," Noah said, snapping his head higher to glance at the door before returning his focus to Jazy. "You're about to meet Clarke. He's a friend but can be cantankerous and a general pain in the ass. "

"Dude, when did you get back to town?" Clarke's booming voice came from the front of the diner.

He watched Jasmine as she peered over her shoulder. He noted the large man approaching their table with six other people following close behind. It appeared she was meeting the gang today.

"We got back late yesterday and crashed," Noah said, embracing his friends with hugs and back slaps. "Okay, everyone, go easy on Jasmine."

After the group had sat down, he introduced his family. They might not share blood, but the bond was as strong as if they did. He went around the table one by one. "Trent's the town's sheriff married to Maggie, who teaches fourth grade. Clarke's a pain in the ass and a US Deputy Marshal. He's engaged to Aimee, who is an assistant to the sheriff. Lastly, Kane's an architect and married to Annika."

A chorus of hellos followed before Noah filled everyone in on his companion. Light conversation filled the table for a minute until Sally dropped off more coffee and took the remaining orders.

"What happened?" Trent asked, taking a sip of his coffee. "I'm guessing Jasmine's not a deep-cover agent?"

Jasmine jumped on that one. "I can't confirm or deny that statement...just kidding. I can tell you that I was innocent, but the whole thing was my fault. I upset someone's boss and they had me taken to a prison-like thing. I'm a photographer and freelance journalist. I'm working on a story, which is why I was there in the first place."

Trent flashed a big grin on his face. "Well, I can tell by your face that you had some complications. Was it a setup?"

"No, I triggered an alarm tied to a pressure pad buried in front of her door. It was dicey at times, but we made it. Jazy is very resourceful and can think on her feet. I learned an interesting fact about Waltzer. She tracked him from Holmberry Hill in the UK to Mexico City."

Clarke stopped mid-sip and nearly choked on his drink. "Wow, that's a lot to absorb. Cyber God isn't good at being stealthy, and she–the non-spy– tracked Waltzer, who's like a super solider. Are you sure she isn't CIA? Let me guess, you pissed off the cartel––isn't the Garcia Family running that area of Mexico?"

Noah leaned back in his chair and rolled his eyes. "Ha ha, yes, that's my assumption, but we'll know more once we can access her photographs. And, no, she's just resourceful with a crap ton of luck on her side."

"Who's Cyber God?" Jasmine asked?

Noah pointed at himself. "You didn't get to witness that skill set. The whole escaping and evading part interfered with my ability to dazzle you."

"Trust me, I was impressed, but it seems like Mr. Analyzer is more accurate."

The table erupted into laughter at her name, but it was Clarke who added his two cents. "That's just one of his annoying traits. The man does have top-notch hacking abilities when it comes to keyboards and networks."

Noah had opened his mouth to say more when Maggie cut him off. Her face was as white as a ghost. "*He's* back in business?"

Trent put his arm around his wife. "You're safe, Maggie. If Waltzer wanted to cause trouble, he would have already. In this case, he helped Noah rescue Jasmine."

Maggie looked at Jasmine. "I'm glad he helped you, but I don't trust him. My brother, Dalton, who was my husband's partner back in the

FBI, lost his life working on the Falcon case, which Waltzer was tied to."

"I'm so sorry, Maggie," Jasmine said in a soft voice.

"So, are you doing a story on that man, about how he's a super solider?" Kane asked.

Clarke slapped Kane on the back of the head. "It's called Special Forces, dumb ass."

"It's unacceptable to hit, Clarke. You're going to teach our future child so many bad habits." Aimee made a tsking sound with her tongue.

Jasmine rested her elbows on the table. "No, my story isn't about him. He just happened to be leaving a church I was researching due to a lead from my source. The pastor I met with mentioned he hadn't seen this much interest in their adoption records in years, so I trusted my instincts and followed the other man there. In hindsight, it wasn't the best idea I've ever had."

"We may finally have a picture of Waltzer?" Trent asked.

"Yes," Noah said.

"Do you think you'll recognize him? It was dark, and you saw him for what, like, five seconds before he shot you?" Maggie asked, leaning forward in her seat. "I can confirm his identity if you need a second opinion."

"Thanks, Maggie, I'll keep that in mind," Noah said.

Sally approached the table with her arms full of plates and her apron full of condiments. Once everything was distributed, she returned to the window to serve more food.

Aimee unrolled her silverware. "Who are you researching for your story, Jasmine?"

"Senator Michael Dubin," Jasmine said, focusing on her food.

Noah cut a large bit of pancake with his fork and popped it into his mouth. He glanced across the table to see Trent staring at him. He appreciated the fact that Trent kept his questions to himself. He wasn't ready to reveal the sordid details of his childhood or that the senator was his father.

Under the table, Noah felt Jasmine's hand rest on his leg. That simple touch calmed him. Reminding him that he wasn't alone and that he had her in his corner. He'd worried that meeting everyone this morning might overwhelm her, but he'd been wrong. She fit right into this group. That shouldn't have surprised him because that was her. She adapted.

His mind raced ahead, creating a checklist of everything he and Jazy had to do. The first was to pull up the pictures to see what she'd captured and what had made its way to the cloud. He found himself wanting to begin the research. It was the first time in his life that he was willing to make himself vulnerable on this subject. To get to the bottom of all these unanswered questions that had pestered him over the years. Who was this supposed family friend? Why did they want to take the senator down? Not that Noah minded. His father should be held accountable, but the unknown made him nervous.

Five

ON THE WAY TO Noah's house, they made a pit stop by the town's hotel to get Jasmine a room. They had been so tired last night that she'd opted to crash at his place. He showed zero hesitation in paying for her room or even the supplies and clothing from yesterday, which she appreciated. She needed to start a list of what she owed him to pay him back. Getting her wallet replaced couldn't happen fast enough. She despised being dependent on someone for everything.

Afterward, they climbed back into his truck and rode in companionable silence. When the engine stopped, she opened her door and followed him inside his home. She was eager to get the ball rolling on the investigation. Both dread and excitement fought for attention in her gut. The last thing she wanted to happen was to cause him any more heartache, but deep down, she would wager a large sum of money that a story lurked with the potential to stun. The biggest question was if they could work through the webs of lies to uncover the truth.

He stood at the refrigerator. "Want anything to drink before we get started?"

"No, thanks," she said, taking in the style of his home.

Last night, she hadn't noticed much. She liked his kitchen's gray and blue tones, the marble countertops, and the stainless-steel appliances.

"I loved meeting your friends. They're a colorful bunch and care a lot about you."

"I've known Trent the longest, but they're a great group. I consider them my family. My house is your house, so make yourself at home," he said, walking down the hallway until he reached a closed door.

He twisted the handle, pushed the door wide, then allowed her to enter. Her gaze darted around the room. In her head, if this were a movie, an orchestra would be playing an awe-inspiring tune in the background. The space could only be described as a computer person's empire.

In the center of the room was a big glass table shaped like a U, with two large monitors on the left side. A leather chair sat in the middle of his desk, which looked like something out of a science-fiction movie. A huge flat-screen television was attached to the wall in front of the desk, and another monitor was to the right.

"It's awesome, I know. I call it my lair."

"Uh, I hate to break it to you, but you should call it your command center." His boyish smile made him look even sexier, if that was possible. "Where do I work? Let me guess, the small desk in the corner?"

His laughter filled the room. "Nah, I'll let you use the corner of my desk. Grab that chair."

He plopped down in his captain's chair, and before long, his remote and keyboard were doing his bidding. A soothing ocean image was displayed on the big television. This space was incredible. In a flash, he had her logged into a laptop and the display mirrored the monitor attached to the wall on the right.

"Here, you're logged into the system. Type in a username and password so you can access it on your own. Just be aware that every keystroke and page is tracked," he said as he approached her. The subtle scent of his cologne, a smoky rosewood and sandalwood, surrounded her.

"So, avoid all the naughty websites?" she asked while she typed in information.

"Exactly." He smiled and returned to his seat.

She played with a strand of hair. "Okay, this space is damn cool. You must come to Chicago and set me up when this is over."

"Deal, but now you have to show me your photography website since your work saved my life."

She wasn't entirely sure why his request made her happy, but she liked that he wanted to know more about her and that he was interested in the work she loved. She opened a browser window and entered her address. In a flash, her main page with her favorite photo was displayed on the screen.

"Wow, that picture's breathtaking," he said, the awe in his voice matching the intrigue on his face.

"Thank you. I adore elephants," she said, warmth spreading over her. "A conservation group hired me to take pictures of Molly and her baby for their marketing materials. Only one of the photographs wasn't used by them. Then, an art dealer commissioned it. You can purchase this one from two galleries in New York, and Chicago."

She clicked a button on her website to launch a scrolling display of her photos. She'd taken almost every type of photo, except nudes, in her short career, but that could change too.

Photography requires skills beyond understanding just how to operate a camera. You had to understand the balance and importance of light, color, composition, and subject. There was also the raw, elemental nature of finding the unique connection between subject and purpose. She equally loved the untold story of a photograph.

"How'd you get started?" he asked, his gaze glued to the display as her photos danced across the screen.

"I bought my first camera at a yard sale in first grade. I loved it and never stopped taking pictures. I'm not sure my family had the same affection for my hobby. I always had a lens in their face. This passion has followed me throughout my life. It's how I make my living, and I've been very successful."

"You have a great eye. Maybe you can give me a few pointers?"

"Absolutely. We'll find many opportunities between the forest, mountains, and wildlife around here," she said.

"I'd like that. Then I'd have a direct link to your heart. My deep dive into a person I find intriguing," he said, his gaze locked on hers.

She took a quick breath. The intensity of that moment threw her off balance. Wanting to create a deeper connection with him, she asked a question that had been on her mind since they last spoke about his family. "What you shared about your mom is horrific, but I sense you didn't share the world's view," she said, not even blinking. "Is that true?"

He paused, making her worry that he might not answer. "I adored my mom. She had a big heart and always had time for us. We were the center of her universe. I can't think of one person, aside from my father, who met her that didn't hold her in admiration. She was the heart and soul of my father's senatorial campaign. When she attended events, crowds were larger, and his polling numbers increased. I barely got to know my baby sister. She had just turned three, but she made me smile."

"Wow, that's young," she said, her voice a mere whisper.

"Yes, and every little thing fascinated her. She would ask a million questions. I was only seven, and after a while, it started to annoy me. But now, I'd give anything to hear them again.

"You sound like a typical big brother, and I know she was fortunate to have you."

He broke their connection and stared at the wall behind her. "I sure hope she knew I loved her. Deep down, I've never thought Mom was capable of such a heinous act. Even the note she left for me is confusing. If she did snap, my father's cruelty should be blamed," he said.

"Why do you say that about your father?" she asked, her eyebrows pinched with indecision of how hard to push. "Grief and tragedy are difficult to handle, so are you mad at him for that or something else?"

His smirk told her everything. "As you know, my father isn't known on Capitol Hill as a nice guy. His motives are always about what benefits him or makes himself look good. Mourning my mother or sister wasn't something I saw him do. Talking about either was off-limits and a big no-no in our house. Then he shipped me off to boarding school to make handling the situation easier."

She covered her mouth with her hand to hide her surprise. "Wow, I couldn't imagine being unable to talk about my family or rehash memories. I don't know what to say to that. When he visited, was it better? Maybe he needed time to grieve individually?"

She caught what she thought was a flash of pain in his eyes before he suppressed it. "No, not once did he visit. I did come home for Christmas a few times, but my father was never available. I spent the holiday with his assistant and security. After a while, I stopped coming home at all."

Her hand clasped his, desperate to soothe the wrongdoings in his life by letting him know she cared. "That's awful. He was a grown man and should have known better. You need family, especially when things are crappy. My mom always had things planned for us to do and try when we were on break from school. Every year, we took a family vacation. We baked, decorated, sang carols, and played in the snow at Christmas. Those memories were magical. It makes me sick to my stomach that you were robbed of those. Where did you end up spending your holidays and summer vacations?"

He linked their fingers together. "The first few years, I stayed at school with other kids. In the summer months, I took extra classes and electives. When I was older, I was allowed to go home with friends if I got permission. I worked better this way since I didn't want to be with him."

She kept holding his hand. No one should have these types of conversations without support. They might have just met, but she cared about him. A protective streak she'd never felt for anyone outside of her family surged front and center. "What did he do to your mom? Was he abusive?"

"Never any physical confrontations, but he was the king of emotional pain. After graduating from the Massachusetts Institute of Technology, I contacted one of my mom's best friends to get some answers about my parents' relationship. That's when she told me my mom was helplessly in love with my father, how she had trouble conceiving, which of course was all her fault. My father accused her of damaging his image and sabotaging his career. All good senators had a family."

Jazy's mouth parted and then closed before she found her words. "Oh, Noah, I don't even know what to say. I feel like I've exhausted the use of horrible, but it's the only word that comes to mind."

He nodded his head and continued. "When she finally became pregnant with me, according to her friend, their marriage improved, and Mom had never been happier. It was sometime after Lisa, my sister, was born that Mom broke down and finally admitted that her marriage was a sham to her best friend."

"Barbara Porter? Is that the friend you're referring to? I got her name from my source and spoke with her too. Okay, this isn't very nice to say because I haven't met the senator, but he's an ass. That reflects poorly on me, but I don't care. And you went to MIT?"

"I did, and I graduated with a dual degree in computer science and political science. My father disapproved of my love for computers. His vision for my education and career centered around a military academy. Again, he believed it would look better for his career."

This gave her a new perspective on her father. He might be opinionated, stubborn, and old-fashioned, but she knew deep down that he loved her. She wished he had expressed it more by believing in her dreams and abilities. Knowing that he was proud of her mattered, but after hearing Noah's story, she could accept their agreement to disagree about her life choices.

"Okay, you ready to see if any of the photos you took in the market uploaded to your cloud?" he asked.

His change in direction didn't go unnoticed, but she agreed with the switch in tactics. Her fingers flew over the keyboard until she was logged into her online storage. She crossed her fingers briefly before she clicked on one of the three images. The first one showed the three black Range Rovers and two men shaking hands. She recognized the big man right away. It was the man they called Waltzer. The other, she had no clue about.

Jasmine circled the man's face with the mouse. "That's him, the man I followed." She clicked on the other two images, bringing them side by side. "Do you know who the other two are? These aren't as clear."

"Yeah, I can enhance that image, but I recognize him. I need to upload this image into the FBI database. Now we finally have a face to attach to his name. I'm almost certain this one is the head of the Garcia family. Not a clue on the other."

"What do you mean? You've never seen or had a picture of Waltzer before? How's that even possible?"

"The FBI knows of him, but we label him a ghost. We've never been able to link a picture to his name. Give me a second to access a folder with the cartel's hierarchy. We can run this photo against the images we've on file. Afterward, I'll upload these too," Noah said.

"That makes sense, but also seems so difficult in this day and age."

In short order, he now had two enlarged copies of the image on his desktop to review. "Bingo," he said, pointing to the screen after a few minutes. "That's Marcelino Garcia, the leader of that syndicate. He's known for arms and drug trafficking."

Great, she'd made an enemy with the cartel while in Mexico. Pinpricks of trepidation traveled down her spine. She'd unknowingly captured a meeting between the two men. Her mind zigzagged. Did Waltzer work for the cartel?

"So, is Waltzer like a mercenary soldier? Will this cartel guy forget about me, or did I screw up my life?" she asked, her stomach plummeting with her following line of thought. "Oh God, my family. He has my identification, Noah."

"I'll have my boss call in increased patrols in their neighborhoods until we better understand how far the cartel is going to push. Waltzer was working as a mercenary for Falcon, so I can only assume he's doing the same thing here. The Garcia family is well known for drug and arms trafficking, and that fits into Waltzer's expertise."

She clicked on the other two images to bring them to the forefront. "Marcelino Garcia brings his family to meetings like this?" she asked, the hairs on her neck bristling.

"I'm not sure who the females in that shot are. We only have them from behind and a partial profile since that man I don't recognize is blocking them. The rest scattered in the background are his security."

"I don't recognize any of them as the one who kidnapped me from the market," she said, scanning each image several times.

His eyes scrunched together. "No, he probably had a portion of his detail in various locations around the market. They'd communicate on earbuds. Once you were identified, the command was given to apprehend you and destroy your equipment."

She clicked on another item. "Here's the photo of that adoption record I photographed."

He leaned forward to study the certificate. "Tell me what compelled you to head to Holmberry Hill to visit that church?"

She opened her email program and navigated through her inbox until she got the message she wanted. "My source indicated that Senator Dubin traveled to this area early in his career. He visited several times from the middle of 1982 to early '83, then the visits stopped. This hospital had a program that provided complimentary care to orphaned children who lost parents in geopolitical conflicts. Dubin donated to the hospital and even researched the logistics to see if it would be a good program for the US."

"This source sounds like someone in the senator's inner circle, like an assistant or aide who could share this knowledge."

She tapped her finger against her upper lip. "Yeah, that makes sense, and that person could be viewed as a friend to the family. I get the impression that uncovering these *secrets* could assist an opponent in defeating a long-tenured senator. Or maybe this person thinks your father used this facility to hide an unwanted child since infidelity was mentioned. I did check to see if his name is listed on any of the records, and zero results were produced."

"Well, that's a relief, I guess," he said, flicking his fingers upward to share his screen. "Or maybe it just proves that no records exist. What was Waltzer doing at that church, though? We don't know for certain that he asked to see the adoption record you photographed on the father's desk. The file could be completely unrelated."

"All very true, so I guess we need to identify the people on the birth certificate from the father's desk and see if we can link them to social media to get some pictures," she said.

"Now, you're speaking my language. I'll work my magic on the names on the certificate and see what I can dig up." Access to multiple databases was a perk of working for the FBI.

Jasmine flipped through some pages in her notebook. "Oh, I did learn something interesting about the hospital. I knew all the birth, adoption, and death records were transferred to the church. While on site, I discovered that the hospital privately catered to individuals with sensitive conditions or treatment needs, provided they were willing to pay for exclusive care that did not adhere to the same protocols as public or government healthcare facilities."

"Hmm, that's interesting. Okay, check this out," Noah said, displaying this information on the wall monitor. The names of the adoptive parents on the certificate are John and Mindy Waltz. Surely that's too similar to Waltzer to be a coincidence. They were stationed in Germany at the time they adopted a baby boy from the hospital in Holmberry Hill. Unfortunately, they've both passed away, so we can't contact them."

Noah had started working in another database when his phone rang. He slid it off the table and answered on the third ring. "Hello," he said.

"Glad to see you made it out of Mexico. The ocean route was smart."

Noah placed his finger across his lips and put the call on speaker. Then, he mouthed the name, Waltzer, letting her hear the conversation.

Waltzer continued. "The man who held you and the woman captive is no longer breathing. All seized identification and any digital evidence in that makeshift camp have been destroyed. What do you have for me?"

"Appreciate you tidying up the house. She's not an agent. She's a freelance journalist working on an independent story. Since you both visited the same church on the same day to view adoption records, she followed her instinct and shadowed you. She has no interest in Marcelino Garcia. Want to tell me why you were at the church? Or why you're hanging out with Garcia?"

"Relax, I made her at the airport. I need to know why her nose was in my business, a place it doesn't belong. What I do in my free time or why I'm with Garcia is above your security clearance, so stand down, Parker. Who's her assignment?"

"You have clearance. Figure it out," Noah said, enjoying the satisfying silence on the other end before he ended the call.

Her pulse beat harder, fluttering against her chest. "Do you think Waltzer's going to be a problem? And what did tidying the house mean?"

"No, I don't think so. He took care of loose ends—your identity documents and your possessions. Bottom line, you and your family are safe."

She let out a deep breath. "I don't know why he did that, but I appreciate it."

"Agreed. Now I need to call Guzman," he said. Once his boss was on the line, Noah relayed everything to keep him current. After several minutes, he put the phone on speaker and placed it on the desk. "You're on speaker."

"Hi, Jasmine. I've expedited new copies of your passport and driver's license. As soon as they arrive, I'll forward those to Noah," Guzman said on an exhale. In the background, a car door closed. "If you haven't already, you'll want to contact your bank and cancel your credit cards. I appreciate you partnering with Noah on this. Waltzer and the cartel are important to the FBI."

"Thanks, Mr. Guzman," she said into the phone.

"Hey, Guz, have you gotten anything back on Orion? Maybe you can shake the government tree a little harder with Waltzer's implied comment regarding his security clearance. He could have been busting my balls about his former military service, or maybe we've examined him through the wrong lens. It would be nice to know for sure."

"I'm working the channels," Guzman said, and the din from a crowd echoed through the line. "We'll connect later."

After he disconnected, she propped her head in her hand. "I need to call my sister. I'm late checking in, so they have probably filed a missing person's report. Do you have any wine?"

"I'm not really a wine person, but I have whiskey and scotch. Both are great for dulling the aches. Don't worry, if they filed a report, I can get it canceled for you.

"You're not funny, but I guess you're good to keep around—a human version of a Swiss Army knife. Can I use your phone?" Sat his yes, she dialed her oldest sister and put the call on speaker. "Olivia, it's me. I'm sorry—"

"Where the hell have you been? Dad is seconds away from a total meltdown. We've barely been able to keep him from calling every agency," she said, her voice an octave higher than normal. "Good God, I even lied and told him you were having phone problems. This whole time, I was worried you were dying in a ditch somewhere, and I'd be the one he'd blame. Do you know what that stress does to a person? It's called serious heartburn and gray hair, Jasmine! Gray freaking hair!"

"You've made your point, and I'm sorry. The truth is that I was kidnapped, but a man came to aid in my rescue, and we escaped."

"That's not funny, Jasmine. What's going on?" her sister choked out between sobs. "I was scared when we didn't hear from you, and Dad would never forgive me if anything had happened to you."

"Olivia, listen to me. I'm fine. I swear. But I'm not kidding about the kidnapped part. You're going to have to tell Dad you heard from me, but I'm going to be out of pocket for a while. I'm involved in something that's gone a little sideways, but I'm committed to seeing this thing through. I'll tell you everything when I get home."

She heard her sister's stuttered intake of breath. "It's a good thing I love you, but I'm going to kick your butt when you get home. This is the last time I'm covering for you. Promise me you'll stay safe."

Noah snagged Jasmine's attention, trying to ask for permission to speak. She shoved the phone closer to him and gave him the okay sign with her hand. He squeezed her shoulder. "Olivia, I'm Noah Parker, and I work for the FBI. I promise I'll watch Jasmine's back. Although, I have to admit, she can handle herself quite well. Don't worry, we've got this."

A lump formed in her chest from his words. He believed in her. Just like that, he made her feel precious and capable at the same time. No one had ever made her feel this way before. Her body hummed with an awareness that tingled throughout. She listened to him end the call with her sister while wearing a big sincere smile on his face that made the corners of his eyes crinkle. Man, was he sexy, and damn it, she wanted him to kiss her again. This time because he wanted to, not to maintain their cover.

T HE NEXT MORNING, NOAH rang Jasmine's hotel room to say he had good news and planned to pick her up in an hour. He'd received Darren Rosen's birth certification overnight but waited to open the file until she was with him. It only seemed right because they were a team.

Last night, before Noah had taken her back to the hotel, they'd reviewed all the information she'd organized and made a list of what to research next. Her thought process and attention to detail impressed him, but it was her colored markers that sealed the deal. She had a color-coded system that made all her notes colorful—like the woman herself. Who was he kidding? He liked her organization.

Taking her to the hotel last night hadn't sat well with him. When he'd returned home, he didn't like the emptiness of his place. He missed her presence. Maybe he'd just gotten used to having her around. He'd never clicked with a woman so easily, and together, they made a formidable pair.

He couldn't put a finger on why all these thoughts swirled around in his head, but he'd spent a good chunk of time processing them. He thought back to the promise he'd made to her sister. He meant every word, but the part he'd kept to himself was that he'd give his life to ensure Jasmine's safety.

When he turned into the parking lot of the Mill Creek Hotel, she stood outside waiting for him. She jumped into the truck's passenger side. "Good morning. Can we stop for breakfast and coffee on the way back home? I didn't sleep well last night, so I need a jolt of caffeine."

"Why couldn't you sleep?" he asked as he pulled out of the drive.

She clicked the seatbelt into place. "This will sound pathetic, but I'm having nightmares. Honestly, I think my subconscious knows I'm safe when I'm with you. Being alone in the dark seems to unleash it all right now."

He reached across the cab and rubbed his thumb across her cheek. "Thanks for sharing that with me, but it's normal. I'd be worried if what happened to you didn't cause a reaction. If it makes you feel any better, I didn't sleep that well either."

She turned into his hand and smiled. "I knew you missed my snoring. And thanks, I'm relieved I'm not the only one. Okay, now about my belly. Who has the best breakfast sandwich and coffee in this town?"

"I can't choose one, but I know where to take you today. Then we'll head home to get started. I want to look at the birth certificate."

"You haven't already?" she asked, snapping her head in his direction.

"No, you're the lead, so we'll do it together," he said, liking the look of surprise on her face.

He pulled into the parking lot of PB&S Café, and fifteen minutes later, they were headed to his house with two bacon and cheese sandwiches and coffees. The inside of his truck smelled delicious, making his stomach protest the wait.

Once inside his garage, he opened the door to his house upon them leaving his truck and led her straight back to his lair. No words were spoken as they both took their seats and tore off the wrappers to their sandwiches.

"Mm, this is yummy," she said around a mouthful. "Thank you. Now, pull up that document."

He enjoyed the enthusiasm she had for everything. He wiped his fingers clean on a napkin before he operated his mouse and keyboard. In a flash, the copy of the official paper was displayed on his wall monitor like a poster. Her gaze lifted, and for a moment, the last few bites of her sandwich remained untouched.

He highlighted the space for the birth father. No one was listed. Then, he highlighted the mother's name. Cynthia Rosen

"So have you seen that name anywhere in your research?" he asked, leaning back in his chair with his arms crossed over his chest.

"No, I haven't seen the mother's name on anything. I find it interesting that the father isn't identified, so that's a bust. Well, the other information matches, right down to the hospital," she said, jotting some notes in a bright pink pen.

"The mother may not have wanted the father listed, or his name was omitted for another reason," Noah said, rubbing his forehead.

She waggled her eyebrows at him. "Okay, Cyber God, work your magic and dig into Cynthia Rosen's life. I'll scour social media."

"Challenge accepted," he said.

The only sound in the room was the keys clacking as they typed. She worked on her computer while he accessed some different official sites. Occasionally, they would stop and confer on whatever had caught their eye. He found himself staring at her as she worked. Her hair had been wound up in some ball on the top of her head. A few wisps of her hair had fallen down and framed her face.

The subtle scent of her orange lotion filled the space, and the fact that she wore almost no makeup made her look young and innocent.

"I meant to ask you the other day. What's your official title at the FBI?" she asked while still working on her laptop. Thankfully, she hadn't caught him watching her.

"I just received a promotion. It's a new position created by my boss. I'm now the special assistant to the agent in charge, Tim Guzman."

Now, she turned her head toward him. "So, you're like, what, his administrative assistant?"

"Something like that, but with the freedom to operate independently and with minimal oversight. I sometimes have autonomy over my assignments and may be assigned to other cases by my boss or collaborate with other agencies. I get to be involved in a wide range of operations. The position is still evolving, but so far, I like it.

"How cool, and Mr. Guzman must think you're pretty *special*," she said.

He smiled at that statement. "All I can tell you is that he's a great boss. You can call him Guzman. The mister makes it strange."

The room fell silent again while they continued to work on gathering information until Noah spoke. "I've narrowed the list of people named Cynthia Rosen to a handful of names, but I'm not finding any connections to Waltzer or my father."

"Well, I may have found something using a family heritage site. These websites can be beneficial at times. I found a Catherine Rosen who married Mark Miller and had a baby girl named Cynthia Miller. I tried social media for her but found nothing except two articles. Are you ready for this? Cynthia worked on your father's campaign in 1979 as a campaign assistant. I found another article mentioning that she resigned the summer of 1982 and moved to England. I think she used her mother's maiden name to add another layer of anonymity."

"Holy shit, okay, let me call in a favor. Hold tight for a second," Noah said as he placed a call. Several minutes later, he thanked whoever he'd contacted and turned to face her.

"You ready for this? Cynthia Miller, aka Rosen, is dead, and her place of death was the St. Paul Hospital in Holmberry Hill. She died of a heart attack in March of 1983. I should have her death certificate in a minute," he said.

Her eyes went wide. "Wait a minute, Darren Rosen's mom is Cynthia Miller, who worked for your father and died in the private hospital known for taking care of delicate situations? Oh, where are my notes?" she said, flipping through multiple pages of paper. "Found it. Yes, Darren was born in February 1983, and according to my source, the senator visited a few times late in 1982 and in early 1983."

Noah sat back in his chair, his arms folded behind his head, with his eyes closed. "Cynthia died in March of 1983, and Darren was adopted in April of that same year. That's when his name changed to Darren Waltz. I don't know what to think. I mean, my mother's best friend said Mom thought he was having an affair. Darren Waltzer could be my half brother."

"Yeah, that's a distinct possibility. I mean, we won't know until there's a DNA test or unless your father admits it. You'll need to talk to Waltzer too," she said.

Noah sat up. "Another option is to see if we can track the money. Email your source and ask if they have more information about his donations, like the amounts, dates, and frequency. If he were involved in taking care of a pregnant woman, that would be costly at a private medical facility."

He stood, then walked out of his office. He needed some fresh air and a moment to gain his composure. His gut churned with anger and disbelief. Could it be true that he had a sibling? One thing that became clearer as he worked with Jazy was that his family had secrets.

He had to talk to Waltzer and gauge his reaction to this news. There was a reason Waltzer had been in Holmberry Hill that day. The only way to verify any of this was to send in DNA samples from both him and Waltzer. Noah had to have proof before taking this to his father.

He stood in front of the kitchen sink and stared out the window. His mind raced with the possibility of what they discovered, and that thought both excited and appalled him.

The slight shuffle of footsteps alerted him to Jazy's presence. She slid warms arms around his middle and held him tightly. When her head rested against his back, a sense of peace fell over him. She righted his world, not with her words, but with her touch. The hug was a simple gesture that showed him she had his back. When he was ready, he'd share his thoughts. But first, he needed to process this little nugget of *what the fuck.*

The strangest part was that he kind of wanted it to be true. Losing his mother and sister had gutted him. Losing his sibling had robbed him of getting the chance to navigate life together with someone as they grew older. His mind drifted back to what Jasmine had told him.

Senator Thomas Dubin and Secrets of the Mangled Family Tree.

Six

J ASMINE'S HEART SPLIT WIDE open for the pain and confusion Noah had to be experiencing. She wanted to soothe his heartache. A child of any age didn't deserve this type of anguish. Inside that man stood a boy who'd had his family ripped to shreds. They were bonded by the experience they'd shared and survived. Her motivation remained on the story, but maybe she could help Noah get some closure. To put this to rest so he could peacefully move forward with his life.

She returned to her chair to start the process of requesting Senator Dubin's records from the Federal Election Commission. This would allow them to audit his campaign donations and expenditures from that period.

The door to his office opened, and a voice she'd recognize anywhere filled the quiet space. "Hey, Jazy, you ready to dive into the deep end?"

"Always with you," she said, holding her hand out to him. Warmth traveled down her arm the moment his fingers curled around hers. "What's the plan?"

She stood, giving him access to his chair. After he took her place, he snagged her hand. "Thanks for earlier. Your support matters. Okay, I'm ready to see what you've been researching while I sulked about the whole half brother thing."

Pursing her lips in concern, she studied him for a minute, contemplating how to respond. Half of her wanted to smack him for trying to downplay his emotions, while the other part understood his self-preservation. "Don't do that. You're entitled to your feelings. That doesn't make you anything less than human. We received a reply from our source on the email I sent. They didn't have much information on donation dates or amounts, except for this one. The senator made a personal donation in June of 1982 for $250,000. I just requested the FEC to pull his records from January 1982 through May 1983. It made me wonder if he may have used his funds for other payments—or donations—during that time frame."

Noah stared at the screen. "That's a solid theory. He could have used campaign funds to hide Cynthia's pregnancy in the hospital. It makes sense that he would have tried to cover it up because the tabloids would've had a field day over the possibility of a love child between the senator and Cynthia. It wouldn't matter if it were fact or fiction. The amount of time they spent together would help fuel the speculations. We must find out if my father and Cynthia had a baby."

Jasmine turned back to face him, her hands on either side of his jaw. "If your father did use campaign funds, that's illegal. Do you have a way to contact Waltzer?"

Noah pursed his lips, then answered. "No, he didn't give me his number. That's something I'll have to work on."

"That brings me to another question. You mentioned that your mom left a note for you. I know it's personal, but would you be willing to share that with me?" she asked.

"Sure, I'll go get it. It's probably good to get a neutral opinion on it."

His blatant trust and willingness to share something deeply personal to him moved her. When he returned with an envelope, butterflies fluttered deep in her belly. This was the last communication a mother had with her son before she died. The sound of paper crackling drew Jasmine's attention to his hands. She accepted the fancy pink stationery with an embossed floral border. When she read the cursive text, tears welled up in her eyes.

Son,

Lisa and I love you to the moon and back. Don't worry, I'll take care of your sister until she's old enough to care for me. I'm proud of you. All my love, Mom.

She handed it back to him and wiped her eyes. "That's a beautiful note. It's perplexing because it sounds like she's going away on a trip instead of leaving permanently. I know you mentioned that they never found their bodies. Have you tried looking for them since you joined the Bureau?"

"I tried once with no results. The agony of waiting for those search results and the enormous letdown of finding zero information was too much to bear. I haven't tried since that first time. It's not like I can't accept the fact they're gone. It just never made sense to me," he said, stuffing the letter into the envelope.

"I can't even imagine," she said.

"It's funny how time fades some memories but makes others more prominent. My sister was only three, and I struggle to remember events with her in them. I do have one that's crystal clear in my mind. She had a stuffed unicorn she carried around with her everywhere. It was white with a rainbow-colored horn. She loved that toy and named it Sparkles."

"That's so cute. She sounds like a happy little girl. My favorite toy was a stuffed dog named Fred. I've always wanted a real dog someday."

Noah's smile reached his eyes for the first time in a while. "I love dogs and would have one in a heartbeat if it weren't for my day job. Anyway, I've got to figure out how to get hold of Waltzer."

She raised her palm and rolled her wrist in a half circle. "Um, how about trying caller ID? That sometimes works."

"Oh, you're a funny girl. That would normally be a good idea, but I can guarantee he called on a burner phone. He'd never use his real number. That's what we call in the business NTK—need to know. I will try to search for a military record under what we now think might be his real name: Darren Waltz."

"Excellent idea. It would be helpful to know that they are the same person. If not, that makes all of this even more complicated."

"Hmm, I just tried to get into Darren Waltz's military record and was denied access. I expect that will trigger something. The person who locked the records will get a message that I tried to access them."

She widened her eyes, giving him her best what-are-you-talking-about face. "Yeah, whatever that means. Why would they be locked?"

"Typically, they aren't, but there are a few reasons when it happens. The most common is that he's Special Forces or doing clandestine work. I'm hoping he'll be asked if he knows why I did this, then he'll call me. You know, the equivalent of sending up the bat signal?"

"Gotcha, that helps," she said, flashing him a goofy smile.

An alert chirped on his cellphone, interrupting their banter. "Hey, good news, your cellphone just got delivered. I can't believe that model was back-ordered for this long. I'll go get it."

"No kidding, try being on the receiving end of that statement. It's so difficult not to have one these days. Hey, will you grab me a soda on your way back?"

She practically clapped when he handed her the box. She accepted the drink and popped the tab, releasing the hiss of the carbonated drink. The first thing she did with the phone was start the setup process.

"I had a thought while you were getting the package. If the FEC audit is a bust, we should see if we can access the senator's bank records to look for the original donation and any others. Do you know any of that information?"

Noah cracked his knuckles. "I do. He's used the same bank forever. I forget the exact story, but he's known the bank president for a long time. It would be easier and faster if I hacked into their system. If we find out later that we need this information legally, I can always follow the proper protocol."

His phone rattled on the desk's surface, and he put the call on speaker. "Hey, boss, you're on speaker. What did you find out?"

Guzman got right to the point. "Jasmine, since you've been privy to this information, I'm fine with you hearing this update because it doesn't reveal specific details. That said, to cover our asses, I'm going to have you sign an NDA before we continue. If you're uncomfortable with that condition, I'll have you drop off the call, but I also have something I would like you to look at if you're willing. I'll get to that later."

"Sure, I'll sign an NDA and help in any way I can," she said. Noah printed out the form his boss sent and gave it to her. She took a moment to read the contents, then scrawled her name. "Okay, done."

"Noah, upload that and send it back after our call. Okay, about Orion and Waltzer, I just got off the phone with Lieutenant General Banks, who educated me in a terse exchange on the merits of rank having its privileges, to which I have none. He commanded that we stand down on anything related to Waltzer and Orion, which is NTK.

So, as pleasant as that call was with the lieutenant general, I don't want a repeat performance. We've learned two helpful things. Waltzer's active duty and is one of the good guys—even if that statement stings. The second, Orion is top secret, so that's as far as we go."

"Understood," Noah said. "I plan to finish assisting Jasmine on a few open items."

"Care to expand?" Guzman asked in a clipped tone.

"After I obtain more information," Noah said.

"Tread carefully and be prudent. If this lieutenant general calls me back, it's your ass on the line," Guzman said, his voice firm. The sound of papers being shuffled filtered over the line. "Jasmine, I've overnighted your license and passport. They should arrive tomorrow."

"Thank you, I appreciate you doing that for me," she said.

"You're welcome," he said. "Okay, I'd like for Noah to show you the file we have on the Garcia Cartel and see if you can identify any of the men from that day—either from the camp or the market."

"Sure," she said.

"Now, I have something for you, Noah. There's a concern that we have a traitor in Congress. The other day, a shipment of SAMS, M4 carbines, and mortars were stolen from a truck after a convoy was forced off the road in Mexico. Those shipments are classified and tightly monitored. I'm sending you the file, satellite coordinates, and images to review. Work your magic and get me a working theory ASAP."

After his call, Noah leaned back and put his feet up on the corner of his desk. "Okay, I'll set you up to review those photographs, and then I'll get to work on all my tasks," he said, placing his keyboard across his lap and jumping into it.

"Are you doing that hack thing?" she asked.

"Yup," he said, his focus entirely on his screen.

Her stomach growled, reminding her that they'd skipped lunch. "How about I make us some dinner while you do your thing? I'll check out those images later."

His head didn't move, but she heard him mutter, "Sounds good, thanks."

Noah's kitchen had everything. It was far better than the small one in her apartment in Chicago. She wasn't a gourmet cook, but she had learned a lot from her mother. The pantry was more stocked than the refrigerator and freezer, and she found the necessary ingredients to make spaghetti and garlic bread. Her mom always emphasized the importance of fresh herbs. Since that was a hard no, she would have to settle for dried ones.

The sauce bubbled on the stove while she put water on to boil. Next, she had to preheat the oven, ensuring the bread and pasta would cook simultaneously. Although this dinner wasn't a date—much as she might wish it were—it could still be a memorable occasion. After everything they had faced together, they were worthy of a home-cooked meal. As dinner neared completion, she went to fetch him.

"Wow, you've set the table, and I like the candles. If the smell is any indication, dinner will be delicious. What do you want to drink? Whiskey, scotch, or beer?" Noah asked from behind her.

She topped the noodles with sauce and placed the bowls on the table. "Beer is fine. Do you have a potholder or something for the bread pan? It's too hot for the table."

He grabbed a trivet and retrieved two beers from the fridge before twisting off the caps. "I accessed the archives and found a deposit. My father transferred $250,000 on June 4th to St. Paul Hospital. I didn't find any other deposits in that time frame, so I'm unsure what that means. I guess we'll have to see what the FEC records show. So far, your source has been correct."

She spun the pasta around her fork. "Wow, Cyber God is good. That was quick."

He winked. "It's a common reaction to my legendary skills."

She held her fork right in front of her mouth. "And modest. Well, maybe we shouldn't jump to the worst-case scenario where your father is concerned."

"You haven't met him yet," he groused. "Thanks for making me dinner. That hasn't happened in forever. Plus, when the chef is this beautiful, it's breathtaking." His eyes sparkled with sincerity and something she couldn't quite place.

Her body heated from his words. "Thank you. You're not so bad looking yourself. Hey, afterward, if you can step away from your work, I thought watching a movie or something might be a good mental break."

"Or something." His gaze locked onto hers. "There are so many I've missed, so we can surely find something we both haven't seen."

After dinner, they washed and dried the dishes before heading to his family room. Her cellphone chirped with another text message from her sister. It seemed her dad's patience had waned, and he was demanding she get home.

Jasmine's chest tightened from guilt. She'd put this burden on her sister, which wasn't fair. She'd have to check in with him sooner than later, but she just needed a little more time. When Noah's palm nestled on her lower back, he interrupted her thoughts as he directed her toward the family room. Stretching out on the sofa, he offered his hand and tugged her against his side.

She rested her head against his chest, enjoying the strong beat of his heart. When his arm draped across her shoulders, the world melted away. Her body hummed with pleasure, and her mind raced with the anticipation of what might come next.

This man would always have a special place in her heart. Could anyone define how a relationship should start or progress? Life was unexpected and chaotic. She'd recognized that forever was earned, not granted, and every adventure started with a first step.

They had a connection that was worth exploring. In the end, no matter the outcome, she'd treasure the experience. All the secrets and questions they hunted would be waiting for them tomorrow.

NOAH'S EYES POPPED OPEN, and it took him a minute to get his bearings. The movie had ended and gone to a screen saver. Jasmine snuggled deep into his side, and her light snores told him she was out cold. Her inky lashes rested against her skin. She looked angelic.

He flipped his wrist to check his watch. It was almost one in the morning. A part of him wanted to let her sleep, but he needed to wake her so he could take her back to the hotel.

"Jazy," he said, nudging her body. "Hey, sleepyhead, it's late. Do you want me to take you back to the hotel?"

Her eyes fluttered open, and she snuggled even closer. "Not really. I'll sleep better here with you. Do you mind if I stay?"

Silly woman, didn't she know he liked having her here with him? "It's fine with me, but I want you to be comfortable."

"Oh, I'm right where I want to be, but there is one thing I've been wondering for a few days now," she said, treating him to a coy smile.

"What's that?"

"Did you like that kiss the other day as much as I did?"

He scrunched up his nose. "What kiss? I think you'll need to refresh my memory."

He barely had a chance to shift his body when her lips pressed against his. Soft and warm, she nibbled her way along his bottom lip. The part of her that fascinated him the most was that she was an open book.

When you asked her a question, she told you what she thought. When she wanted something, nothing stopped her. No games were being played. She put everything on the line, and he found that intoxicating. He angled his head and claimed her lips in a deep, long kiss.

When he pulled back, he glanced down, loving how her eyes were dilated, and her lips were swollen from his kiss. He'd tried to hold himself back, but that had only frustrated him. He wanted her in his life and by his side.

"I could become addicted to kissing you," he said.

She laid her palm on his cheek and reached up to kiss him again. "Yup, and I'm happy it was you who came to rescue me."

"I'm pretty sure you were about fifteen minutes away from breaking out of there on your own. But for what it's worth, meeting you was my favorite part of that ordeal."

She snuggled into his side, and before long, her breathing had evened out again. Since she'd dropped into his life, he'd found himself wanting to keep her close. Somehow, that fireball had altered his views on life and had him thinking about the future. Marriage didn't have to be in their future, but they could be together.

There was something magical about his Jazy. He needed more time to figure out why she had flipped his switch. She even had him contemplating every fail-safe he'd created for his life. Even then, he found himself adjusting his life and views to include her. Those realizations floated around in his mind like a sucker punch to his gut as he drifted back to sleep until the sun brightened the room.

She stirred beside him and raised her head. "Good morning. I slept great. No bad dreams."

"That's good, and the same to you," he said, unwrapping himself from her and stretching. He cut the motion short and grabbed his side with a wince. "I need a shower and coffee. You can shower in the spare bathroom. Do you want me to find you a pair of sweats and a T-shirt to wear until we can swing by the hotel?"

"Yes," she said. "I'd prefer to stay here with you. It also makes sense since we're working together, and it'll save some money."

"I'm fine with that, but if you do, full disclosure– I want you to know that I'm going to try to put the moves on you," he said with a wink.

He motioned for her to follow him down the hallway. When he reached his room, he opened two dresser drawers, removed a few articles of clothing, and handed them to her.

"Good God, I'd hope so," she said, exiting his room.

He stood there wanting to roar like a lion. He wanted that woman more than he wanted his next breath. All the blood in his body traveled south, making him as hard as a rock. So many ideas popped into his head, but he needed to slow down and do this the right way, which meant using his big brain. This mattered to him because he wanted to build on their relationship, not just have this be a quick hit.

After they showered and dressed, he took her back to the hotel to check out and then to Knotty Pine Tree to grab breakfast. The last stop before they headed home was the market. A trip to the grocery store had never held much appeal before, but he liked the thought of cooking together and hanging out. He couldn't quite wrap his head around the fact that he enjoyed sharing his sanctuary with her. When he'd left school, the first thing he'd looked forward to doing was getting his own place that would serve as his refuge.

Once they returned, he unloaded the bags from the car, and she put everything away. The doorbell chimed, so he turned to head in that direction. When he approached and opened the door, he greeted a delivery person and signed for a package from Guzman.

"Your identification is here," he announced, handing her a cardboard envelope.

"This is such a relief," she said, pulling the tab to retrieve the two items. "It's almost like that whole scary part didn't happen. Now, I need to get a new camera. Not having one around bothers me. When I get stressed or need a break, I like to explore and take pictures. You never know what you'll find."

"Like the Garcia cartel?" he said in a mocking tone.

"Exactly," she said.

She headed to the office, shaking her head at him as he trailed behind her. She logged into her email program and scanned the contents. "Okay, sitting and waiting for information to be compiled or delivered sucks. There's no email from the FEC. Do you think we should update our source and let them know that we've verified the 250 grand and are still working on others? At some point, we need to share what we've found out about Cynthia."

"Do the first, but hold off on the second. We need to arrange a meeting to find out more about who's pulling the strings. It needs to be a virtual call. I want to know more about this person, this family friend. I mean, what's in this for them? Revenge? Is it political?"

"That's fair, but I don't know if they'll agree," she said.

"Maybe we use the information on Cynthia as leverage to convince them to agree," he said, then returned his focus to several satellite images that he'd run through a program last night to enhance them. There were two in particular that caught his eye.

"Do you have a second to look at this? What I'm about to share is tied to national security, but I think you have a unique perceptive based on your experience in Mexico."

He flicked an image onto the big monitor and heard her sudden inhalation.

"Th-that's the man who kidnapped me at the market. They also drove black Range Rovers like those. Are they behind those weapons being taken? That means the Garcia cartel is involved."

Noah sent an email, then grabbed his phone to call Guzman. He'd finished his supposition. "Hey, boss, I just sent you two pictures, and my report will follow. It's the Garcia cartel. To what end, we don't know, but they took the weapons. Jasmine confirmed that they drive black Range Rovers like the ones in the satellite images you sent me to analyze, but more importantly, she identified one of the men in the photo as one of her kidnappers in Bonita Verde. He's the one who brought her to that prison."

"Fear and stress can just as easily obscure a person's memories as crystalize them," Guzman interjected. "How sure is she?"

Noah looked right at Jazy. "Zero doubts. She also identified him in the cartel file you had her review. Also, when I compared the purchase invoice to the bill of lading, only half of the weapons were on the truck. I called the company to get the reason, and they said it was due to production delays at the manufacturer. Garcia's men only jacked half of what was expected. I recommend that we monitor chatter in the area and check in with our assets to see what they're hearing. I also think we should set up a fake delivery, feed inaccurate route information through our normal process, and see what happens."

"There's no guarantee we'll catch who's behind the leak," Guz said.

"No, but it will prove the leak is real. It would provide a compelling argument to obtain warrants to review the phone records of everyone who knew about the shipment," Noah replied at the same time his phone beeped with another incoming call. The display read unknown caller. "Hey, I've got to take this call. It's all in my report."

He accepted the incoming call, hoping it was Waltzer.

"Why can't you follow directions like a good boy? I told you this is above your pay grade. Now, you've pissed off my boss. He didn't appreciate that you were searching for my military record. Imagine my surprise when he called me wanting to know who the hell you are and what you trying to dig up."

"It sounds like you survived," Noah said, his stomach queasy with unease. He'd wanted Waltzer to make contact, but now that he had, Noah felt like running in the other direction. Did he really want to know if his father had betrayed his mom and the family?

"I just told him the truth, that our paths keep crossing." Waltzer's nonchalant attitude irked him until he added. "I also mentioned that I respect you."

"Since you didn't give me your number, I had to improvise, hoping it would prompt you to reach out. My plan worked," Noah said.

"Well, you've got me," Waltzer said.

Noah froze for a second. What if he was wrong and they weren't half brothers? What if Cynthia wasn't Waltzer's mother? That the senator had forced her to go to England to handle an unplanned pregnancy.

Noah's mind raced with random thoughts and concerns. This was serious shit. Good God, there could be many reasons he'd been at the church that day. Noah had thought he was prepared for this call, but now he didn't know how to even start the conversation. His father was a selfish bastard, and the thought of having another person, a brother, witness his cruelty bothered Noah.

A simple touch from Jazy's hand had him lifting his gaze to her. She mouthed the words, "Stop analyzing and just tell him what you suspect." The warmth from her hand settled against his own.

"No bullshit, Waltzer, this is important. Why were you at that church?"

A long pause followed then, "This is off the record, Parker. I'm adopted, and I'm looking for my biological parents. My adoptive parents passed away, so I can't ask them these questions. I'm interested in medical history and that type of thing. Why?"

Noah scrubbed a hand over his face. "Your adoptive parents are Mindy and John Waltz. You're Darren Waltz, right?" He heard a woosh of air on the other end of the line. "It's a long story, but here's the nuts and bolts. Your birth mom is Cynthia Rosen. I think she had an affair with my father, Senator Michael Dubin, which means we might be half brothers."

"What the fuck? Repeat that?" Waltzer asked in low, measured voice.

Noah repeated what he'd just shared and added, "The senator will never admit to it, so we need to do a DNA test to prove or disprove this assumption. The only people who know this are you, me, and Jasmine. Trust me, shocked is a relative term. Considering you shot me, I'm not thrilled with this discovery."

"Shit, you're right because that would make me an even bigger asshole. No one wants to be the guy who shot his brother. What do you need, a hair sample?" Waltzer asked

"Yes, with the follicle attached on the end. We can use nail clippings as a secondary source. Send it to my home address," Noah said.

"I'm going to send you a number that you can use to contact me, but that's it. Don't use it to communicate any information. Ever. You'll have everything by tomorrow. I only ask that you don't go through the FBI. Use a third-party company. How long does the test take?"

"Agreed. Three days, give or take," Noah answered.

"I'll be waiting," Waltzer said before he ended the call.

The moment Noah lowered the phone, Jasmine followed with a question. "That sounded like it went fairly well?"

"I guess it did," he said, filling in the blanks. "I think we're both in disbelief."

"Now we know Darren Rosen is Darren Waltz, also known as Waltzer. That's a lot to process. How are you?"

"Relieved because the facts are on the table. I don't know what I hope the DNA test reveals. I wouldn't wish my father on another person."

"I hope we get the FEC records so we can see what that reveals, if anything," Jasmine said.

Noah rubbed his temples. The tension in his neck had crept upward to his head, which now throbbed. He needed some ibuprofen. His mind whirled with how he should approach his father if the test returned positive, which he knew was highly probable. That would mean that not only had the senator been a horrible husband who was estranged from his legitimate son, he'd probably also forced Cynthia to hide her pregnancy and put their baby up for adoption.

A darker thought crept into Noah's mind. Had his father gone the extra step to ensure Darren's mother would never leave the hospital alive so their love child would remain a secret?

A private hospital to handle delicate situations.

Seven

ON MONDAY MORNING, JASMINE awakened and showered and was surprised to see Noah already in the kitchen. Last night, he'd excused himself from watching television to work in his office.

Around midnight, she went to bed in the guest room while he continued to work. She'd been torn between wanting to bang on the door and invade his space and allowing him to process his feelings. Life never stopped moving forward. If you weren't careful, it could swallow you whole.

After breakfast, he filled out the form for the DNA testing company and prepared his samples. She watched him check his work three times while glancing at his watch throughout the morning. Instead of asking how he was doing, she decided to let him approach her, knowing that no one liked to feel pressured. Today was going to be painful enough until that package arrived.

She noticed her sister had left her another voicemail, and her stomach tightened. It was time to face her father and let her sister off the hook.

She unplugged her new phone from the charger and dialed Olivia. "Hey, sis, I'm sorry it's taken so long to call you back. What's up?"

"Plenty, thanks to your exploits. You need to call Dad. He will do something erratic if *you* don't check in with him. He wants you home," Olivia said.

"Okay, I'll call him, but he's not going to like what I'm gonna tell him," Jasmine said.

"No, he won't, but at least he'll hear your voice. It will also allow him to chew some hide from your backside. I think you've pushed him too far this time."

"I'm sorry, but I appreciate your support. I'm sure I have, but he's just angry because he can't control what I do, which bothers him. Dad won't be happy until I live down the street with a husband and 2.5 kids," Jasmine said in a sardonic tone. When she looked up, she saw Noah watching her with a frown on his face.

"That's not true—well, maybe a little. The good news is that our street has zero homes for sale. Come on, sis, you know he loves you, so he worries about you. He only wants his girls to be home and safe."

Her older sister always defended their dad. They were really two peas in a pod. She was more like the free-range chicken of the family. Her goals and wants in life were different, and she hoped that one day, her dad would understand.

"You win, but I'm telling him the same thing I told you. You both will have to trust me. I've got everything handled," Jasmine said, ending the call and dropping her head into her hand.

She hated that her sister was in the middle, but she needed time to focus on the job in front of her. A part of her also needed time to swallow her pride so she could talk to her overprotective father without losing her temper.

"A little family drama erupting over there?" Noah asked, leaning back in his chair.

"Yup, now the hardest call is coming."

"I'm going to point out the obvious here," he said, heading toward the door and stopping before he exited the room. "Talking to him probably won't change his opinion, but you know he loves you. His opinion isn't stopping you from doing what you love, but he knows you love him. So, just be *you* and focus on the important parts."

"That makes sense, and ignoring him isn't making this conversation easier," she said, her thumb scrolling downward on her screen.

He smiled. "Exactly. Do you want a drink?"

"Sure, a soda would be great." She moved the phone to her ear and took a deep breath. "Hey, Dad," she said as he answered on the first ring.

"Where the hell have you been? I want the truth. I know your sister is covering for you because she's a horrible liar."

Jasmine choked down a groan. "She didn't lie, Dad. My new project hit a few bumps, but I'm fine now. This assignment is complicated and requires my complete dedication. That's why I told her I couldn't talk until it's wrapped up. I also didn't want to hear all your objections."

The snap and grind from the lid of the cola made her look up into beautiful eyes the color of the Caribbean Ocean. She accepted Noah's offer and poured the liquid into a glass of ice he had brought to her.

"You're hell-bent on pursuing anything that keeps you away from your family in some ridiculous desire to prove some point to me."

His words hit her like a sucker punch. Sucking in a deep breath, she stiffened her spine, ready to give him a piece of her mind. "You and I will never see eye to eye on my future. I'm working on building a career that excites me. That makes me proud. I'm needed here because of my job. I'm okay and just wanted you to know I probably won't be able to check back in until it's finished. I love you."

After she ended the call, Noah sat on the edge of the desk next to her. "I only heard half the conversation, but it sounds like you handled it with dignity. Much better than I would have done."

"I had some good advice." She winked. "What good does fighting do? It makes me miserable, and we still end up on opposite sides."

"Team Jasmine will always be my choice," he said with a big smile. She'd noticed that some of his pent-up energy had abated.

He moved his right hand and placed an overnight envelope before her. "Guess what came while you were talking to your old man?"

"Holy cow. Open it so we can send it off to the lab," she said.

She watched him grip the tab at the top of the thin cardboard container and rip it free. He reached inside and retrieved a bubble-wrapped packet. A little grin escaped before she could suppress it. Waltzer and Noah had some commonalities already. Waltzer also labeled both samples with the sample type and initialed the tape on his sealed package like Noah had done earlier.

He carefully packed all four samples and the paperwork into the new package. Then, he ripped off the seal, pressing down to ensure it stayed closed, and added packing tape across the lip. All that was left was to initial the tape and mail it.

"You ready? I'm going to send this next-day express," he said. His long strides already had him clearing the threshold of the room.

She grabbed her phone and followed him to the garage and into his vehicle. They sat in companionable silence as he drove toward town. A handful of minutes later, he parked in front of the Mill Creek USPS.

"I'll be right back," he said.

While she waited, one of her favorite songs started playing, so she increased the volume. A small rap on the passenger window had her jumping out of her seat. When she turned, she saw a familiar face, but she couldn't quite find the name. She pressed the button on the door to lower the window.

"Hi, Jasmine. I'm sorry for startling you. It's Aimee," she said.

"Oh yes. Hi, Aimee. You're Clarke's better half, as Noah puts it."

Aimee's snort of laughter had her laughing, too. "Yes, that big boy is all mine, but he really is charming when he wants to be. Hey, everyone is having dinner tonight at Maggie's house. She's trying out a new recipe. You and Noah should come over. It would be fun."

"Sure, let me run it past Noah when he—"

The door to the truck swung open, and Noah slid in the driver's seat. "Hey, Aimee, what's happening?"

She smiled and waved. "I wanted to invite you and Jasmine to dinner at Maggie and Trent's house. She's making a new recipe, and there will be plenty for two more to join."

He touched Jasmine's arm. "You game?"

When she nodded, he replied to Aimee, "Sounds good, what time?"

"Six. I'll call her and tell her to expect two more. Don't forget to eat a hearty lunch," she said before she turned and walked away.

"What did she mean by eat a hearty lunch?" Jasmine asked.

He flashed her a lopsided smile. "Maggie is a beautiful person, but she's a horrible cook. Aimee has tried to teach her some culinary skills, but it's still a work in progress."

"Oh yeah, I remember now. It's sweet that she tries. Cooking isn't for everyone," Jasmine said, smacking herself in the forehead. "We can't come empty-handed. What should I bring?"

"How about we hit the market for wine and beer?"

"That will work, but I think we need to bring both white and red since we don't know what she's serving."

The rest of the afternoon flew past. Noah had to finish some work after they returned home, and she'd checked her email every so often see if anyone had bothered to respond. Instead of wasting time, she started drafting some ideas for her story with the information they'd gathered to this point. She glanced at her watch and realized they had about thirty minutes to freshen up before they had to leave for dinner.

"Hey, it's almost dinner time," she said, tidying up her workspace.

"Hold on, Guzman just sent the list of names of everyone who knew about that weapons shipment." He motioned for her to come closer. "Look, here's the list. What name stands out?"

She knelt so she could see the list of names. "Holy moly, your father's on this list."

He shook his head, a quirk in his lip. "Yeah, he's been the appropriations committee chair for some time. I didn't realize he also sat on the subcommittee for defense. I need to look into the names on this list. This puzzle keeps growing in size and scope. God, I hope he's not the traitor."

"Did your boss get the green light to access phone records?" she asked.

"Not yet. That's a delicate and highly complicated request. Most of the people involved will protest, saying it's a national security risk. It'll take some time and lots of meetings," he said, his face scrunched in disgust. "I do have another angle I'm working on, but it'll take a little time."

Her mind processed the latest tidbit of information. It wasn't something she'd write about since it fell outside her story parameters and went against the NDA she'd signed. Noah's job fascinated her. He had so much knowledge of situations happening in the United States and around the world. How did he turn it off and function? She'd be a basket case worrying day in and out.

She hurried to her room to change into a pair of stylish jeans and a soft sweater. On her way to meet him in the kitchen, she snatched her compact and lip gloss. She took care of that step on the ride over to Trent and Maggie's house. Once they arrived, Noah rested his hand on Jasmine's lower back and escorted her into the house. She liked how he always touched her in some way.

Laughter and chatter could be heard, growing louder the closer they got to the kitchen. When they crossed the threshold, all gazes landed on them. A mixed chorus of greetings was followed by hugs and handshakes. Aimee and Annika sat at the island, cheering on Maggie as she worked on dinner. The men disappeared to another room, leaving them alone to chat.

Jasmine placed the two bottles of wine on the counter next to the beer Noah had carried. The smell of cooked meat and seasonings made her hungry. "Maggie, is there anything I can do to help?"

"Not a thing. Aimee and Annika helped me set the table, and we're just about ready," Maggie said, even though she looked frazzled.

"How long are you staying here in Mill Creek?" Annika asked.

Jasmine added a wineglass in front of her. "Noah and I are still working on some things from Mexico, so I'm not entirely sure."

"Red or white?" Aimee asked, standing with a bottle of each in her hands.

"Red, please," Jasmine answered.

Aimee filled the other two glasses with the merlot and held hers up. Once everyone had their glasses raised high, she toasted the group. "To Maggie's culinary masterpiece and another great night with friends," she said, and the women all clinked glasses.

When the oven timer dinged, Maggie went to work getting dinner set up on the counter so everyone could serve themselves. In minutes, they had the meatloaf, baked potatoes, green beans, and salad ready to serve. She hollered for the men to join them, and in short order, plates were filled, and everyone took a seat in the dining room.

Trent pulled out Maggie's chair. "Looks good, baby," he said to his wife, kissing her temple as she sat.

"Don't let the food get cold," she said, adding butter to her potato.

The conversation lulled a little as the sound of forks and knives scraping across the plates took over.

"Maggie, you've impressed me. This meal is actually delicious," Clarke said with a big smile, but his eyes looked confused.

"Don't sound so surprised. And, maybe your wife helped me a little, but I did all the actual work," Maggie said, winking across the table at Aimee, her smile a mile wide.

"Thanks, Aimee," Trent said. "Maybe we should host weekly dinners so you can practice and learn to cook other dishes?"

Maggie shot a look at her husband that had him frowning. "Thank you for volunteering to do the dishes tonight and every night afterward."

Laughter erupted at the table, followed by funny stories and a little town gossip. Jasmine enjoyed the banter. It was obvious how much everyone cared about each other. They were a fun bunch, and if she lived in Mill Creek, she could see herself being friends with all of them.

Who was she kidding? She wanted to date Noah because he made her feel alive and supported her dreams. After dinner, Maggie and Aimee cleared the dishes and retreated to the kitchen. After several minutes, they returned with a decadent chocolate cake and coffee.

Noah draped his arm across the back of Jasmine's chair. The slight touch of his fingertips dusted her shoulders. She twisted her head and flashed him a smile. His simple touches warmed her insides and made her heart beat faster. Did he even realize he was doing this with his friends present? She glanced at Maggie and Annika to see if they noticed his gesture too. Not that she could tell, but if they did, she'd have some explaining to do.

Noah cleared his throat but didn't move from his position. "Since everyone is together, I want to share something. I trust it won't leave this table. It's only a matter of time before it becomes public knowledge, but I wanted all of you to hear it from me."

The room fell silent, and no one moved a muscle. All focus was directed toward Noah, including her own. "My father is Senator Thomas Dubin. We're not close, which is why I decided to take my mother's maiden name for my surname. I was born Michael Noah Dubin, but I changed my name to Noah Parker at eighteen. As you know, Jasmine is doing a story about the senator regarding his mangled family tree."

"What does that mean? Is he living a double life or something?" Clarke asked, his brows drawn together.

Jasmine folded her hands on the table. "We're in the middle of doing our research, but we've uncovered a few rabbit holes. My source claims to be a friend of the family and has provided information we've been able to verify."

"There's a strong chance my father has additional offspring roaming the earth. I'll know more in a couple of days."

Kane flattened his lips and shook his head. "That's difficult news to find out. If you ever want to talk, Noah, I understand very well that not all fathers deserve to be called Dad."

Trent exhaled. "Whatever you need, you let us know."

The table erupted into echoed sentiments of support. This had to be one of the reasons he considered this group his chosen family. They showered each other with unconditional love, support, and a healthy dose of sarcasm. They might not be blood, but they stood behind him.

"Appreciated. I should know more soon," Noah said.

When the night ended, he escorted Jasmine to his truck. The strength and unconditional love that had flowed around the table tonight had moved her. Like her family, this group had a strong bond, but the vast difference was unlimited support. That was what she shared with Noah—unconditional acceptance and support.

A surge of emotion flooded her system. This man at her side understood who she was and treated her like an equal. He valued her opinions and solicited her input. Driven by warmth and love, she cupped his cheeks and kissed him.

It wasn't a chaste kiss. It was a deep, hungry kiss that she poured her heart and soul into. Crackles of energy pulsed through her body. She needed him to know that she wanted him. That she cared about him. That he mattered to her. That he made her world brighter because they were a team.

When he slid his hand into her hair and tugged on her scalp, she moaned. He changed the angle of her head and devoured her, kissing her like she held the secret of life. He slid his other hand down her arm, stopping just above her elbow. His thumb stroked the side of her breast, and liquid need pooled in her center.

Sighing, he broke off the kiss and rested his forehead against hers. "You're incredible, Jazy. You ready to head home?"

She nodded. When he opened the passenger door, she slid into her seat and fastened her seatbelt tightly over her lap. Her lips tingled from his touch. Tonight had made her realize several things about her family and what she wanted in life.

Simply put, she wanted to be happy, to live within the parameters she defined for her life. If she and Noah could do that together, even better.

NOAH WOKE UP EARLY, wanting to get a head start on the day. He had an idea that he wanted to research. Last night had been perfect. He'd enjoyed having dinner with his friends, but the key component had been Jazy. Having her as a part of his life was as natural as breathing.

God, that kiss they'd shared had wound him up tighter than he'd ever been with another woman. Stepping away from her had taken a Herculean effort, but that wasn't the time or place to lose control. She deserved better from him.

After returning home, they shared another kiss but ended up in separate bedrooms. Deep down, he knew it was the right decision, even if he didn't like it. Jazy was worth the wait, and he planned to turn up the heat between them until he had her where she belonged in his life. Unsure what the extent of that thought meant, he decided to focus on the present moment. The next thing he had to do was take a cold shower to take the edge off his desire for a woman who'd taken him by surprise storm.

Once showered and dressed, he found a steaming cup of coffee and a plate of peanut butter toast on his desk. His fingers pounded on the keyboard as he accessed flight manifests stored on the FAA's servers. This idea had come to him last night. He could have gone through the proper channels, but he wanted to see if it would be worth the red tape. If he could link at least one of the members of the defense subcommittee to any trips to Mexico before or after the heist, it would give his boss additional evidence to support his request to access phone records.

The moment Jasmine entered his office, his body tingled. He was hyperaware of her presence and didn't need to see her to confirm that she was in the room.

"How'd you sleep?" he asked as she walked past him toward her computer with a cup of coffee in hand.

The wheels from her chair scaped across the floor. "A little restless at first, but then I slept like a baby." She glanced at him over the brim of her cup as she took a sip.

He flashed her a big smile as he enjoyed the flirtatious vibe. "There are several good ways to relieve tension."

Her eyes widened a moment before she caught herself. "Really? Speaking from experience here, or are you willing to share some tips?"

"Absolutely, it depends on the mood and person, but there are many ways. See, last night, I had to take a cold shower before even attempting anything as docile as sleep. You had me hard as a rock," he said, deciding to push the boundaries of this conversation.

The reddish stain creeping up her neck and cheeks looked adorable on her. "I worked a little magic of my own, and I believe it ended with me whispering your name as I came."

Holy shit, that admission made him hard all over again. He just got schooled by a very beautiful woman who drove him crazy. He adjusted himself, aware she had turned her focus back to her computer. The openness she shared with him not only surprised him at times but also relaxed him. She had no ulterior motives, and that was refreshing. Instead of saying anything more, he let her comment hang in the air between them, savoring the images he conjured before returning to his screen.

He finally found what he'd been looking for and downloaded the information to forward to Guzman. Only one member of both committees had traveled to Mexico City before the stolen shipment—Senator Martin Decker. He'd traveled to and from Mexico three times in two weeks. Now, Noah had to find out why he'd flown there and with whom he'd visited.

Jasmine gasped and clapped her hands. "Noah, look, I got the campaign records from the FEC. It covers May 1982 through to March of 1983 for both donations and expenditures."

"Cool, send me half of the files to analyze," he said.

The room fell silent as they reviewed every bit of data. It was amazing how many line items were keyed into these reports. The entries varied from dry cleaning to lunch and everything in between. She had her colored pens out and had started making notes. He preferred a paperless approach.

The crick in his neck made him roll his head from side to side to alleviate the pain. The rumble in his stomach made him check his watch. They'd been working for a while, and lunch had blown past.

He stood to stretch his legs. Walking up behind her, he gripped her shoulders and kneaded the tight knots there. Her small moan of appreciation hit him low and hard. "Need a break? We've been at this for a while."

She lowered her head, giving him more access to her neck and back. "Not when you're making me drool. Besides, I found something, but it isn't very clear. Did you find anything?"

Noah moved his hands to her neck, working in small circles. "Yes, the senator listed several travel expenses to London and Holmberry Hills in June, July, October, and February. He tied the trips to one of his campaign strategies regarding a fostering program for orphans from geopolitical hotspots. What did you uncover?"

"I found one withdrawal for $1 million in the beginning of July of 1982 from his campaign earmarked for St. Paul Hospital. So that's a personal donation of $250 grand, several expensive flights, and now a million-dollar withdrawal."

"That's something because campaign funds can't be used for donations. That would have to go through the appropriations committee and come from a different budget," he said.

She craned her neck to see him. "So that's illegal? What about the travel? That's got to be linked to Cynthia since the time frame would be during her pregnancy."

He nodded. "It's an obvious connection, but proving the purpose behind the flights will be difficult since he linked it to a political endeavor he openly discussed. The biggest find is the $1 million. Have you heard back from your source?"

"Let me check. I saw the email from the FEC and dove right in," she said.

Looking down, he watched her elegant finger tap the buttons on the keyboard. His mind whirled with the implications that his father had stolen money. His old man had his issues, but not once had Noah considered he might be corrupt. His stomach churned with apprehension. Was there any part of his father that was good? What the hell had he done with that money?

After a few seconds of scrolling, Jazy clicked something to display its contents. "Hey, my source replied."

They both read the message, and she broke the silence first. "They indicated that more payments were made around that same time, but it doesn't appear to come from the senator's personal accounts."

Noah pinched the bridge of his nose. "I looked, and he didn't make any other donations to that church after June in any amount, so your source's statement is correct. I also don't see a lump sum for a seven-figure deposit. We can't check under Cynthia's name since she's deceased. Let's review the files again and see if we can find a pattern—the same name or amount."

"What if someone else used that money to pay the hospital?" she asked.

Noah gripped the back of her chair. "This is the frustrating part of analytics. One moment you're so damn close to the answer, and in the next, you're miles away with more questions. No Scooby snacks today for a job well done."

The ding from his email alerted him that he'd received an email. He pivoted and sat back down at his desk. His gut clenched when he saw the message was from the DNA company. The results were in. He was about to find out if Waltzer was his half brother. If Noah's father had strayed from his marriage like his mom and her best friend speculated. Paying to expedite the results had paid off.

He closed his eyes for a few seconds and clenched his fists before he reopened them both. "The DNA results came back."

She stood and came up behind him so she could see his screen. "Already? Holy cow, that was fast. Do you want me to read it first? Or should I leave to give you some privacy?"

"No, we'll read it together."

He clicked on the file and flicked it toward the big monitor. He digested the chart and read the synopsis, fighting to contain his mixed emotions. His hand shook, and chills crept up his spine. The graph stared back at him, mocking his life.

All this time, he's had a fucking brother.

"Oh my gosh, Noah, what now? What can I do to support you?"

He had no fucking clue what he should do next. A rush of adrenaline burst through his body. He jumped up, almost knocking Jasmine over, barely able to steady her. "Sorry, but I've got to go—"

"No, I'm not leaving you alone. How about we take a walk or go for a hike? We don't have to talk, but I'm not leaving your side," she said, and her hand zipped out to grab his arm.

The only thing he managed to do was nod. They headed toward the front door. The sun was close to setting, so he changed course to the mudroom to grab their coats and a flashlight. He held hers so she could slide her arms into the openings, then slipped into his.

When they were outside, he locked the door and grabbed her hand. They set a brisk pace and walked hand in hand for close to an hour. Finally, the need to pummel something ebbed from his body, allowing his mind to work over every detail as they headed home.

Inside the front door, she turned and hugged him. "I can't imagine your or Waltzer's feelings, but I'm here for you. I'll kick anyone's ass for you, even your father's for being such a callous jerk. What can I do? Are you hungry? Want a scotch, or maybe the whole bottle?"

A laugh erupted from his mouth, surprising him. Jazy had made him laugh, not because what she said was funny but because she was willing to protect him. Her silent support empowered him to have his meltdown, while her strength kept him grounded.

They stood in his entryway, wrapped in each other's arms, and he had zero motivation to move. He liked how her soft curves felt against his hard angles.

Finally, he pressed a kiss to the top of her head. "I need to tell Waltzer. He deserves to know the truth. I only hope my father didn't have anything to do with his mother's death. I'll take two fingers of scotch and bring a glass of wine. We have a call to make."

When she returned with drinks, he motioned for her to sit beside him. He called his brother's phone, and his brother answered on the first ring. His voice resonated around the small space since he was on speaker.

"You have the results?"

Noah didn't answer the rhetorical question and didn't want to prolong anything. "Twenty-five percent match on both samples. We're half brothers."

Waltzer had to be in a nightclub because the loud Latin music in the background made it hard to hear him. "Daddy dearest is Senator Dubin––super."

"Yes, that's what this test is telling us. I won't be able to prove it beyond a shadow of a doubt until I get a sample from him. I had the lab retain a hair sample from each of us for a second test if I can get a sample from our father."

"A family DNA test. Fucking great. Don't expect to be on my Christmas card list," he said, then shouted to someone that he'd be right there. "All of this is need-to-know. I gotta go."

The call dropped, and so did Noah's stomach. He'd come to one conclusion. His father had some explaining to do. God, what if he was behind Cynthia's sudden death? Noah knew at a young age that his father was a piece of work, but he'd never thought it would end with anything like this.

He remembered how his father had chastised Noah for wanting to talk about his mom and sister. *They're dead; leave it be.* The next school year, he'd sent Noah away to boarding school so he could live without him.

A private hospital to handle delicate situations.

Paybacks were a bitch, old man. This time, they would talk. All of his pent-up anger would be unleashed while he peppered him with every question he had. If his father dodged or refused to anything, he'd just threaten to take it all public. That would motivate his father the most because his precious stature could be tarnished.

His father had no clue who he was up against, and Noah had his own reputation to maintain. Leverage was the key to this confrontation masked as a conversation, and filing charges on the misuse of campaign funds would hold his attention. It wasn't like his father expected jail time if he were convicted, but it would hurt his public image and make his reelection bid difficult. That in and of itself would be satisfying.

Eight

J ASMINE SHOULD BE HAPPY that her article was coming together, but instead, dread was a more accurate description of
what churned below the surface. Noah had already suffered from
a traumatic childhood, and now all these new revelations were
being slapped in his face.

Last night, after the call to Waltzer, Noah had guided her to the
family room and started a movie. They'd lain on the couch while
he held her. Neither had moved all night.

The next day, his demeanor was reserved. He'd focused on his
work and hadn't really said too much. She'd spent the morning
organizing her notes and creating an outline for the second part
of her story.

Now, she sat next to him as he navigated his truck into Clarke's
driveway. Noah had setup a meeting in his bunker at noon. This
meant Trent could join them during his lunch break.

"Afternoon, Jasmine," Clarke said, opening her door. "You
look like shit," he chirped at Noah, who flipped him the bird.

The crunch and pop of gravel told them Trent had arrived in his
official vehicle. In a matter of seconds, they entered Clarke's house
and marched down a set of stairs hidden underneath a trapdoor
in his laundry room.

Her gaze zipped around the space. Clarke had so many gadgets, including a computer with a large monitor. Above that was a row of three more monitors stacked double. There were also cages filled with weapons and supplies, including a large empty one. She wondered if that was supposed to be a holding cell but decided she didn't want to know.

Clarke's face radiated happiness as he spread his arms. "This is my command center, or as Maggie says, my Batcave. The most important thing to remember is it's not common knowledge—only you, Noah, Maggie, Trent, and Aimee know about my sanctuary."

When she nodded, Clarke continued with his overview. "My aunt had a bomb shelter built into the basement during the original construction. It has its own ventilation system, air filtration, and reinforced walls. It even has an emergency exit. I have everything in here for all types of situations. You can see my weapons locker, medical supplies, bug-out gear, food, and other gadgets I've acquired over time."

Trent smiled and took a seat at the computer. "Yes, he even has the entire property rigged with cameras, so don't ever trespass or toilet paper his house because he'll know."

Clarke folded his arms across his massive chest. "Why did I miss lunch with Aimee for this meeting?"

Noah ran his hand through his hair. "I wanted you both to know that Waltzer is my half brother."

"Shut up," Clarke barked.

"What?" Trent muttered. "That's not funny. He shot you and tormented Maggie."

Noah stared at the two of them, so Jasmine jumped in to fill the gaps. "Uh, it's true. We have a DNA test to prove it. The results were conclusive that Noah and Waltzer are related."

A heavy silence filled the room. Trent bent to rest his elbows on his knees. "Maggie's going to flip when she hears this. Have you confronted your father?"

Noah massaged his temples. "Nope, that's the next step in my plan. It gets worse. It appears that he used campaign funds to take care of the woman he knocked up. He wanted to keep his name and reputation away from a scandal. I just hope he didn't cross another line with his mistress. She died of a heart attack at the hospital in Holmberry Hill a month after she gave birth."

"Shit, man, that's a lot to handle. How did *he* take the news that you're his brother?" Clarke asked.

"I would say he's shocked, although he's not one to share his feelings or go into lengthy discussions," Noah said.

"Are you worried he may do something rash? Like go to your father?" Trent asked, concern written across his face. "He may not be directly responsible for Dalton's death, but he worked for the man who is."

Noah leaned on his forearms and steepled his fingers. "I trust you three with my life, so this doesn't leave the room. Waltzer is active in the military and does deep-cover operations. His lieutenant general got his panties in a wad when I started digging around too much on the guy. He's solid, even though that statement chaps my balls."

"He saved my life when he called Noah," Jasmine interjected in a low voice.

Clarke ran his hand over his bald head. "True, and he did only maim you that night instead of killing you. Truth be told, that shot was precise or maybe damn lucky, but I'd put my money on the first."

Noah put his arm around Jasmine. "You're both right, but he's inflicted damage along the way, but that's on his conscience."

"Collateral damage is a bitch when it's tied to a mission or assignment. It's something you never forget but learn to compartmentalize," Trent muttered. He rubbed his forehead. "I'm not sure Maggie will see it that black and white."

The risk, reward, and sacrifice these men and women made to do their jobs humbled her. It was not a career Jasmine would want or could handle day in and day out.

"So, what now?" Clarke asked.

"Jazy and I continue with our research. I wanted you to know the latest and give you time to digest it. If Waltzer comes to visit, I'm not sending him away. He's innocent of my father's bullshit, and I owe him a second chance."

Trent looked at Noah but didn't say a word. He had to be thinking about how Maggie would take the news when Trent told her. Jasmine wasn't sure how she'd feel if the man who'd kidnapped her in Mexico suddenly turned out to be part of her life. Clarke grabbed Noah's shoulder and tugged him into a brief, manly hug.

"Keep standing and fighting. We're here for whatever you need," Clarke said before he turned to hug her. "You're included in that statement. You've both been through a lot, but you're not alone. We watch out for our own."

The drive home happened in a blink of an eye. Jasmine's offer to make sandwiches allowed Noah time to eat while he worked. She removed four slices of bread and started to add the spread. On automatic pilot for lunch, she shifted her focus. It was time to email her contact requesting a face-to-face meeting. The information she'd gathered so far would serve as the bait.

It was a delicate balance because she didn't want to share all of it, but she also didn't want to risk losing her contact. She agreed with Noah—it was time to find out who this person was and learn what their intentions were. Since he planned on calling his boss to give him the news regarding Waltzer and the senator, the timing was right.

Two plates were balanced on her arm, and she held water bottles in her other hand as she headed toward the office. Once his turkey and cheddar on rye landed before him, he picked up half the sandwich and started eating. "Have you made your call to your boss?"

"No," he said, taking a bite and chewing.

"I had a thought, and it's a little extreme. Do you think that the hospital had a pay-for-death model? I don't know what else to call it. You know, medically speaking, a drug that could kill someone outright or make it look natural, like a heart attack? I mean, that place doesn't exactly scream high moral standards."

He took another bite and chewed. Then he washed it down with a sip from his bottle. "Yeah, that thought had crossed my mind. That's why I want to meet with my father. I want to interrogate him, express my disdain, and threaten his old ass. See what I can get him to admit to while we collect a DNA sample."

"How will you get him here?" she asked.

"Easy, I'll pique his curiosity by saying I may have something a tabloid would devour," he said and grabbed his phone.

She turned her focus back to her tasks and ate her sandwich. She sent off her email to her source and started to look at cameras online. When her stress levels were elevated, going out to find a subject to photograph calmed her. She immersed herself in capturing the raw and natural environment of whatever theme she had in her sights. Noah had been on his call for quite some time discussing the weapons situation, and by the time he finished, she had her camera ordered.

"Hey," she said, flashing him a big grin. "Long call?"

"Yes, my update on Waltzer and my father rendered my boss speechless, at least for a minute. Guzman agreed with my assessment that my father could be behind the leaked information regarding the weapons due to his position in Congress. Now I have some homework because he got permission to monitor the call records for everyone who sat on the defense subcommittee. We've got the green light to run the bait-and-switch operation. I'll be able to review the call records for the next forty-eight hours."

"What does that mean? I'm not up on my superspy slang."

Noah kicked his feet up on the desk and crossed his ankles. "The second half of the shipment is going to move in two days. It's being announced tomorrow. That should force the mole to make contact so they're ready to seize the weapons. I'll monitor the call records to see who makes an international call after it's announced. My money is on Senator Martin Decker."

"Why would you just give them more weapons?"

"We're not. That's where the switch comes into play. The trailer will be empty, but we'll watch on satellite coverage and a camera mounted to the trailer."

"Oh, got it. That's devious and doesn't put anyone at risk. Well, I sent the email to my source asking for a video conference so we can officially meet, so the ball is in their court."

"Perfect, now I have to call my father to get him to fly out to meet with me tomorrow. As the saying goes, I'll make him an offer he can't refuse."

She stood and perched herself on the corner of his desk. He dialed the number, putting the call once again on speaker so she could hear. It only took two rings before she listened to the senator's voice for the first time. It sounded oddly similar to Noah's, a little deeper and more gravelly.

"Son, what a nice surprise. I honestly didn't think you'd ever call me."

He rolled his eyes and pinched the bridge of his nose. "You mentioned you had a target on your back during our last call."

"Yes, but now isn't a good time for that conversation. Perhaps we can schedule a time we can talk without interruption?"

Noah fisted his hand on the desk in front of him. "I have a better idea. Why don't you come to Mill Creek tomorrow? We can talk in person. There's some information that's come to my attention that might enlarge that target. It's troubling and urgent we talk."

There was a long pause on the other end, and for a minute, she thought the senator might refuse. The sound of paper being shuffled and arranged came over the line. "I can clear my schedule. Do you want to move the meeting to Boise?"

"No, you should come to my house in Mill Creek. I'll text you the address."

"Okay, I'll see you tomorrow around one in the afternoon."

Noah ended the call and grimaced. "Well, tomorrow will be a whopper of a day. I haven't seen my father in many years. I don't even know the number off the top of my head. Anyway, I hope I'll be able to get him to purge his sins and admit what he did all those years ago."

Apprehension burned her veins at what could happen tomorrow. So much could go wrong, and he stood at the center of it. As far as she was concerned, he had the most to lose. His father obviously only cared about himself.

She hoped off the edge and turned his chair so she could straddle his lap. What she wanted was to show Noah that he mattered to her by giving him something to concentrate on rather than his pending meeting with a man he never called Dad.

"Make love to me, Noah Parker," she whispered, nipping his earlobe as she ground down on his growing length.

She loved his sharp intake of breath and how he'd hardened beneath her body. Even his eyes had dilated and darkened to a deep-cerulean blue. He was a gorgeous man with a heart of gold. The power that flowed through her body at her boldness, combined with his reactions, intoxicated her.

From the moment she'd met him, she'd been direct. She hadn't held herself back or hidden her intentions. Just like he didn't shield her or hold back. He treated her as an equal partner, and that was so sexy.

"Jazy, I'd love nothing more, but you must be certain. Once we go down this road, there is no turning back. I'm not looking for marriage, but you will be mine."

"And you'll be mine," she said, wrapping her arms around his neck. Nothing could be clearer in her mind.

In a fluid motion, he stood and carried her out of his lair and into his bedroom. Kicking the door closed with his foot, he slid her down his toned body until she stood at the foot of his bed. He stood a foot higher than her, which made her tilt her head upward to see his face. He rubbed the back of his knuckles down her cheek to her throat, then across her collarbone. Tiny bumps erupted across her skin, which made her shiver in anticipation of what came next.

"We may not have met under the best of circumstances, but I will never regret it. You have rocked my world," he whispered in a deep voice a second before he claimed her mouth.

His tongue dueled with hers until he stepped back and sucked in a ragged breath. His fingers traced the delicate softness of her lower lip.

NOAH WANTED HER NAKED and on his bed. Her uttered plea had left him speechless. He'd never wanted anyone this intensely. She was a fantasy and reality all in one package. The moment he'd witnessed her bravery and resolve, he'd been hooked. Her inner strength radiated brightly, and she did nothing half-assed. She was a worthy ally and partner who had slipped under his skin.

He'd developed feelings for his little ball of fire who didn't shy away from anything. She fought for what she wanted and spoke her mind unabashedly. All she'd done was utter four simple words, and it had unleashed a torrent of desire within his body. He wanted trace every square inch of her skin with his lips and tongue. Gripping the hem of her sweatshirt, he pulled it upward and tossed it off to the side.

Warmth radiated off her bare skin along with the subtle scents of orange and sunshine. Sliding his hand down her chest across smooth skin, and he went lower until he was running his fingertips along the edge of her waistband. A low moan escaped her throat, encouraging him to continue. His knees hit the floor in front of her, and he pressed his lips against her belly. He nipped, sucked, and licked his way up her supple skin until he reached her breast. His mouth sucked on her tight bud through the lacy material of her bra. Then he moved to the next.

"More, oh yes, more," she murmured.

Reaching around her back, he skimmed his fingers across her skin until he could unhook her bra. The lacy material slid down her arms and fell to the floor. This experience with Jazy had to be committed to memory because everything was perfect. She was worth the wait. He gazed at her with rapt hunger as he palmed each perfect breast, squeezing and tormenting each tight bud with his tongue and mouth. Her whimpers and encouragement to move faster fell on deaf ears. He wanted time to slow down so he could savor it for longer.

"Shh, Jazy, let me explore you. I promise you'll get what you need, but I'm in no hurry."

Her body quivered under his touch. Satisfied that she understood, he stood and pushed her backward onto the bed. He shed his shirt and discarded it behind him. Then he crawled over her, leaving enough room to tug her yoga pants and panties down her shapely legs. Her slender but toned frame made him feel like a giant next to her.

He pressed a kiss to her stomach and navel and nipped her left hip bone and then the right. His mouth trailed lower until he nipped the inside of her thighs with his teeth. A series of low, garbled sounds filled his ears, and a set of fingers gripped his hair. At her core, he pressed a kiss to her clitoris before flicking it with his tongue. When he added the pressure of his thumb to the mix, she thrust herself against his mouth, riding the edge of her rapture.

"You're going to kill me. My hands don't work like yours do. It's been so, so long, and this feels way too good," she said in a gravelly voice.

That admission went straight to his head. He wanted to be the only man who made her sing. Biting down on her tight bud harder, he slid to fingers into her slickness. The guttural noises that flowed from her mouth made him harder than granite. Determined to make her see stars, he kept up the movement. When her legs gripped his head like a vise, he knew she couldn't take much more.

"That's it, give me everything," he whispered, his body primed for the next step.

She clenched around his fingers and lost her control. Her hazel eyes glowed with satisfaction. She panted and twisted through every last aftershock. When her gaze locked on his, the slow smile she gave him heated his insides.

She threw her arms over her head with her long, dark hair bunched around her head. Her skin was flushed from her orgasm. Never had he seen such a beautiful sight. It was one he'd never forget.

"I need more skin. Plus, I'm dying to know if my fantasy will come true," she said, pointing toward his package.

"Trust me, you won't be disappointed."

She rolled her eyes in an exaggerated way and huffed. "I'm not taking about your penis. I want to know if you wear boxers or tighty-whiteys."

His deep laugh filled the room because her answer wasn't even close to what he'd expected. This was how things were with her—exciting, transparent, and unconditional. Now his control slipped with the need to be connected to this woman. Unlatching his belt, he pulled the leather through the loops, letting it snap in the air. Next, he forced his jeans down his legs, loving how her eyes sparkled with her surprise and lust.

His length bobbed and pointed directly at her before she found her voice. "I did not see commando coming, but I like it–very efficient, for an overthinker."

Palming his cock, he stroked himself from root to tip, watching her take in every movement. It was beyond hot, and the fact that she openly ogled him made his temperature rise even higher. She would never be boring, that was for sure.

"Sometimes underwear is overrated, but when I do, it's boxers all the way."

He crawled over her, kissing his way up her body until his erection almost poked her in the nose. The fact that she licked her lips and opened her mouth almost made him come right there. She was a natural wonder who lived life with boldness and innocence. He retrieved a packet from the nightstand drawer and placed it between her breasts.

Tonight wasn't about physical release. It was about something more profound than he'd ever experienced, and he wanted to brand himself on her forever. The warmth of knowing that she cared about him bubbled deep in his chest. It radiated like the brightest star, guiding him forward in a moonless night.

HOLY MOLY, SHE WANTED to pinch herself to ensure this wasn't a dream. She was about to do the horizontal tango with Cyber God! Unable to resist his rather sizable member as it bobbed in front of her face, she opened her mouth and sucked on his tip.

His head fell back with an audible moan, so she did it again.. A mesmerizing balance between velvety softness and hardness slid deep while she tongued the underside. He was so damn handsome with all his brains and muscles, but even sexier was his heart.

He moved his hand into her hair, lifting her head as he thrust his hips. She opened her mouth and took him even deeper. He didn't rush her or thrust too hard, but the pace curled her toes. This erotic image was worthy of a photograph—only for their eyes—but instead, she'd lock it away in her heart.

She never knew sex could be this mind-blowing. Her only other sexual experience she had been nice, but when she compared it to this, it sucked. And they hadn't even gotten to the best part. Yup, if she looked out the window, she had no doubt a rainbow arced over his house.

The grip on her head tightened, causing her scalp to tingle. Her eyes lifted to see a devilish grin covering his face. "I love that mouth, but I want to sink into your depths and never leave. Use it." He nudged his head toward the square packet on her chest.

In no time, she had the condom out and was rolling it down his erection. In only a handful of seconds, they would be joined together. They might never end in marriage, but she wouldn't complain because she was getting a piece of him. He scooted backward and made room for his body between her legs. The head of his cock rested at her entrance, and with a roll of his hips, he penetrated her. He paused long enough to lean forward and kiss her. A long, seductive kiss that made every nerve ending in her body tingle.

"Thank you for this precious gift," he said and thrust hard and fast.

She fisted the comforter behind her back and curled her legs around his waist. Every last thought in her head fled. Only blinding pleasure gripped her. Unable to hold back, she cried out at all these new sensations. Small ripples of arousal detonated deep within her core. Her muscles tightened, and a guttural moan ripped from her throat.

Oh, Noah...I can't believe...amazing," she rasped, panting between words, loving how sweat glistened across his shoulders and face.

"Just feel, let yourself float, Jazy," he said, hiking her legs higher and plunging deeper, driving her closer to the stars.

Meeting him thrust for thrust, a sensation of ecstasy washed over her. He drove her closer to the stars with each press. Energy burned between her hips, riding the line of her spine. If she didn't know any better, she would think she might just explode right here in his bedroom. Her body went liquid, and her soul shivered in contentment. Her orgasm was a blade that severed her from reality.

His movements slowed a fraction and seemed shaky right before he buried himself deep and stayed. Growling out her name, he collapsed on her, nuzzling her neck with tender kisses.

"There are no words other than spectacular," he whispered against her ear. He moved so he wasn't crushing her.

"That was the best sex of my life. We need to do this again. You know, to test that theory, or whatever you analysts call it," she said, wrapping her arms around him.

He bit the tender space between her neck and shoulder. "For sure, and that's just called a fact."

The moment he rolled away and off the bed, a sense of loss hit her squarely in the chest. She didn't like the feeling of emptiness. Oh man, she was in deep. When he returned from the bathroom, he scooped her up and pulled back the covers. Once they were lying nestled together, her world righted.

Yup, this might be a problem. Well, that was a thought to consume her brain on another day. Right now, she needed to focus on what was in front of her—or rather beside her. She curled into his body and closed her eyes, content and happy. All good things had to start with a first step, and so far, they'd shared many together.

Nine

J ASMINE LEANED AGAINST THE kitchen sink, needing a distraction from Noah. The tension in the house could make a volcano erupt. The pending meeting with his father rivaled that of standing in the center of a frozen pond with the distinct sound of a new crack hissing and popping. Her body ached in the most delicate of places, reminding her of how they'd spent last night. She grinned because now she had a whole new meaning to hump day.

They'd run to the PB&S earlier to get some sandwiches and salads. As soon as Noah had opened the door, her stomach had rumbled from the delicious smells of freshly baked bread. She'd met the owner, Lauren Granger, and loved how she'd decorated the inside as country chic with big chalkboard menus and fresh flowers in old milk bottles on every table. Jasmine's heart ached for the man who barely had a grip on his emotions as the time ticked closer to the senator arrival.

Now, as he paced somewhere in the house waiting for the confrontation, she watched the big puffy clouds move across a deep-blue sky out of the window above the kitchen sink. Even the pine trees dotting Noah's property were a bright green. When he entered the kitchen, she felt his energy bouncing off the walls.

A heartbeat later, he slid his hands around her waist and pressed his front against her back. Her body softened, and all she wanted to do was soothe his angst.

"I think you've got magical powers. Your touch calms me. It's like all the stress from the world melts away during these moments," Noah said."

Touched by his comment, she turned in his arms and laid her head against his chest. A small giggle escaped her lips, making her cringe because she didn't want him to misunderstand what had caused her reaction.

She lifted her finger and pressed them against his lips. "Before you ask, I feel the same way. This is different somehow and so intense at the same time."

His chuckle vibrated within his chest. "I can agree with that too. Thanks for making me laugh. I needed that."

"No matter what today brings, I've got your back," she said.

He didn't respond with words because actions always seemed to speak louder. He tightened his arms around her body, and his hug told her everything she needed to know. The crunch of gravel had them both turning toward the window. A black sedan approached the house. Her heartbeat against her chest, and her stomach fluttered.

She expected the real version of this man to appear more sinister, with horns coming out of his head. Instead, as his photos had detailed, Senator Thomas Dubin was an attractive older man. His gray hair was shorn short, and his physique was trim. The only thing betraying his age was his face. He had the same blue eyes as his son. If she were being honest, his father was attractive, and it gave her a glimpse into Noah's future because there was no doubt they were related.

He opened the front door after he made his father ring the doorbell. "Senator, you made good time."

"Son, it's so good to see you. You look good," the man said, holding his hand out to Noah.

He extended his hand for a brief shake. "This is Jasmine," Noah said, canting his head in her direction.

The senator's smile softened his features. "It's nice to meet you, miss," he said, taking her hand into his larger one and patting it twice. "Are you two an item, or whatever you younger people call it?"

Noah didn't provide an answer. Instead, he hitched his thumb toward the kitchen. "I have sandwiches if you're hungry. Would you like something to drink?"

A flash of disappointment washed over his father's face before he masked it. "That would be nice, but I could use a bathroom first."

"It's down the hall," Noah said, pointing behind them. "It's the first door on the left."

Noah strode toward the kitchen. She stood in the hallway as his father walked down toward the bathroom. Well, this was off to a great start. She followed Noah into the kitchen and helped him set the table and arrange the sandwiches. A few minutes later, his father appeared, and Noah motioned for him to take a seat.

"I've got soda, orange juice, scotch, or water," Noah said.

His father surveyed the room before sitting at the head of the dining table. "Your home is nice. Thanks for inviting me. Soda is fine."

Jasmine moved the assortment of sandwiches to the table, followed by the macaroni and potato salads. She'd let Noah handle the drinks.

Three cans were placed on the table before Noah sat opposite his father. "I'm still updating the house."

The kitchen was filled with an awkwardness that was difficult to describe. If she had to describe the mix of feelings, she would say there was apprehension, hope, and dismay. His father cleaned the rim of his can with a handkerchief before flicking open the tab.

Needing something to do, she slid into a middle seat and took half of the turkey, brie, and arugula with a balsamic jam. The first bite melted on her tongue from all the delicious flavors, but her appetite had waned from all the tension.

The senator returned his sandwich to his plate and swallowed his bite. Then, he turned a kind face toward her. "So, Jasmine, what do you do here in Mill Creek? How long have you and my son been together?"

She took a moment before she answered his question. Lying wasn't her style, but she'd only give the bare minimum. "Not too long. I'm mainly a freelance photographer, but I dabble with some writing projects. Isn't Mill Creek charming?"

The senator wiped his mouth on his napkin. "The town is modeled after the good old days of the past. I can't believe I'm eating a fried banana, peanut butter, and huckleberry sandwich. It's unique and amazing. I've never had fried bananas."

"It's a food lover's paradise. Wait until you try the Knotty Pine Tree. It's another culinary masterpiece."

Noah pushed his plate back and tossed his napkin onto his plate, his sandwich only half eaten. "I appreciate you coming on short notice. I'm sure your schedule is packed full, so I'll get to the point of my call."

"I think it would be best to discuss this matter in private," the senator said, tossing his napkin on his plate, then taking another sip from his can. The senator appeared casual and relaxed, but she'd bet his insides were churning at full speed.

Noah sat back in his chair, stretching his legs out under the table. "Jasmine knows what I want to discuss, so there's no reason to leave the table."

The two stared at each other for a matter of seconds, and a veil of dread fell over the kitchen table—thick and heavy. She almost excused herself but decided that wasn't fair to Noah, who wanted her to be a part of this discussion. Plus, this was her investigation.

The senator finally gestured with his hand. "Proceed, I'm all ears. What's so urgent?"

"I'm sure you're getting ready to start your campaign for the upcoming election cycle. I thought it fair to warn you that some information has come to light. It seems you had an affair years ago with a campaign assistant."

His father took that statement with ease, not even breaking a sweat. He was in full politician mode. The only tell she caught was the muscle clenching in his cheek.

"That's ridiculous, and that rumor is as old as I am. I thought you were a better analyst, but it's clear that you didn't do your research before wasting both of our time. I thought you had something important to discuss. Is this your doing, Jasmine? Are you trying to worm your way into my son's life with lies? Let me guess, you're a journalist trying to make a name for herself?" he asked, shaking his head in disgust as his gaze went between them both.

She cringed at his words and demeanor but wouldn't back down. "Yes, and I can assure you the research is thorough. As for Noah and I, we're partners in this endeavor, so––"

"You don't get to toss out insults. As for research, let's see if any of these clues will ring a bell in your righteous mind. Holmberry Hills and Cynthia Miller, or Cynthia Rosen, since she used her mother's maiden name. That's the name listed on the adoption record. I know about the son you forced her to give up."

The senator pointed at Noah. "How dare you insinuate that I'd cheated on my wife, your mother, whom I loved."

Noah shook his head in denial. "I'm not implying anything. I'm pointing out facts. You sent her there to hide the pregnancy, forced an adoption to keep your image squeaky clean, then Cynthia died of a heart attack. If I had to guess, which I'm not, the going price for that type of problem solving is $1.25 million."

Jasmine sat forward. "The best part is the one million was withdrawn and earmarked for St. Paul Hospital from your campaign funds. That's illegal."

"Do we have your attention now?" Noah asked.

The senator crossed his leg and folded his fingers around his knee. The pose was regal and confident. "Random facts can paint an inaccurate picture unless you have all the facts. I would have thought that'd be lesson one for the FBI. Cynthia took the money from my campaign before she left for London. She knew the rumors were circulating and didn't want to add to the drama or risk the press assuming the child was mine. I think she chose Holmberry Hills because of my work. I flew across the pond to meet with her several times to get her to return the money. I filed an official incident report to ensure I complied with our policy and procedures."

"I wasn't aware you'd filed a report. That's very upstanding of you. I'm sure your peers and constituents appreciated your candor and transparency," Noah said. "I met your son. And before you say anything, I have a DNA test proving that we are, in fact, half-siblings. So, I guess those pesky rumors are true."

She itched to grab Noah's hand but wouldn't in front of his father. His composure and strength while he navigated this conversation were impressive. Her heart beat hard against her chest as she waited to see if his father would finally admit the truth. Her family had its issues, most stemming from her own wants, but they were nothing compared to this type of betrayal. Noah's head turned toward the kitchen window, and she saw his chest expand in a slow, steady manner.

After an excruciatingly long pause, his father responded, "Darren Rosen is my son. I regret many things about my marriage, but I need you to know that I loved your mother. "His raspy voice was filled with an emotion she couldn't label. "What does Darren want? Is he threatening to take all this public?"

Noah snapped his head back toward his father. "Are you that cold of a bastard? You just admitted you have another son. The first question you ask is what does he want? Not, is he okay? Or, am I okay? Nothing that demonstrates compassion or responsibility, only how this nugget of truth could hurt you. Well, fuck you."

The senator stood and ran his fingers through his hair. "Now you have your answer. I think it's best if I go. I'll see myself out."

She saw Noah's father turn and walk toward the front door without so much of a glance over his shoulder. Noah sat motionless while his father walked out of his life again. Leaving a trail of devastation in his wake.

The silence stretched between them until his father's car engine turned over, followed by the crackling of gravel underneath the tires. There were no words she could utter that would help. Instead, action was what drove her. She enveloped him in a crushing hug.

"Now you've met my father," he said, grabbing her arms. "He's a gift that keeps giving."

She pressed a kiss to his cheek. "He's in a league of his own, that's for sure. I don't know if I would have been able to keep my composure like you did. You're impressive."

"I've had years to perfect it," he said, tugging her into his lap. "The part that bothered me the most was his comment about loving Mom. All I remember is how much they fought. She was not a happy woman in that marriage. How could that be love?"

"At least we don't have to send in his saliva sample to the lab. He admitted it."

"Yes, but I'm still going to do it. It won't hurt to have ir- refutable proof. Since I had the lab retain hair samples, it just makes sense to do it."

"Do you believe he filed a report on the funds Cynthia suppos- edly took?"

"There's no doubt in my mind he manipulated the system for his gain. Obviously, the issue was closed out and never went public. That sucks because I was looking forward to filing those charges against him."

"What now?" she asked, resting her head against his shoulder.

"We wait for your source to respond and hope they agree to a meeting. We'll share our information and see if they have any more items to share regarding this mangled family tree. Tomorrow, I'll have all the phone records on the members of the defense subcommittee."

"What about for the rest of today?" she asked, wiggling on his lap and giving him her best bewitching smile as he hardened underneath her.

He nipped her nose. "Are you trying to seduce me, Miss West?"

"It depends. Is it working, Mr. Parker?" she demurred.

"Mmm-hmm," he said right above her mouth, his breath warm against her lips.

"Then, yes, I want to get in your pants."

His laugh made her grin right before her world went upside down. He flipped her over his shoulder and strode toward his bedroom. She smacked his back, demanding that he put her down. He reciprocated with a smack to her bottom.

Great, now she'd unleashed the beast inside this man. She couldn't wait to see what he had planned. Tomorrow, he could put his cape back on and save the world. Tonight, she wanted the beast.

T HE FOLLOWING MORNING, NOAH scooped up his cellphone on the second ring, happy for an interruption. He'd been working on the call records for two hours. "Hey, Aimee, what's up?"

"Sure, hold on a second. She's sitting right next to me," he said into the phone before pressing the speaker button so Jasmine could hear. "Okay, we're both here."

"TGIF, you two, tonight's Friday Fresh at Two Stepping Bar and Grill. It's the best night to go because they showcase local bands. It happens on the second Friday of every month. We're all heading over. Wanna join us? We'll be there at 6:30 PM. The band starts at 7:00 PM."

Jasmine's eyes twinkled. Her enthusiasm was palpable as she waited for his reaction. How could he deny her? He gave her the thumbs-up, and the sheer joy that radiated across her face warmed his chest. He liked making her happy.

"Count us in, Aimee. Thanks so much for inviting us. What do you all wear? My wardrobe is a little limited at the moment," she said.

"It's a casual environment. Maggie, Annika, and I will probably wear jeans. The only fashion diva of the group is Kane. He'll wear some sort of dress pants and an Oxford. Unless Annika puts her foot down and makes him wear jeans. He's learning, poor guy. He struggles with taking the New York City out of his wardrobe. We all think he had tailor-made diapers because he's all glamor and style." A hint of a giggle leaked through her words.

Noah laughed. Jasmine leaned closer to the phone so the speaker would pick up her voice. "Jeans, I can do. We'll see you there."

"Is Kane stuffy? Because I've never gotten that impression," she asked after she ended the call.

"No, but his family is another matter. He comes from old money—like with servants and drivers. But he's different. Do you want to take the truck and head to Rayna's to buy something for tonight? We've been holed up in this house all week."

"I appreciate the offer, but I'm fine. I just didn't know if the girls wore dresses and stuff. Can I help with the records so you can finish before we have to leave?"

"No need, I'm running an algorithm to parse the data into country codes and prefixes. Then, it'll be sorted by each person's number. Once that's finished, I'll deep dive into any calls made to or from Mexico. This will be ready in no time. It was getting the records that took forever."

"Does your job ever depress you? I mean, how do you handle all the bad stuff that the rest of us are oblivious to?" she asked, her eyebrows scrunched together.

"Sometimes, especially when we lose agents. You learn to compartmentalize while reminding yourself that you're doing this for the greater good. "Check this out, it's ready. This list goes by subcommittee member and is separated by country code and so on."

They scanned the list together. "I'm only seeing two people who made or received calls from the Mexican country code. My father received a call and made a call from this number earlier today." He pointed to the screen. And Senator Decker made three between yesterday and today."

Noah opened another window and started to search the phone numbers to see who they belonged to.

"Isn't Senator Decker the one who also traveled to Mexico recently?" she asked.

"Yup, you're right. His calls were made to a man who works at the embassy and one to a restaurant. My father's calls were to a lawyer, Miguel Reyes, who works for the Embassy of Mexico in DC. But those happened today, so that technically eliminates him as the traitor. The next logical deep dive would be Decker because of those recent trips to Mexico. We still don't know who tipped off the cartel about the weapons, but we should see why Decker traveled to Mexico just to be sure."

She tapped a pen against her lips. "At least it wasn't your father, but he did miss the meeting that spread the false data when he traveled to meet with you."

"I agree with you. Now, I need to send this to Guzman. He gets the fun of explaining and finding out how to proceed. At the end of the day, we still have a leak."

"Maybe the person responsible wasn't at the meeting or got cold feet," she said.

Noah opened his email file and typed a message. "My boss makes the big bucks, so he'll have to push a little harder to get the clearance to do a deep dive into Decker. At this point, he's the best lead based on the limited data."

"Right," she said, then she got up and headed toward the door. "I'm going to shower and get ready. It'll be nice to get out and have a little fun."

Once Noah backed up his data and sent his findings to his boss, he powered down his system. His mind rolled over her question. Had his father missed the new shipment window because of his trip there?

Noah couldn't see his father deliberately hurting the country he loved and had served for so many years. This was why Noah hated doing half-assed analysis. Partial information meant you weren't seeing the bigger picture. Not being able to review the phone records for the past month like he wanted meant he was trying to stab a fish in a pool with a spoon.

WHEN NOAH AND JASMINE entered Two Stepping, the place was packed. He glanced around the room until he saw Clarke standing toward the front. It helped to have tall friends when you were trying to find them in a crowd.

Noah laid his palm against Jazy's back, steering her toward the group. Having a chance to unwind with his friends while sharing some laughs sounded pretty damn good. Not to mention dancing with Jazy would be fun.

"Hey, everyone," he greeted Clarke, Aimee, Kane, Annika, and Maggie while the girls hopped up and hugged Jasmine.

After all the hellos and hugs, the women piled back into the booth, leaving the men to stand around the table. Girl talk had taken over the table, so he turned his attention toward Clarke and Kane. "Where's Trent?"

Clarke flicked his wrist, checking the time. "He had a conference call pop up that he had to take. He should be here soon. We picked up Maggie on our way here."

The band began their warming up routine while Noah and the other guys ribbed each other and eavesdropped on the women, who were talking in full animation. Jazy fit right in like she'd known them her whole life. That was one of her skills. She could adapt to any situation.

Noah turned in the direction Clarke pointed toward to see Trent approaching the group. His first stop was to give Maggie a big kiss. Noah envied his friends in that moment because they'd found the women who made them happy and were building their lives together.

Noah didn't begrudge their happiness, so why did he suddenly want what they had? That thought confused him. He always avoided that road because wanting a wife and family would make him face his deepest fears. It was easier to avoid it altogether because his head and heart had different opinions.

He shared the same DNA as his father and mother. Both had made a mess of their marriage, and if he listened to the news, his mother was unhinged, and his father was narcissistic. So, where did that leave Noah? Both his parents possessed the skill to manipulate. He was destined to fail. It was in his blood.

The lights illuminated the stage, and the band launched into their first song. It was an upbeat number that had the dance floor filling fast. Aimee, Maggie, Annika, and Jazy flew past Noah, holding hands to claim their space. Sheer pleasure radiated off each of their faces, and they twisted their bodies and worked their assets on the floor.

"What's the latest?" Trent asked, taking a seat at the now-empty booth.

Noah told them the latest from his meeting with his father. He also stepped back to fill Kane in on his half brother.

"Did the senator shit himself when you laid it all out for him?" Clarke asked.

Noah rubbed his forehead. "No, but that would have been satisfying if he hadn't been sitting in my house."

"Good point. No one wants foreign poop in their chair."

"Uh, I'm pretty sure it's just no poop, like ever," Kane said.

The men laughed, and Kane flagged down the approaching waitress. He ordered the first round for everyone—beer for them and wine for the ladies.

"Jasmine's very cool. Are you two doing it?" he asked, dodging an incoming elbow from Trent.

"Um, seriously, if I were, I wouldn't tell you," Noah answered, giving them his best what-the-hell expression.

"Wait," Clarke said. "Dude, did you just say *doing it*? Are you ten?"

Clarke and Kane held their hands to Trent, who pulled two twenty dollar bills out of his wallet, then threw one at each of them.

"You three fucking bet on if I'm having sex with Jazy?" Noah spat out.

"Oh, hell yeah, and we were right," Clarke said, slapping Noah on the back before doing some strange dance move. "Trent said you wouldn't mix business and pleasure, but we knew better."

When a slow song started, the women returned, and one by one, they dragged Kane, Trent, and Clarke toward the mass of sweating bodies. Jazy stood in front of Noah with flushed cheeks and a goofy smile. She'd extended her hand and asked him to join her.

Yup, all she had to do was ask, and he'd deliver whatever she wanted. Once they stood in the center of floor, he circled his arms around her warm body. He snuggled close to her, not caring that his friends were watching him. This was his girl, and he had no reason to hide his attraction from anyone.

She grounded him. She also scared him. Because for the first time in his life, he wondered if he could do marriage. Or would they follow the same path as his parents?

When this song ended and another slow number started, he shoved all those thoughts out of his mind. All Noah wanted was to enjoy the slow, sweet torture of having her soft curves plastered against him.

They moved rhythmically to the beat of the music. Tomorrow would come soon enough, and he'd have plenty of time then to figure out why she somehow challenged all his convictions.

Ten

Jasmine fiddled with her hair as she scanned her inbox. She'd made plans to meet Annika, Maggie, and Aimee at the Knotty Pine Tree because it was Saturday, which meant Sally's famous fried chicken. Why couldn't these women live in Chicago? Her sisters would adore them. Maybe the better question was if Jasmine could live in Mill Creek.

She'd only known the girls for about a week, but it seemed like she'd known them her whole life. They clicked and even shared similar interests, and somehow, through all of this, the friendships were organic. These women were sincere and protective of their family and friends, qualities she admired. A deep dart of longing hit her square in her chest because she missed the chaos of her family—even her overbearing father.

Last night had been so much fun. She'd seen how life could be in Mill Creek if she and Noah were a couple. The only thing that nagged her was that when they returned home, she sensed that he was preoccupied because he'd distanced himself from her. Had something happened at the bar last night, or was the strain of all these events weighing on him?

Her mind focused on one email that made her stomach flutter with butterflies. She didn't want to interrupt him because he had an interdepartmental high security meeting this morning. She'd taken her laptop to the family room where she could watch her favorite morning game show and work. The screen on her laptop darkened as it went to sleep.

When the snick of a door opening grabbed her attention, she turned to watch the hallway. Soon, she heard the shuffling of feet right before Noah wandered into the room.

"Is your meeting finished or are you just taking a break?" she asked.

He sat next to her and laid his head on the back of the sofa. His deep exhale worried her. When his hand landed on her knee, he squeezed. "A bank robbery went south. Two of the five men escaped. One entered an empty elementary school playground and was quickly apprehended. The other man went to the streets, so the FBI wanted all available analysts to scour surveillance and traffic cameras to find him."

"And?" she asked, seizing his hand.

"He's being apprehended now," he said, rubbing the bridge of his nose with his free hand.

She scooted off the sofa and looked back at him. "Two or three ibuprofen tablets?"

"Two, and you're an angel. Thank you."

When she returned, his eyes were closed. She put a bottle of water with his two pills onto the coffee table. As she turned to leave, he snaked out his hand and snagged her wrist. Her heart fluttered at his touch.

"Don't leave," he said, "I'm just resting my eyes. What time is your lunch with the girls?"

She looked at her watch. "In forty-five minutes. Are you sure you don't mind me taking your truck?"

"Nope, but you could always surprise me by bringing home a Saturday special."

"Do you want to have that for dinner tonight? I can get something else to eat and bring you a true surprise?"

His eyebrows lifted. "I like surprises. If you're willing, that's a great idea." His child-like exuberance made her laugh. He was such a handsome goof who made everyday life more fun. "I'm pretty sure you're thinking with your other brain. As for the big one on top of your head, I'll bring home food."

"And dessert. You should never desert dessert," he said with a wink.

"Oh, I almost forgot, my source replied and is willing to meet. I offered to send a video conference request for tomorrow at ten in the morning. That way we can get their IP address, and you can do your superspy stuff."

"You hear it, don't ya, the theme to *Inspector Gadget* playing in the background?" He hummed the tune briefly before chuckling. "Good job, and that kind of rules out criminal intent, so that makes me feel better. I'll look up their geolocation. Have fun at lunch. Guzman has new orders on this weapons situation, and I have to wrap up my surveillance report from this morning's madness. I'll see you when you get home."

JASMINE SCORED A PARKING space right in front of the diner. She hoped out and opened the door, remembering the first time Noah had brought her to the diner to meet his friends. It took her eyes a moment to adjust from the bright sunlight. She saw the girls in a booth in the back.

Annika and Aimee waved their hands, and Jasmine went over to them. As greetings were exchanged, she slid into the booth next to Maggie.

Sally rushed over to the table and pulled up a chair to sit on the end. "I'm sensing a gossip session. What's happening, ladies?"

"Trent and I are good, still working at growing our family. I hope I get pregnant soon," Maggie said, making a pouty face.

Sally grabbed Maggie's hand. "It will happen when it's time. I have no doubt, sweetheart."

Maggie squeezed her hand. "Thanks, Sally."

Annika added her hand to the stack. "You two just need to practice more, but it will happen. Kane and I are flying back to New York tomorrow to finish some holiday shopping and to visit his brother and niece."

"How long will you be gone?" Aimee asked.

"We'll be back the day before Christmas Eve. We want to invite you all over for dinner and carols. It'll be the first one in our new home," Annika said, with a big smile plastered over her face. "Sally, this invite extends to you and Peter, and to Irene too."

"Oh, how sweet. I'll ask Peter and get back to you. It should be fine since we close the diner at noon that day. Your invite will also make Irene's day. She loves any holiday and gets a little sad around them since her husband died," Sally said.

"That's for sure, and it's why I love my big boy more every day. He assisted Irene with Halloween decorations last year, and it's going to become a tradition and not just for Halloween. He's taking Irene shopping for a real tree. Then we're having dinner at her house to begin a decorating tradition," Aimee said.

"And to think those two were archenemies." Sally giggled.

"Why, she's so nice?" Jasmine asked.

Aimee snorted. "That's a l-o-n-g story, but the gist is that Irene can be a bit of a busybody. She thought Clarke had some unusual tendencies and might associate with criminals."

The table erupted into laughter, and Sally stood and pushed the chair back. "Okay, ladies, give me your orders."

She efficiently went around the table, capturing every detail before she dashed toward the computer to input everything. Silverware, iced teas, and one lemonade were dropped off a few minutes later. Jasmine unrolled her utensils and placed her napkin in her lap. Aimee and Maggie asked Annika what they could bring on Christmas Eve, and a pang of regret hit Jasmine squarely in the chest. She wouldn't be at that dinner, and she wanted to be.

Aimee leaned forward and pointed at Jasmine. "We had an ulterior motive for inviting you to lunch today. We–"

A lump formed in Jasmine's throat at the intimidating remark.

"Don't get us wrong," Maggie said, momentarily speaking over Aimee. We wanted you here because we enjoy your company, but on the other hand, we worry about and protect our extended families."

"Sorry, I sometimes forget to add the fluff. I'll blame that on Clarke. His gruffness is rubbing off on me," Aimee said, flashing Jasmine a lopsided smile. "Are you using Noah for additional information about his father? We all sense some vibes about you two, but we don't want to see him be manipulated."

Jasmine couldn't be mad at either of them for asking that question. They were protecting the people they loved. Hope bloomed in her chest from their comment. She tried to remain optimistic that Noah would change his mind about marriage, but a realization dawned on her. Why did she have to be married? If they loved each other, everything would sort itself out.

Was marriage her father's ideal, or was this her hard line? Could she live with a man and see how it went for however long it lasted? Let time and their love sort itself out? "No, I've been upfront with him from the beginning. I feel horrible because this information has hurt him. We met by accident, and if I'm honest, I've fallen for him. Could you imagine if we ever became an item? The whole how'd-you-meet conversation would be epic."

"That's what we all thought, but you know, we still had to grill ya," Aimee said.

Annika took a sip of her tea and swallowed. "At times, you really do remind me of Clarke, Aimee. It's a little scary."

"Well, it hasn't escaped our notice that Noah seems very interested in you. All his touching and how he calls you Jazy," Maggie said with a whimsical note to her voice.

Annika let out a catcall whistle. "I like the idea of our group growing by one. You stay after him and don't let him hide. Our men seem to have jaded ideas about love at first. All you need to remember is that, at times, you'll have to fight for what you want. Or withhold sex until you get their attention."

Jasmine laughed and thought that maybe she should take Annika's advice. "Annika, you just surprised me. I thought you were the nice, reserved one of this group."

Maggie leaned into Jasmine. "God, no, she's the inner voice we need to hear sometimes."

Aimee laughed before she lowered her voice and added, "If the other suggestion doesn't work, I've found that withholding sex until they are willing be more agreeable. You could say it gets them focused and listening."

The table erupted into giggles just as Sally appeared, her arms loaded with plates and condiments in her apron pocket. Once all the dishes were handed out, she went to grab a pitcher of iced tea and lemonade to refill everyone's drinks. "Enjoy, ladies."

Jasmine's phone vibrated. She grimaced when she flipped it over to see who had sent her a message. It was a text from her older sister. *Heads up, Dad is on the war path. He expected you home days ago. When are you planning to come home? It's only thirteen days until Christmas. Miss you and love you!*

"Everything okay?" Annika asked, her voice showing her concern.

"Yeah, it's a text from my sister. My father wants to know when I'll be home. He's not a fan of me traveling alone or being away from home. I guess you could say we're going through a rough patch. It's my fault, but if I don't stand up for what I want, then I'll always be miserable." Jasmine made a mental note to text her sister after lunch because heading home wouldn't happen until she wrapped up her story.

Putting her phone down, Jasmine lifted her glass of tea, and when Maggie, Aimee, and Annika followed, she toasted her friends. "You're the best, and I love that you've included me in this family. Which I promise to protect. Someday, I hope to introduce you to my family, especially my sisters, because you'd love them."

A chorus of clanks followed before everyone returned to their food. They ate, laughed, and shared stories for the rest of their meal. Jasmine learned more about their pasts and how they'd met their men. Maggie also shared what happened to her and why she was so leery of Waltzer.

Annika shared a bit about her past, but most of her stories focused on Kane. Aimee listened attentively and occasionally threw in a funny story about Clarke. This eclectic group of women was strong and supportive. Their camaraderie brought a smile to her face and made her miss her sisters. Why couldn't her father meet her halfway?

Time had flown, and she wished she could stay longer, but she needed to get home to prepare for tomorrow's call with her contact.

S UNDAY MORNING CAME MUCH too quickly. Noah had gone to bed alone after working late into the night. His love for his job motivated him, but it wasn't a nine-to-five, Monday-through-Friday gig. His muscles were tense and protested every movement from a restless sleep. When he rolled his neck from side to side, it helped a little, but what he needed was aspirin to stop the dull headache he had from progressing.

He wanted this damn call over with already so he could see who was behind the exposé. The unknown bothered him because more unsavory fun facts about his family could be revealed that he didn't know. This whole thing sucked.

The other thing chapping his ass was the more time he spent with Jasmine, the more his heart and head were at war with each other. A part of him didn't want to let her go, but the other half didn't want to make the same mistakes as his parents. In the end, they were a caustic pairing, and he shared their DNA, so anything was possible, and not recognizing that would make him an idiot.

What was love? A marriage certificate didn't guarantee a happy ending. Even if you thought you had a grip on the abstract emotion, it could evaporate, leaving devastation in its wake.

Jazy strolled back into his office, dressed and ready for this video conference with her source. There was nothing she wouldn't try, and her confidence was sexy. They arranged her workspace to be nondescript. Her attention to detail never ceased to impress him, right down to the impressive list of questions she'd prepared for the call. He reviewed how to mirror her monitor so he could watch the exchange without announcing his presence.

"You ready to do your spy magic?" she asked, turning back to look at him over her shoulder. She started the conference and shared her screen.

"Yup," he whispered, watching Jasmine as she stared at the monitor, waiting for the other person to show up.

They sat in silence for eight minutes past the meeting time. Just as she was about to terminate the connection, a woman wearing a Mardi Gras mask that covered her from forehead to upper lip appeared. "I'm sorry I'm late. I had a slight distraction, but I'm finally alone now."

Jasmine smiled to reassure the woman. "No worries, things happen. Thanks for meeting with me. As you are aware, this story is unique and targeted, and it could impact a man's career and reputation. Understanding why this is important to you and being able to meet you is important to me."

The woman suddenly twisted her head to the right before returning to the camera. In a lower voice than she had started the conversation, she answered, "I have my reasons. The most important thing is that Senator Dubin must be held accountable for his actions. He can't just ruin people's lives and get away with it. Decisions and actions have consequences."

Jasmine took a second to jot down her response in her notebook. It would be a good quote for her story. "Do you have any other information you want to share?"

"Maybe, but I want to hear what you've learned first."

"That's fair, but I want you to know that the more you can share, the stronger the story will be. So, back to your teaser about the mangled family tree. He has an illegitimate son from an affair with Cynthia Miller, his—"

"Campaign assistant from early in his career," the lady said in a monotone voice. "What's his name?"

"Darren Waltz. His mother died shortly after giving birth in Holmberry Hill."

She sucked in a sudden breath. "Is he alive?"

"Yes," Jasmine said.

She shut her eyes for a moment. "Does he know who his real father is?"

Jasmine nodded. "He does now. I tracked him down."

"Is the senator's name on the birth certificate?"

Jasmine rested her chin in her hand. "No. Only his birth mother's name. Although she altered it a little by using her mother's surname—Cynthia Rosen."

A loud, muffled male voice made the woman snap her head to the right again and yell to someone, "Hold on, I'll be right there."

When her face returned to the screen, her eyes were wide. She spoke at a rapid pace, barely taking a breath. "You need to check into a man named Miguel Reyes. He knows about the $1 million used by the senator. I didn't know until now that it was for that boy. Shoot, I've got to go. Send me another invite when you're ready to talk."

The screen went black. Jasmine ended the conferencing application and stopped the camera on her screen. They both sat in silence, no doubt processing what they'd just heard. Finally, the creak of her chair caused Noah to look her way.

She rotated her chair to face him and grabbed her notebook. "I don't know what to think. She's younger than I anticipated. This story is personal to her. That came across loud and clear. Are you thinking she's another illegitimate child?"

He ran his hand through his hair. "Yup, and her logic is sound. My father should be held accountable. She knew Cynthia. It's a little creepy, but I don't sense deceit from her. Maybe she's speaking big-picture accountability, or maybe my father hurt someone who mattered to her along the way."

"I didn't like the abrupt ending to the call. She didn't want to be caught talking to us."

"Yeah, I got the same impression. That name she mentioned sounded familiar. What was it again?"

"Miguel Reyes," she said.

His fingers flew across the keyboard, and in a matter of seconds, he'd shared his screen on the wall. "This is the approximate location of her IP address. It's Mexico City."

Her eyes were wide, and her mouth dropped open.

He stood and paced the floor behind his system. The urge to hit something flooded his system. "What the fuck is it with Mexico?"

"I don't know, but do you think she's computer savvy and maybe bounced the IP signal, or whatever they do in the movies?"

"It's a possibility, but no because it's not as easy as the movies make it appear. In real life, you have to have the knowledge, access, and equipment. She could've just used a VPN or proxy, but she didn't," he said. The abrupt snap of his fingers followed. "I remember where I've seen that name."

"Miguel Reyes?"

"Yup, my father received a call from him," he said, tapping into his system and pulling up the call records from that day.

"That's right, and she just told us he has knowledge of the $1 million. How do you want to dig into that lead?"

Noah straightened. "Go right to the source. I'll call my father and ask. We've already rattled him by knowing as much as we do, so let's see how he handles this fact."

"When?" she asked.

"No time like the present," he said, dialing a number he detested. The sound of the rings filled the silent room. On the fourth, a gravelly voice came across the line.

"What could you possibly want now, son? I thought we cleared the air the other day?" the senator asked. The sound of paper being shuffled filled the background.

"Nope, I think you spun a story about being a victim to save your ass. I think we need to revisit that matter based on some new evidence," Noah said.

"Son, I'm a busy man, so get to your point. I have actual issues that need my attention," Senator Dubin said.

Noah's blood heated from his arrogance and dismissal. Warmth heated his flesh, which had him reaching to switch on the small desk fan and take a deep breath. "We need to discuss Miguel Reyes and the missing million."

He hated that he couldn't see his father's reaction. "I already told you about the money. As for Miguel, he and I were friends a long time ago. When our paths cross now, it's regarding political matters."

That answer rolled off his tongue too quickly and with vague detail. Noah scrubbed his hands through his hair. A textbook reply by a skilled senator to sound credible without committing or revealing anything.

Now was the time to shake the tree. "Nope, I'm not buying that answer. I've discovered a few other items, but those would be best discussed face-to-face. If you can't make the time to come back here, I'll have no other choice than to call Mr. Reyes myself and—"

"No," the senator roared into the phone. "I'll figure out when I can get there, but do not do anything rash until we speak."

"You have forty-eight hours to be here, or I'm making that call."

"I'll be there," the senator said, slamming the phone.

"He didn't like the idea of you contacting that lawyer," she said, her lips twisted into an ugly line.

Noah couldn't stop the hysterical laughter flowing from his mouth. "God, I'm losing my mind. This isn't funny in the least, but I can't seem to stop myself either."

"It's surreal, that's for sure. What do you think he's going to reveal?" she asked.

"Who knows, but I'm guessing that his past friend—whatever happened there—has information. The bigger question is whether my father will tell the truth or try to spin another tale."

"Well, your father was very insistent about not contacting him. That must mean something important."

"Family sucks," Noah mumbled under his breath, tossing his head back and looking at the ceiling.

Whatever it meant, he didn't have a warm, fuzzy feeling about it. This whole situation seemed to worsen with every discovery.

His heel tapped as he churned over the latest series of events. Jasmine's source was in Mexico City. Waltzer was in Mexico City. Jasmine was kidnapped and held in a suburb of Mexico City. Noah's father was connected to a lawyer who worked at a Mexican Embassy. Senator Decker had business in Mexico City. The only thing that made sense was that nothing made sense.

Eleven

J ASMINE STOOD IN THE laundry room, folding the last few items from the dryer. Her limited wardrobe meant washing more frequently, which she detested. She and Noah had spent Sunday afternoon doing laundry and lounging around watching television. Her usually quick-witted, funny man had devolved into this pensive, stoic person.

It wasn't like she could blame him for everything that had happened. The part that bothered her was the growing distance between them. He wanted her by his side, but he'd closed himself off and had gone silent.

Today, she'd made pancakes and bacon for breakfast earlier so Noah could jump on one of his standing Monday conference calls. Instead of eating with him like usual, she'd opted to eat her meal in the kitchen. This whole thing was stupid. She wasn't helping the matter by playing by his rules.

No, she needed to invade his space and shake the low-hanging fruit from his trees. The breath she expelled could have blown a house down, but she refused to give up. He had to talk to someone about all of this, or he'd explode.

Many steps later, she stood outside his office, squared her shoulders, then entered. No more hiding.

Damn him for making me love fall in love with him.

She smacked herself on the forehead and smiled. She did love him, which was why her insides were twisted up in a knot and her heart hurt. At some point, her love had blown past the friend category and morphed into a deep, palpable need.

"Thanks for breakfast. I needed that today. All these conference calls are killing me," Noah said when she entered his office.

"You're welcome. I finished folding the final bits of laundry and put a stack of clothes on your bed. I'm sorry I have to do laundry so often," she said.

He cleared his throat. "Well, you're living out of a suitcase now, so it makes sense. Besides, I'm more than spoiled because you add mine into the mix. I hate doing laundry."

"Me, too, but you'll have to resume that chore when I leave to head back to Chicago," she said, hating how those words sounded full of regret. She didn't want to leave, but at some point, they were going to have this discussion.

"Well, there's no rush for you to leave. Hey, on a serious note, I owe you an apology for being a grumpy bastard yesterday. I didn't mean to push you away. I just don't know how to put all of this into words. I'm struggling with how vulnerable all of this makes me feel."

He managed to right her world in five sentences. "I think under these circumstances, you're allowed to have a tiny mood swing and to feel exposed. Your life's history is being rewritten," she said, realizing that pushing him to make decisions about their relationship would be selfish right now.

He didn't need the added pressure. Knowing that he wanted her here was enough for now.

Her cellphone vibrated, alerting her that she'd received a voicemail. She'd forgotten to move the ringer off silent. Raising her phone to her ear, she listened to the message and bristled when she heard her father's voice.

Jasmine, don't bother coming over for Christmas if you're not home by tomorrow. I don't understand why you put this job ahead of your family. It's time you settled down and quit traipsing across the country pursuing this so-called career. Your place is here with your family, preferably married, and starting your own family. I love you, honey, but this insane need to chase adventure is childish. It's time to grow up.

The sob stuck in her throat broke free, and a deluge of tears poured down her face. She didn't mean to lose her composure, but her father's voicemail broke her. Why couldn't he understand that she didn't want what he wanted?

She loved her sisters and supported their choices to start their families, but she wanted a career. Her dad made it sound like she was out partying across the country, which couldn't be farther from the truth. His lack of understanding and support really hurt her. He was judging her life based on his ideals. She'd admit that she hadn't handled any of this right, but she'd never been involved in anything this important, and it consumed her. Her desires and wants in life were not wrong. Why couldn't he see that?

A warm hand slid down her back, tugging her against a solid frame. The moment she turned into his chest, Noah tightened his hold. His cologne, a combination of smoky sandalwood and rosewood, filled her senses with its exotic fragrance. Time seemed to stop, and all she knew was that he made her feel precious and safe.

He pressed a kiss to the crown of her head. "What's upset you?"

She couldn't utter the words and handed him her phone instead. "Listen to the first voicemail."

She watched as he pressed the device against his ear. After a few seconds, his eyebrows knitted together, his jaw hardened, and the small muscle at his temple pulsed.

"I know he's your father, and that message was hard to hear, but he loves you. That's why he worries about you. You've got to sit him down and tell him how you feel. Ultimately, whether he can accept it is his choice, but you have to have the discussion–not the screaming match. You make him understand that he raised a strong woman who doesn't know the word quit."

Her fingers whisked away a few more unshed tears. She feared that she and her father would never see eye to eye. Hopefully, in time, he'd forgive her because feeling like an outsider in her family hurt. Her mind drifted back to everything that had happened since she'd left home to work on this story. As if a rubber band had snapped inside her head, her mind clicked to an image.

"Noah," she said with an edge to her voice. She rushed toward his computer and heard his footsteps behind her. "I just remembered something."

The sound of furious clacking followed as she went in search of the photos she wanted to show him. Damn it, she was too eager and kept botching her password to her cloud account. She pounded the keys slower and squeezed her fists when it worked.

She palmed the mouse and scrolled until she found the picture and double tapped. "Look, this photo had two females in it. It's not much to go on with only their backs and a profile captured, but do you think this ties to all of this somehow? They were with Garcia, that cartel guy, along with this man. Maybe one of them is Senator Decker."

Noah snatched her mouse. He adjusted the image and made it larger. "It's a possibility, but I don't know any of them."

"Could you call Waltzer to find out who these people are since he was there that day?" she asked. "He probably has some knowledge that would be useful."

Noah nodded. "Reach out to your contact to see if we can meet ASAP. I want to get more information about what she knows about Reyes and his connection to my father before he comes to meet us."

Jasmine scribbled some notes. "Done, but what if the girl we spoke to and the one in this photo are the same person? I also think we should tell her we're meeting with the senator to provide a sense of urgency on her part to accept the meeting."

Noah pursed his lips before he responded. "Okay, let's do it."

She opened her email program and fired off the email to her source. If she accepted, Jasmine would send another invite for a video call. All these rabbit holes were hard to manage, and the emotional up and downs on what would reveal a strong, valid lead were difficult.

He worked with a photo editor, made two clippings of the females and the other man, and sent them to his workstation. She sat with her arms crossed as he worked, letting her thoughts drift. Could this girl be connected to the cartel? More importantly, what was her motivation for holding the senator accountable if that were true?

The ringtone from Noah's phone blasted into the silent room. He answered, then mouthed to her that it was his father. She listened and watched his expressions change as they spoke. The call didn't last long, so she hoped he'd gotten what he wanted and another visit was on the horizon.

"The senator will be here tomorrow afternoon. I got the distinct impression he isn't happy about coming back to Mill Creek so soon," Noah said.

"That's fast. I guess you motivated him sufficiently. Now we'll have to see if he will share something worthwhile. Like why he and the lawyer are no longer friends. What drove them apart?"

He leaned back in his chair, straightening his legs. When he folded his hands across his abdomen, the gesture pulled his T-shirt taut across the muscles of his arms and pecs. She wanted to tell him to stop distracting her with his sex appeal because it made it hard to think. Then she thought better of it because what would be the fun in that?

She glanced down at her screen and smiled. "Good news, Noah, we're meeting with our contact at six tonight. Apparently, she's heading to the coast for the rest of the week. I'll send her the invite for the video meeting, then I'll head to the kitchen and whip up something to eat for dinner."

NOAH COULDN'T EAT ANOTHER bite even if Jasmine had made dessert. The lasagna for dinner tasted so good that he ate a second serving. Rubbing his bloated belly, he regretted the decision. Admittedly, he liked how she put the salad inside her dish. He hadn't been entirely sure when he saw the shredded carrots and spinach folded into the layers of cheese and sausage, but it tasted great.

Maybe he should have her explain this trick to Annika, who insisted that salads had to accompany every meal—even pizza. Then Kane would owe him one.

They had just finished loading the dishwasher and were headed back to Noah's office. He needed to focus on the call. The view of Jasmine on the big screen while she sat on hold mesmerized him. She was so competent and beautiful. When she lifted her head, she smiled at him.

A warmth deep inside his chest bubbled upward. There wasn't a damn thing she did that annoyed him, and that irritated him. There are times in a person's life when a particular someone crosses your path and fundamentally changes you. It could be for the better or worse, but when it happened, the exchange was profound and left you altered. This was how it was with Jazy. And that reality scared him.

The rattle of equipment surged into the room through the speakers, and a moment later, the young lady came into focus. Today, she wore a masquerade-style mask reflecting the celebration of *Día de Los Muertos*. It appeared she was taking this meeting in her bedroom. There was an innocence about her that he'd missed the other day when they'd spoken.

"Sorry, sometimes getting twenty minutes to yourself is a hassle," she said, moving her laptop to the left a little. "I'm sorry about bailing on you the other day."

"No worries." Jasmine's upbeat voice had the young woman's shoulders relaxing. "As I mentioned before, I'm meeting with the senator tomorrow. He was not pleased that I brought up Miguel Reyes's name. I was hoping you could give me a little insight into their relationship. Anything to keep the senator off-balance."

The girl tapped her pen on the table. Was that nervous energy or a sign she was pensive? The silence stretched, and then she spoke. "There's a larger issue I can't speak about, but their friendship ended when the senator took advantage of Reyes and lied to him. I'm sorry, I know that's vague, but I can't get into specifics. The part you need to focus on is what Reyes did with the money."

Jasmine had a furrowed brow as she listened. "Are you related to this lawyer?"

"Absolutely not," she said, and the conviction of her words came through loud and clear.

Jasmine raised her hand. "The thought occurred to me, so I had to ask."

"He's not the bad guy here. The senator holds that honor," she said, pointing at the screen with her pen. It escaped her fingers and bounced off the monitor.

The girl ducked to retrieve her pen, exposing the back of her room, which her body had blocked. Noah gazed across the space and spotted a stuffed unicorn with a rainbow horn on a shelf. His stomach dropped, threatening to expel his dinner. His chest constricted, squeezing his heart.

Sparkles? His blood rushed his through his system, making it hard to concentrate.

How was this even possible? He was losing his shit. There was no way this girl was his baby sister. The note his mother left all those years ago. The one that had bothered him for all these years played in his head.

Son,

Lisa and I love you to the moon and back. Don't worry, I'll take care of your sister until she's old enough to care for me. I'm proud of you. All my love, Mom.

A whimper tore from his throat. Speaking in low tones so only Jazy could hear his command, he told her to call the girl Lisa, his baby sister's name. Stars flashed in his eyes as he held his breath until his chest burned, and he felt dizzy.

Jasmine shifted in her seat. "Lisa, you okay over there?"

"Yah, sorry, I had to get my pen," she said, popping back onto the screen.

Her face contorted with shock and then panic when she realized her mistake.

She'd responded to her name like she'd probably done her whole life. "How'd you know my n-name?"

"I'm good at research. It's why you trusted me with this story," Jasmine said in a soft, calm voice, trying to keep the girl from severing the line. "Your identity is safe with me."

The girl sputtered on the other end of the line, which kicked Noah into gear. He had to know for sure if she was his sister. On wobbly legs, he moved to kneel beside Jasmine so the girl could see his face. His heart cracked his chest in anticipation of her answer. He didn't want to scare her with what he was about to say.

It all crystallized in his mind. This story was personal to her. She wanted the senator to be held accountable for his mangled family and to expose his secrets. God, he needed to hug her and hear about her life. Where had she been all this time? What happened to their mom? Was she alive, too? *God, please don't let this be some cruel joke.*

"I recognized Sparkles, Lisa. You never went anywhere without that stuffed animal. I'm Noah, your brother," he said, his voice cracking with his heart.

Lisa's hand went to her mask, and she yanked it off her face. Tears flowed freely down her cheeks as she stared at him through the camera. "I've seen pictures of you when you were younger. Mom has told me a ton of stories about you."

He started to shake. When Jasmine wrapped her arm around him, he couldn't stop leaning into her embrace and taking the silent strength she offered. "Is Mom alive too?"

Lisa closed her eyes and bit her lip for a moment. "It's complicated, Noah. I should never have contacted Jasmine. My anger got the best of me, and now it will put us at risk."

"Risk from who?" he asked, his voice raw from his pain. He couldn't believe he was speaking to his sister. "How's Mom? Is she healthy? Does she know you're talking to Jasmine about our father?"

Her eyes went wild, her gaze darting all around, "No, God, no. She'd kill me for being so reckless. Yes, she's fine."

"Who are you hiding from, Lisa?" Noah croaked out. "Mom didn't kill you or commit suicide. What the hell happened?"

"Our father wanted to win an election more than have a wife and daughter. We were collateral damage for the betterment of his campaign. A grieving husband/senator gets lots of sympathy votes. Their marriage was miserable, and he was unfaithful. He put a hit on us to better his life.

It was Miguel Reyes who saved us. He staged the murder-suicide scene, complete with our blood, and he whisked us away to Mexico before the real hit happened. That's why they're no longer friends. We've lived in Bonita Verde at Reyes's house ever since."

Noah's mind raced with how to take his father down and vindicate his mom. He had always known she could never hurt herself, let alone one of her children. "I have so many questions. Are he and Mom together? Do you or Mom have any proof of what the senator did? Like whom he paid or the name of the hitman?"

"I don't, but Miguel told Mom everything. I think to reassure her that she was safe with him and to ensure she severed all ties to her old life. We kept our real first names and changed our last names to Reyes. As I got older, she finally opened up and told me about my past and what happened. So that's why I want to make our father pay. He destroyed our family."

Noah stared at the screen, processing what she'd said. His brain had turned to molasses, and he couldn't formulate a thought to save his life. He had to know what hold that man had over his family. He ran his hand over his face and sighed. "You didn't answer my question. Are Mom and him together?"

"No, but Miguel has always had a thing for her. We're just his pretend family, but he's always treated us right. I want my life back, Noah."

"Do you have a phone number?" he asked. When she nodded, he continued, "Email Jasmine your number, but don't tell anyone what we figured out today—especially not Mom. I need a little time to work on some loose ends. The less people who know, the better. I'll call you soon."

Lisa took a deep breath. "I'm going with Mom to Miguel's beach house for the rest of the week while he travels back to the States for business. Promise me you'll help us take our father down. He must be brought to justice. I love you, Noah."

"You have my word. Now that I know you two are alive, the world isn't big enough to keep me away. I've missed you, Lisa, and I love you too," he said as the screen went black.

His shoulders slumped, and his head dropped. Seconds turned into minutes before he lifted his face and turned to Jasmine.

"Oh my God, Jasmine, my mother and sister are alive? I-I don't even know what to say. I'm happy, but at the same time, I'm at my breaking point with all these lies and deceit," he said in a grave tone.

The agony of every word was like a knife slicing into his skin. He wrapped his arms around her and held her tight against his body.

Twelve

Jasmine's heart broke for the man she loved. Everything he thought he knew about his life was an illusion or a lie. How did a person reconcile all those lies to move forward in life? A desperation deep in her soul had her wanting to do something to ease his suffering, but there wasn't anything she could do.

What she'd heard tonight blew her mind. The depths the senator had gone down to win a stupid election made her sick to her stomach. How horrible of a person do you have to be to do something like that?

Noah's face was as white as a ghost. He stood and kissed the top of her head. "Will you call Clarke and Trent and tell them I need to talk? Say it's urgent. I just need a few minutes to pull myself together."

"Of course," she said to his retreating form as he walked out of the room.

She called Aimee first, and in a second, her friend had Clarke on the phone.

"Hey, Jasmine, is everything okay?" he asked, his concern radiating over the line.

Her voice quivered as she said, "No, Clarke, not even close. Noah needs you and Trent over here now. I'll let him explain, but it's devastating on so many levels. Trust me, you won't believe it when you hear it. The front door will be unlocked."

He exhaled over the phone. "I'll call Trent. Go take care of him, and we'll be right over."

She went to the front door and unlocked it. Then she went in search of Noah. It did take her long because he sat on the sofa in the family room with the bottle of scotch hanging between his knees. In his hand, he clutched a small square with two images that she figured was a picture of his mom and sister. When she sat next to him, he didn't move or acknowledge her presence, so she tucked her feet underneath her body and sat beside him in silence. He was not alone anymore. He handed her the bottle, which she accepted and took a big sip. The warm liquid slid down her throat and left a smoky-peaty flavor on her tongue. She was unaware of how long they sat, alternating between taking sips of the amber liquid and staring at nothing. Finally, two distinct male voices issued greetings as they headed to the sofa.

"Hey, man," Trent said, taking a seat in one of the two chairs along each side of the couch.

Clarke sat in the other chair and rested his ankle on his knee. "No matter what, you're not alone. We all have your back, man."

Noah took one long sip of scotch before he placed the bottle on the coffee table. He ran his hand down his face and sighed, which turned into a guttural groan. The next several minutes were spent by him bringing them up to speed on everything. He even told them about the weapons shipment and his suspicions. Trent and Clarke barely blinked as Noah spoke.

"What? I don't even know what to say," Trent uttered in bewilderment. "I'm glad to hear your sister and mom are alive, but I can't even imagine what they've been through."

Clarke just raised his brows and rubbed his bald head. "What's your plan?"

One of Noah's shoulders went up in a shrug. "Honestly, I don't know what to think at the moment. I need your help with Jasmine in vetting my thoughts. I know killing my father isn't an option, but I don't even know if I can do this meeting with him tomorrow without committing murder."

Clarke kicked his legs out in front of him. "Will Jasmine be present when you meet with him?"

"Of course," Noah answered without hesitation.

"Then you'll be fine. The good ones," Clarke began and inclined his head at her, "have a way of keeping us focused and on track. I think you should wear a wire and record the conversation. I know you have some clandestine gadgetry in your closet. Hiring a hitman isn't an ordinary task."

Trent leaned forward with his elbows on his thighs. "You'll have to present the sequence of questions and events in the right order to get him to snap. I have no doubt you can handle that one. You're the best analyst I know and can study people. Have you had a chance to let Guzman know any of this?"

"No, but he knows about Waltzer being my half brother. I want to talk to my father first so I have the full story. Then I'll hand everything over to Guzman."

"What time's the meeting with the senator?" Clarke asked.

"Afternoon sometime. He didn't give an arrival time," Noah said.

Jasmine interjected, "If he learns that your mom and sister are alive, that would put them at risk."

Clarke and Trent nodded.

"I won't tell him that his friend saved them. He thinks they were killed by whoever was contracted to do the hit," Noah said.

"You sure?" Clarke asked.

"According to my sister, Lisa, Miguel made sure my mom knew she couldn't contact anyone from her old life. They even changed their last name to Reyes."

Jasmine squeezed Noah's knee. "Waltzer gained a half sister today too. You'll have to reach out to him to give him the update when the time is right. He deserves to know his family has grown, and his biological father is evil."

Clarke pointed at her. "You have to watch out for this one. She's unraveled a hell of a cover-up with some help from key sources. My favorite is that she followed Spec Ops boy to Mexico City. Not all the ugliness that followed, but she's good and has earned my respect."

"Yes, and the whole paper clip trick was pretty damn smooth," Trent added. "I have to say, that took some courage."

Jasmine smiled at their praise and hadn't realized Noah had shared so many details of their time together in Mexico. They were a damn good team, that she knew without a doubt. When the time was right, she planned to have an open conversation with Noah about what came next.

"We made it out in one piece, so I call that a win," she said. "Well, more me than you. I never want to watch you being pummeled because of me again."

Noah winked at her. "It wasn't that bad, and I'd do it again for you. How long do you think it'll take to bring them back to the US if they want to come? My sister seemed ready, but I haven't spoken to my mother."

"That all depends on how the authorities decide to handle the senator and what charges will be filed. The biggest thing will be getting him to reveal who he hired and/or paid to kill his wife and daughter," Trent said.

"Shit, that could take a long time. He's a long-term senator and will be afforded the benefit of the doubt."

"Hold up, Noah, that's not the focus right now. The senator will be held accountable in the end. It may not happen as quickly as you'd like, but it'll happen. Focus on getting through the meeting tomorrow with him. One step at a time. If your father won't supply the information, you'll depose the friend—Reyes," Clarke said.

"You're right. My brain is muddled. I never thought in a million years that this would be my predicament–getting my mom and sister out alive. I'm grateful, but it's also overwhelming. All right, I'm good and somewhat stable considering all this shit."

She stood with Noah, who accepted backslaps from both Trent and Clarke. Once they exited through the front door, Noah flipped the deadbolt and grabbed her hand. He tugged her into his arms, squeezing her. After a bit, he gripped her biceps to pull her back so he could see her eyes.

"Thank you again for having my back. I'm exhausted, but I sleep better with you by my side. Will you be my angel tonight?" he asked.

Raising onto her tiptoes, she cupped his face to press a sweet kiss to his lips to reinforce that she wasn't going anywhere. She'd be his seatbelt on this wild ride and keep him safe. "I couldn't imagine a better place to be."

No more words followed. She entwined their fingers and led him toward the bedroom. How could she refuse him anything, especially when he asked in such a sweet way? His request came from his heart, and she'd take any chance to comfort him, even if he didn't yet realize it. She would lie awake all night to chase away his demons if necessary.

THE FOLLOWING AFTERNOON, NOAH instructed Jasmine on how to tape the microphone to his chest. He was not overly pleased when she laid a practice strip and yanked it off, giggling. Once she had the device secured, he tested the recording equipment. Satisfied that both were working, he put the unused equipment and devices away.

His skin prickled with unease, but his mind was focused on what he had to accomplish. This was for his family, and he'd get it done.

He strode toward the kitchen and took a water bottle from the refrigerator. His fingers twisted the cap right off so he could take a sip. The cool liquid felt good as it slid down his throat. His stomach had been churning ever since last night. He'd slept better than he thought possible due to Jasmine being by his side. She completed him. Her presence in his life made everything better, but it also turned his life inside out.

His DNA was flawed. When it came down to it, he had trust issues. His heart had been torn out during his childhood and stomped to death. He didn't want to put himself in a position where the past would repeat itself.

When things got difficult his first instinct was to push everyone away and focus on school or, later, work. He took the path of least resistance by isolating himself, but when the curtain was drawn back, he was not different than his father. He didn't fight for resolution. He just shut down and walked away from his old man.

Hell, he couldn't even be sure he wouldn't choose his career over Jasmine. Then, the other concern was if his career would ever put her in jeopardy. His friends were one thing because they understood he had a job that took priority. Marriage was different, and in the end, it would never work because he didn't trust himself enough to do the right thing. God, he was a mess, but these were the facts of his life.

The familiar scrape, crunch, and pop of gravel moving underneath tires had him lifting his head. He checked his watch. It was just after 4:00 PM. Through his kitchen window, he saw a sedan pull into his drive. His stomach flopped like a dying fish.

He closed his eyes and focused his mind on the strategy he'd worked out earlier. The goal was to link the senator to the hitman. The second goal was determining how he'd financed such an endeavor. His leverage was the relationship the senator had with Miguel Reyes, which included the $1 million stolen from that campaign fund.

Noah opened the front door and motioned for the senator to enter. Instead of talking in the kitchen, he moved toward the family room, where Jasmine already sat. It struck him as odd that anger hadn't dominated his reaction the moment he laid eyes on his father. Instead, he was fueled by his determination to uncover the truth and be done with this man.

"I'll get to the point because I know you're a busy man," Noah said, throwing his father's words back at him. He occupied the open chair, leaving the sofa for the senator.

His father sat with a slight groan, and his knee cracked. It wasn't until that moment that Noah noticed his father's age. It wasn't that he looked bad for being in his sixties, but the signs were present. He had crow's feet around his eyes and spots on the backs of his hands that matched his salt-and-pepper hair. What stood out the most were his dull eyes. It made him appear worn out, like there was no life left in his body, which he hadn't noticed before.

The senator cleared his throat. "I have to admit, I never thought I'd be here talking about all of this. You mentioned Miguel Reyes in your phone call. He was a friend a long time ago. We met in college and were pretty tight. I think we got along because we were driven with the common goal of accomplishing great things. After we graduated, our careers demanded our full attention."

"I appreciate the history, but that doesn't scratch the surface. Why does the name Miguel Reyes make you angry? Tell me about his involvement in your campaign funds. If you intend to make me drag everything out of you, I'll just end this meeting and go straight to the man myself."

The senator's cheeks reddened, but he'd give him credit for not losing control. "I would prefer to have this discussion without her present."

"She stays," Noah said, his gaze locked with his father's.

"I'm a part of all of this whether you like it or not, Senator," Jasmine added in a steady voice.

The senator sat quietly, his gaze moving between them while he must have either considered proceeding or leaving. Looking up toward the ceiling, he continued in a gravelly voice, "I hate that you despise me, son. This tension between us has taken a toll on my heart."

"I—"

"Shut up and let me finish. You wanted the truth, and this is part of it," the senator said, his calm veneer crumbling. He crossed his legs like he planned to sit in that chair for a while. "I'm beyond tired, son. Your mother was a great political wife, and I miss her. Hindsight is so powerful. She was pretty, and people loved her. I was a better man when she stood by my side. If our lives were like cats, I'd do many things differently in my next life. Do you have any water?"

Jasmine popped up. "I'll get you some."

"Thank you," the senator said. "Miguel had a crush on my wife back in college. He flirted with her, but she'd chosen me. I think that started the downfall, but I could be wrong. I was reckless. I had an affair with Cynthia Miller. When she got pregnant, it took me by surprise. She had shared her medical records before we became intimate that she was unable to conceive. Well, my sperm defied that diagnosis."

Jasmine returned and handed the senator a bottle of water and a glass with ice in it.

"This is perfect," he said, sipping from the glass. "Anyway, I erupted and directed all my anger and disappointment at your mother because we had so many failed attempts at conceiving. It wasn't until later that we conceived you. Anyway, I panicked because I didn't want the news that I'd strayed to get out. I had a plan in place, and Cynthia had agreed to it. She went to St. Paul Hospital in Holmberry Hill to hide her condition until the baby was born. She would give it up for adoption—a win-win for everyone. My problem is that I was a new senator who had just won the election and couldn't afford the cost of the private hospital at the time. This hospital was expensive, but it provided the level of discretion making it invaluable."

Noah's stomach roiled with disgust because what his father described matched what Jasmine had found out. *A private hospital to handle delicate situations.* He shifted and stretched out his legs. "You made a woman and baby disappear to maintain your public image and legacy."

"Yes, that's the gist of it, but it gets more complicated. Cynthia's idea was to take the money from the campaign fund to pay for the hospital in Holmberry Hill. She wanted to continue our fling. I didn't know what to do, so I called my friend, Miguel, and told him everything because I thought I could trust him. That was the first of two mistakes that I made. Those mistakes ended up costing me everything.

"What the hell does that mean?" Noah asked in confusion. Had he missed something?

The senator waved his hand to shush him. "Life is long and messy, Noah, and so is this story. Be patient. Anyway, Miguel liked Cynthia's idea of using money from the campaign, but the lawyer in him urged me to make it clear Cynthia was culpable. Meaning I put all the blame on her shoulders in an official capacity, which is why I filed the report. That protected me, so I saw no reason not to agree. Miguel even volunteered to make the payments to St. Paul Hospital, which removed me from any distribution of the money. He told me that someday I'd return the favor and help him. So, every month starting in July, he paid a hundred grand to cover her room, board, and care until she went into labor. In February, the amount increased to two hundred grand. The last payment was made in March because she died of a heart attack."

Noah leaned forward, his hands hanging between his knees. "Did you pay for that heart attack?"

The senator's eyes hardened. "I can understand why you asked, but no. I cared about her, and I didn't need to have her killed because she had planned to live in London."

"Did you ever check on Darren after she died?"

"I wasn't listed on the birth certificate or adoption record to maintain my anonymity, but I did keep tabs on him for a while. He was adopted by an American military family stationed in Germany. They were a solid family. I believe he had a good life. He entered the military, and when the time came, I supported his growth, promotions, and assignments. He never knew that, of course, but I used my powers as a senator to help him move up the ranks and obtain certain positions."

Noah flinched at that statement. His father had landed a stab right to his heart. He'd done more for Darren than he had for his legitimate son.

The senator took another drink and stared into the distance as if preparing for whatever was coming next. He folded his hands across his lap and switched his legs, so the other was crossed.

"I want you to have zero contact with Miguel Reyes. The lesson I learned from him is that you can never trust anyone with a secret that could be used against you. Promise me, Noah."

"No promises until you finish telling me the whole story. You mentioned two lessons," Noah pressed his old man.

"I was up for reelection, and my polling numbers were falling like a cement block were attached to them. Your mom flat out refused to stand by my side, and our marriage was unraveling. I didn't want to lose my power. I wanted to keep my position in the Senate. I started drinking in my office. Miguel called and offered to take me to dinner one night, and I accepted. He'd reserved a private room in one of the many steakhouses in DC to talk and catch up. I kept drinking and told him my woes. I told him I was going to lose the election, and I was pissed. In my rage, I stupidly said the only way I'd win was if my wife died, and I got sympathy votes. God, I was rambling."

His father paused. His face had whitened, and he scratched at something on his tie. Noah waited until his father composed himself. There was no doubt that this wasn't an easy story for him to share. After his father cleared his throat, he continued with his story.

"Miguel works at the Mexican Embassy. That night, he excused himself from the table to take a call, and when he returned, he nudged me back into my drunken diatribe. I didn't catch what he was doing, but he got me to confirm my statement that I wanted him to have my wife murdered so I'd get sympathy votes. He'd chastised me that murder was not the answer and that I'd lost my mind. He said I needed to get sober and get my head on straight. Then, as if he'd slapped me, he did a full reversal, telling me I'm brilliant and that he'd help me. Hell, we even toasted to getting me reelected."

The senator leaned forward and put his head in his hands. His voice stuttered. "Th-three days later, your mom killed Lisa and took her own life in our backyard along the riverbed. The evidence and investigation came to that conclusion, even though their bodies were never recovered. The authorities said the swift current of the Potomac carried them away. The forensics team found blood samples that matched the DNA obtained from the house. The news ran with the story of a murder-suicide, and I won the re-election in a landslide."

Noah fisted his hands, trying to force down the sudden rush of emotions threatening to escape from his body like a fissure. Why could he say? He refused to let his father lie. "What are you saying?"

The senator stood to remove his jacket and folded it over the back of the chair. He sat again, loosened his tie, and let the two halves hang on either side of his shirt. "Two days after their deaths, Miguel showed up at my house in the middle of the night with two men while you slept in your room. He made me join him outside by the firepit. He played a recording he'd made of me that night where I asked him to commit murder for my campaign. Then he congratulated me on my win. That's when I noticed the branding iron resting in the fire. The two men restrained me while he told me to be quiet so I wouldn't scare you. Miguel ripped my shirt open and thrust the brand against my skin right over my heart. God, I can still smell the scent of burning flesh."

His father unbuttoned his shirt to show Noah the mark. A wave of nausea hit him. The logo on his father's chest was raised and scarred, displaying a large G with two smaller letters, a D and L in the middle area. "Miguel told me he had it made especially for me. I could create whatever story I wanted, but I was owned by the Garcia Cartel from that point forward. If I told anyone or went against their wishes, they would kill you, son."

Noah's world spun out of control. His chest tightened, making it difficult to breathe. Words stuck in his throat, preventing him from speaking. All he could do was sit and stare at his father. He opened his mouth and closed it several times before he gave up.

"It's a lot to process, I know. This is why I sent you away to boarding school and turned my back on you. I didn't know what else to do. I wanted you to hate me as much as I hated myself. I figured that in the long run, it would keep you safe. If they thought we didn't care about each other, it would be harder for them to use you as leverage. That's why I didn't fight you when you took your mother's maiden name. I love you, son. I've always loved you. I made a horrendous mess out of parenthood and had all my priorities in the wrong order. I'm not asking for your forgiveness because I wouldn't forgive myself if I were in your shoes."

Jasmine asked a question while Noah struggled with his composure. "To be clear, you're saying Miguel blackmailed you and that you have nothing to do with their deaths?"

"Yes, that's correct," the senator said.

Noah needed to focus on the business side of this discussion and compartmentalize the rest, or he'd split wide open. Hearing his father declare his love while confessing he'd made horrible errors satisfied the boy deep inside, who never understood why his father had abandoned him. It also pissed off his adult side because he'd spent his life trying to survive endless lies.

How could his father have been so reckless with his family? Did he not know what he had until he'd lost it all? Or had he thought he could have it all on his terms? No, Noah had to stop these wayward thoughts and remain in the present to stay on track. He had to finish this conversation. People were counting on him, and he refused to let them down.

"How did you help the cartel?" he asked.

His father pursed his lips. "I kept a log in my safe. I knew this day would come, and I wanted to make sure I had a record. There are fewer entries than you would think, but the cartel was strategic with how they used me. Now, my problem is that I want to retire, but they don't support that decision."

"Did you give Miguel the heads-up on the partial weapon shipment last week that were stolen?" Noah asked.

"Yes, and the cartel is pissed. They want the rest of it. It seems they have big plans for those weapons. Miguel has called me several times threatening all sorts of things. I've told him I don't control manufacturer or shipment delays."

Noah rubbed his forehead and sighed. "The alphabets know there's a mole. You just escaped capture because you were here visiting me and missed the bait shipment. Who does Miguel Reyes report to in the cartel?"

His father chucked a humorless laugh. "He's Marcelino Garcia's son. He dropped the last name, so there isn't an obvious connection. Working at the embassy gives him the ability to work on issues at higher governmental levels, and he has diplomatic immunity. They set it up brilliantly."

Noah closed his eyes. His heart beat hard against his ribcage. His sister and mother were living with the enemy. "Where's Miguel now? Do you know who they're selling them to?"

"Miguel is in DC until Saturday. I don't have any information on the buyer."

"You know I will report all of this, right? If you learn anything new, call me. I won't contact Miguel," Noah said.

"Good, I'm ready to end this, and whatever happens to me is fine. I'm going to keep my interactions with Miguel normal for now."

"That's good, and I'll be in touch. Thank you for telling me the truth."

A prickle of fear snaked down Noah's spine. His mom and sister had no clue they were in the viper's den. His father's recklessness had crushed his family and caused so much pain. Noah had never expected to hear his father tell him he loved him. Or that he'd pushed him away to protect him. Nothing in his life made sense. Not one damn thing. His life was now spinning out of control.

He had to contact his sister because the timetable for getting his family out of Mexico had just shortened. His father would have to admit his crimes. The how would be decided behind closed doors by people higher up the totem pole and with better titles.

Noah needed to bring Guzman up to speed. So many things had to happen fast, and Noah was worried he might not be able to protect his family when they needed him the most.

Thirteen

J ASMINE WAITED IN THE family room while Noah walked the senator out. This family had secrets on top of their secrets. She was torn between writing this epic tale of betrayal, love, and misguided sacrifice and allowing them the privacy to process. On the other hand, if she didn't pen the story, the media would, and no one would do a better job because she understood the players.

Her determination to complete this story propelled her forward, and she'd ensure all the details were balanced against the emotional elements. At the heart of this story was a father who'd exercised horrible judgment and had made mistakes, but he had truly loved his family. He'd paid a high price for his sins against his loved ones, and the public and judicial system would mete out the punishment for those crimes.

Her time with Noah had undoubtedly taught her to be true to herself. She hated adding one more thing to his plate, but they needed this conversation. She would need to walk away now if he genuinely couldn't keep an open mind about their potential relationship.

He padded back into the room. "I don't even know what to say. I've formed all these opinions about my family history based on lies. God, I've spent years being angry about things that were fabrications. The scariest part is I don't even know how to move forward from all these deceptions and lies."

She took his hand and pulled him down on the cushion. "Why didn't you tell him about your sister and mother?"

"Although I'm 99 percent sure he told me the truth, I'm not willing to stake their lives on that 1 percent," he said.

"That's a fair point. Noah, this isn't the best time, but maybe it's also the perfect time." Her breath caught in a shuddering gasp. "I love you. I want to be with you because of who you are and how you make me feel. We're great together. Something that's become clear to me is that forever is earned, and I want to work on that with someone worthy of that investment. Marriage doesn't guarantee a happy future. I know that, and I'm willing to be patient while we work toward that outcome. I know you need time to process all this, but I had to tell you what's in my heart."

Noah blinked. His face morphed into a confused look, and his eyebrows knitted together. When his gaze landed on hers, she thought she saw a flash of emotion that she couldn't place.

"I love that you speak your mind. And you're right. This conversation is long overdue. That's my fault. I never expected to find the other half of my heart in that hut, but I'm incapable of anything deeper. I don't even know who I am anymore. I do know that I'm damaged. I don't want to make the same mistakes as my parents. In the end, I'd only hurt you."

She cupped his cheek. "You're not damaged, Noah Parker. You've been hurt, and you're nervous. Please know I will always be in your corner. I love you, and you're worthy of my love and a lifetime of happiness, but you must be willing to fight for it. Thank you for being honest with me. I guess this is where we end."

Noah crushed her to his chest. "Promise me we'll always be friends. I can't lose you from my life."

She hugged him back just as fiercely while she fought to keep her tears at bay. "I don't like your decision, but I respect it. We'll always be friends, that I can promise you. If you change your mind, you know where to find me."

Content to remain in his arms, she let his warmth surround her. Her heart shattered into a thousand pieces. She wanted to be mad at him but couldn't be because he'd only been honest. Deep down, she'd feared this would be the outcome. It was best to reach this conclusion now rather than in a year when she had fallen even deeper in love. Being here with him would be difficult, but she refused to stop being his friend.

Noah dropped his arms. "Hey, I better call my boss, and I need to check in with Trent and Noah. I'm sorry, Jazy."

She leaned into him once more, then straightened her spine. "Don't forget to call Waltzer and update him. He's your ally and deserves to know the latest. Oh, and we need him to identify the other man in that picture."

"You're right," he said, then headed in the direction of his office. He stopped and looked over his shoulder. "Aren't you joining me for these calls?"

She nodded, unable to speak just yet. What she wanted to do was run to her room and cry. "Sure, give me a minute, and I'll be right there."

A few minutes later, she popped into the office with two sodas. At least she didn't worry she'd start crying right in the middle of the call. Noah was in a video conference with his two best friends.

It was Clarke's rough charm that broke through the awkwardness. "Man, your family's fucked up. No wonder you love us so much. Hey, on the bright side, at least your old man told the truth. Did you take a picture of the brand? That could be a signature for the cartel."

Noah shook his head. "No, the thought didn't cross my mind. Besides, he'd mentioned that it's a custom brand. Now that you know everything, I have a plan I want to run past the three of you before I pitch it to Guzman. I still need to talk to my mom and sister, but getting them out of Mexico City has become a priority before Miguel Reyes leaves DC this Friday. In my new role, I assemble teams with Guzman's blessing. Clarke, I want to leverage your position as a US Marshal and your ability to coordinate through a field office to take custody of Lisa and my mother, Diana.

I'll charter an FBI plane to Mexico, but I'll need your connections to get them out and watch my back. That way, if we run into any trouble, having the marshals supporting this operation won't hurt. I would have Guzman clear this officially with your boss just so we're legitimate."

Clarke smiled and crossed his arms across his massive chest. "Works for me. They're always welcome in my shelter until the next part of whatever needs to happen does. So, what's next?"

"Thanks, man, I appreciate it. Jasmine, if you're willing, I'd like you to accompany us to Mexico City. You'll stay with the plane, but once we board, you can help answer any questions my mom and sister may have. The other part of my plan depends on Guzman, but I haven't spoken with him yet. I wanted to get your thoughts, Clarke, before I offer you up."

"One question, what if your sister and mom have a guard detail or if the house is guarded?" Trent asked.

Noah nodded. "Yes, and I hope to get additional details when I talk to Waltzer. Do they keep Miguel's connection to Marcelino on the down-low in Mexico, or is that only in the States?"

Trent scrubbed his hand over his face. "I'm going to point out the obvious concern. When you two pull the women out, you won't have much time before Marcelino finds out and potentially puts whatever operation is being planned at risk. Four days is a super-small window when you have multiple agencies involved."

Noah folded his hands behind his head. "I know, but leaving them is a greater risk. If news leaks or breaks that my father is under investigation, that'll put them at risk too. Either way, the window to extract them is tight."

Jasmine leaned forward. "You know, if Waltzer has the information on who is buying the weapons, that'll help. I mean, he's their hired mercenary, right? Maybe he's already reported that information up his chain of command."

Clarke exhaled. "This is a big *if*, but it could put Waltzer and his cover at risk if Jasmine's story or any of the senator's story becomes known."

"Okay, we need to be prepared to leave Wednesday morning. Do you think you can get your contacts set up that fast? I'll make sure Guzman contacts your boss to take care of the back-end clearance."

"Yup, not a problem," Clarke said. He had a pencil in his hand as he jotted notes.

Trent added, "I'll be your local transport."

"We'll take a helicopter from Boise to Mill Creek when we return from Mexico. A ride from the landing pad to Clarke's house would be great," Noah said.

Trent also jotted something down. "Done, and I'll inform my deputies, so we'll have more eyes patrolling the area once you bring them to Clarke's home."

"Thanks, guys. I'll talk to you both soon. I have several calls to make to get this ball rolling." Noah then ended the call.

"Okay, I'm going to head to my bedroom for the night," Jasmine said.

"Sleep tight, Jazy. I'll fill you in tomorrow after my calls with Guzman and my half brother," Noah said while he palmed his phone.

Jasmine had to escape back to her room and put some distance between them. Tomorrow, she'd be stronger, but she needed to release these tears tonight. His stubbornness and misguided thoughts about his future and what he deserved had to change, but that was on him. Life could be so unfair.

N OAH CHECKED HIS WATCH and sighed. It was late on the East Coast, but way past time to give Guzman an update. Too much had to happen in a small window. His boss answered on the second ring.

A gravelly voice filled the line. "This better be good because I have a meeting early in the morning with the secretary of defense, so is this call worth interrupting my beauty rest?"

Noah smiled at his choice of words. "No, because you need all the help you can get, but I wouldn't have called you at this time otherwise. Here's the big picture of what I've uncovered. I'll get to the details later. My father's the traitor, and the Garcia cartel is blackmailing him. Miguel Reyes is a lawyer at the Mexican Embassy and is Marcelino's son. He's the one my father updates. The kicker is my mother and sister are alive and are living with the lawyer under false pretenses."

"You have my undivided attention." Guzman's voice had sharpened. "Now, back up and give me the details."

Noah spent the next thirty minutes relaying the last few days of hell that he'd endured. There was a giant part of him that wanted to scream and explain that his life as he knew it was one big fucking lie. How did a person get over that and move forward? What type of analyst did that make him? A pathetic one. When he finished, his boss remained silent. It was a reaction Noah had come to expect after working together so many years.

He also floated his idea about partnering with Clarke and the US Marshals to extract his family from Mexico and put them in protective custody in Mill Creek. "The trickiest part will be balancing the weapons' operation and getting them out safely before Miguel catches a hint."

"I'm going to need that log the senator has kept. If you haven't already, send me all this in a report. Once this is reported up the chain, the senator will have to be debriefed, and then charges should follow. What happens next with your father will be out of our hands. You understand that, right, Noah?"

"Yes, and he wants it to end and to take responsibility, which is why he kept the log. We might need him when we get to the final objective. We must keep Miguel Reyes thinking that everything is running smoothly," Noah said.

"I approve your plan with Clarke, and I'll contact his boss and the regional office. I understand you are still working out the logistics. Keep me informed when you leave for Mexico or if you abort for any reason. If it goes sideways, you're working on your own because the United States doesn't want a negative international incident with Mexico brought to light. After all, we sidestepped the Mexican government. Make sure Clarke understands that risk. How do you propose we handle the weapons shipment and whoever the buyers are that the Garcia family has lined up?" Guzman asked.

"Give me until tomorrow morning. I need to call Waltzer off the record and get some additional information. I'll have a tentative plan worked up then."

"My phone better ring first because I have other departments that need to be brought up to speed. I despise this question because it can come out hollow, but are you okay? You're handling quite a load in your personal life, too."

"I'm fine, hurt and fucking upset? How's that for honesty? My focus is sharp because I want my family out of Mexico. I also don't want US weapons in the wrong hands. So don't worry, I won't break down until after this is over."

"Appreciate the temperature check, Noah. You know I'm here if you want to talk off the record. Good job on all of this, but I'm sorry you and your family have suffered. Get me that update," Guzman said right before he ended the call.

Noah dropped his head and groaned. A part of him didn't want to make this call, but Jasmine was right. Waltzer deserved to know his sister was alive. A giant knot sat right in his gut, and he didn't get the feeling that it would abate until all this was over. The hardest part now was to push all these emotions to the side and do his damn job. That included getting Waltzer's help to make all this work. Now, the question of the moment was whether Waltzer would even agree to do it?

Noah dialed Waltzer's number and hung up on the sixth ring, then Noah waited a few minutes before redialing the number. This time, he made it to seven rings before he hung up. He pressed the phone to his forehead, willing his brother to pick up his damn phone. A minute or so later, just as he was about to try again, his phone blasted to life, startling him.

He almost dropped the damn thing. "Waltzer?"

"You're an impatient fucker. Has anyone ever told you that?" Waltzer said in a low, stern voice.

"I need information and your help in that order. It's urgent, like in a situation that affects us both," Noah said, trying to gauge his reaction before going further. "Can you talk?"

"Define urgent. FUBAR? Never mind, you've got my undivided attention."

"I want to send you a couple of pictures. Where do you want them?"

When Waltzer confirmed his phone, Noah sent the images. "The first one is from the marketplace the day Jasmine was kidnapped. What was that meeting about? I've identified you and Marcelino, but who's the other man closest to the Range Rover? Also, who are those women?"

He heard a device receiving the pictures. "That's the Ambassador of Buranda, Marcus Cruz. The two women are with Miguel Reyes, a lawyer at the embassy. He's still inside the Rover and is super tight with Marcelino. They've known each other for a long time."

"I'd say since conception. He's Marcelino's son. They've gone to great lengths to keep it a secret. What was the meeting about?"

"No shit, that's interesting, and it explains why the old man meets with him so much. How do you know all of this?"

"It's a long story. I'll give you the play-by-play later, but here's the shortened version right now," Noah said as he brought his brother up to speed on the situation.

"Hold up, they're alive and have been living with Reyes, who twisted the facts to keep them hiding from Senator Dubin. That's seriously fucked up. Marcelino and Miguel are tight, and now it makes sense why I'm having so much trouble penetrating the inner circle."

Noah rubbed his forehead. "Yes, the cartel knew about that weapons convoy last week because of a tip from our father to Reyes. That partial shipment has caused problems for the senator because Reyes wants the missing weapons for a pending sale."

"How'd you get involved?" Waltzer asked.

"I was brought in to analyze the intel on the convoy and to help find the traitor within our government. So that part's been solved, but we don't know who the buyer is for those weapons, which is problematic considering what's in that shipment. Do you know?" Noah asked, flipping through the photos on his desktop.

"I don't know anything about the buyer. Garcia is tight with information. This op has been difficult because I'm only given directions from him right before my team is needed. It's taking longer to build up my credibility with the group. I've only been working with them for about three months." Guzman reported. Wind in the background echoed over the line.

Noah stopped on a picture. "How's he connected to Cruz?"

"Marcelino's a kingmaker. He loves to entertain and show that he's a team player. Of course, his team has to win, but he likes to make a big production. He's always meeting with people. He's smart in the way that he networks. It also makes it hard to know the true intent of a meeting."

Noah sat back and stared at the ceiling. "I've already updated Guzman on all of this except for what you've just shared. There's another name that jumped out over the last few days. Senator Decker has some ties to Mexico, and I need to dig into that a little more. It could be nothing, but it's worth a check. Does his name ring any bells?"

The crackle from the wind made it hard to hear Waltzer's answer. "No, but maybe he's working with Marcelino?"

"Good point. I'll check for connections between them. So now to the big favor part of my call. I need your help to pull out my mom and our sister. I'm hoping you know their location on the coast and if they travel with guards. We need to do this fast because the second half of the weapons shipment is going to happen soon. I need to get them out of Mexico and into a safe house while Reyes is in Washington preoccupied with cartel business. I'll have one of the FBI planes and a US Marshal assisting me. All I need is for you to escort them to a predetermined meeting place."

"That's a tall order because if things go south, I'll lose my cover and status with Garcia. How fast does this need to happen?"

"Tomorrow or Thursday morning at the latest," Noah answered.

"Fuck, Noah, that doesn't leave a lot of time to plan," Waltzer said in a sharp tone. "Unless something has changed, there's no security. The house is secure and gated in a small, affluent housing community. I'll send you the coordinates. There's also a little landing strip with a hangar just north of the area. God, I can't believe that girl's my sister. Does she know about me?"

"Yes, she knows your name but hasn't seen a picture of you. Do you want me to tell her you're guiding them?" Noah asked.

"No, emotions complicate everything, so leave it be. Speed and safety will be key to getting them out of the country and keeping my cover in place. Make sure they know I can be trusted because they've seen me with Marcelino. Have them go to the market tomorrow afternoon to get food for dinner. Instruct them only to bring one bag, the same size they'd usually take to the market. The point is to blend in and do normal, routine things. I'll intercept them at 1:00 PM tomorrow. I'll have a blue bandanna around my neck and a baseball cap on backward. When your mom greets me, have her use the phrase,

'It's good to see you,' and I'll respond with, 'Join me for an early dinner.' If I'm not there, they're to return home."

"Got it. I'll call you when we're in the air. Thanks, I owe you." Noah said, checking his watch. It wasn't late, so he called Trent and Clarke to give them a quick update.

He dialed Clarke's number, and when he answered, Noah instructed him to hold while he added Trent to the line. "Sorry for the late call, guys. I just finished talking to Waltzer. We're on for tomorrow afternoon. He's sending coordinates for the meeting spot and the airstrip. Once I receive them, I'll flip them to you and file the flight plan. Clarke, Guzman reminded me that we're on our own if this recovery goes to shit."

Clarke snorted. "I've already gotten the lecture from mine. Guzman works fast. We're good to go, and I already have a man who's willing to escort us on this cakewalk. He'll be an extra gun too."

"Perfect, let him know it's happening tomorrow afternoon. Also, Waltzer indicated that no guards are assigned to them, so that's a positive."

"Okay, text me the time to pick you up tomorrow, and I'll drive you to the helicopter pad," Trent said.

After Noah finished that call, he rolled his head from side to side. The hardest call was left. He needed to call his sister and mother to let them know the plan.

"Noah?" Lisa asked in a soft and scratchy voice. He loved hearing his baby sister's voice.

"Yes, I'm sorry for waking you up," he said.

"No worries, I'm up now. What's going on?" she asked, her sleepiness all but gone.

"Can you go get Mom? There's a lot going on, and I need to get you and Mom out tomorrow." Make sure you can both hear me."

The thud of the phone being put down and the rustling of covers filled the space. After a few minutes, a voice his heart remembered flowed over the line. Tears welled in his eyes. The moment was surreal, but he'd have time to reminisce and catch up later.

"Noah, is that you?" his mother asked, tears choking her words. "Your sister broke her promise and told me what she did."

"Actually, that's probably better because what I'm about to tell you will be a shock. I need to get you out of Mexico City tomorrow. Miguel Reyes has been lying to you."

His mom started to protest, but he heard his sister talking to her in the background. She pleaded with her mother to listen and reminded her that he worked for the FBI.

"Mom, I swear this is true, and I have the proof to back up what I'm going to tell you. He's a part of the Garcia family cartel. His father is Marcelino, and he's the one who staged your murder-suicide. He did that so our father would be beholden to him, and he lied to you about it so you'd be compliant and willing to hide. I have to get you out of there now because this cartel is going to deal stolen weapons from the US. If we wait, Miguel will know that our father is betraying him. I need you to believe me."

His mother's sobs broke his heart. She'd been through so much. "Lisa, help me," he said.

In the background, he heard Lisa whispering to their mom, but he couldn't make out all the words.

"Son, I'm scared. Are you sure it's safe? I thought Miguel— Never mind, it doesn't matter."

"Mom, I'd stake my life on it. I can't wait to hug you tomorrow, but for a brief period of time, you're going to have to stay at a safe house. If Miguel calls you, just act normal."

"I trust you and Lisa more than anyone. I want lots of hugs first, but then I want answers," his mom said.

"That's the plan. Listen up because we don't have much time," he said.

Then, he went through every detail about what she had to look for and say when she met Waltzer. Noah made sure they knew Waltzer could be trusted, and just to be sure, he had her repeat it all back.

He ended the call when he was satisfied they understood what was expected. He had to give his mom time to accept the lies and truths, but she had to stay strong until they were in Mill Creek.

Fourteen

J ASMINE THREW THE COVERS back with a determined flick of her hand. Her skin was heated and itchy from tossing and turning. Yes, Noah's words had hurt, but she couldn't be mad at him for telling her the truth. It wasn't his fault that she didn't like hearing it.

Now, the two options she had were to accept what they had or walk away. Somehow, that declaration sounded better in her head because her heart sang a different tune, which made her sad.

She had wanted some space from him earlier, but she'd spent that time stewing over everything. Question after question flooded her brain, so she gave up and headed into the kitchen. She noticed the light shining out under the door of his office. If she was hungry, she knew he must be, too, since they'd both skipped dinner. She made her favorite sandwich for when things went wrong in life. This comfort food made everything better.

Two plates were balanced on her arm as she poked her head into his space. "Is anyone hungry for a when-all-hell-breaks-loose sandwich guaranteed to make something a little bit better? This is my go-to when I need a tasty and special treat."

His hair was mussed from him tugging and running his fingers through it, but his smile melted the ice surrounding her ticker. She dropped off his plate and soda and took her usual seat.

"How can I refuse a miracle sandwich?" he asked.

"You can't. It's as simple as that. Be prepared—it's a mayo, mustard, and potato chip sandwich."

"I see you used the entire bag of chips," he said as he rotated the plate to inspect her masterpiece.

Jasmine picked up her sandwich and took a big bite. A loud crunch and an exaggerated mmm came next. "The chips are the main ingredient. You can't skimp. Now, while you're eating, fill me in on what I've missed."

The next few minutes were filled with crunching and talking while they devoured dinner. She was amazed at all that he'd accomplished, and her chest tightened with worry over the whole Mexico portion of the update. She hoped they didn't run into any armed men. The last thing anyone needed after all this turmoil was a complication.

His lips pursed, opened, then closed again. "Are you still willing to help me tomorrow on the plane with my mom and sister? I understand if you don't want to, but I'd like you there with me."

The undertone of that statement had both a tingle of longing and a dose of awkwardness inching down her spine. "Why would that change? What are safe topics for conversation? I don't want to overstep."

Noah ran his hand through his hair and sighed. His gaze locked on hers. "This suck, Jazy. Keep the discussion light, and if they ask anything deeper, let them know we'll talk later. It's the best I can do for now."

"Got it, now put me to work because sleeping isn't going to happen for a bit," she said, hating the emotion that threatened to engulf her. The bigger question was could she survive these next few days only being his friend? Well, she'd committed to it, so she'd do it because she cared about him.

He smiled and nodded toward the big screen. "I've decided to go back through the phone records that were given to me for that forty-eight-hour period. Since Waltzer identified the unknown man as Marcus Cruz, the Ambassador to Buranda, I want to know if Senator Martin Decker made or received any calls to him."

"That's a good point. Why would an ambassador be meeting with the head of a cartel?" she asked.

"Let's see if we can find out. I've pulled his numbers, and I'm running them against the raw data. He could be using a personal cell I don't have, but I doubt it. We should have the information in a minute."

Noah displayed one number, and under it were eight rows that displayed a number, date, and time on the big screen. She studied each one before directing her attention back to him.

"Interesting. It seems that Decker and Cruz speak quite a bit. All of these happened in that two-day period," Noah said.

She pointed at the screen. "Don't forget the air travel. I don't understand the connections. Senator Martin sits on subcommittees for appropriations and defense, right?"

"Yes, so Martin's been in contact with Cruz, who's the ambassador to a small South American country, and he also had lunch with a cartel leader and his son," he said, massaging his temples with his fingers.

Jasmine tapped her pen against her notebook and spoke more to herself than anyone in the room. "We know from your father and Waltzer that the cartel is selling those stolen weapons soon but is short half the quantity."

Noah dropped his hand. "I'm calling my father. Since he's the appropriations committee chair, he'll know if there is a legit reason for Decker to have business with Cruz."

She held up her hand. "Noah, it's late."

"That's never an issue in my job," he said, his phone on speaker so she could hear the exchange.

The voice of a worn-down man who surprisingly sounded awake answered. "Son, this is becoming a habit."

"I know. We'll be scheduling lunches next. I've been checking on something since you left, and I need your help. Why would Senator Decker be working with Ambassador Cruz?" Noah asked.

Jasmine's chest tightened at the almost friendly banter the two had just shared. It was far from the typical definition, but it was a start. She wondered if Noah even realized he'd done that. Maybe there was a chance they could find a small piece of common ground to build a relationship. His father had made some huge mistakes, but no one was perfect.

The senator cleared his throat. "Uh, Martin worked with Cruz on an aid package for agriculture and medical supplies. It closed this week. The dictator of that country is corrupt and spending government resources on building his military program to keep him in power rather than helping his people. It's in the best interest of the United States to help the people and hope they will overthrow the dictator. Why?"

Noah's shoulders dropped. "Hmm, okay, I wanted to know if there was a legitimate reason for those calls to Mexico. I'm trying to figure out who Garcia is planning on selling the weapons to. Okay, appreciate the information and your time."

After he killed the call, he ran his hand through his hair again. A groan from deep down in his chest rumbled out. "Well, now we're back at square one with who wants these damn weapons."

"Too bad you can't use those dog microchips," she said. He snapped his gaze to hers, but his mind seemed to be miles away.

"Bingo! When the real second half of the shipment moves, we can have RFID tags in them and track them that way for however long they are active," Noah said. His fingers worked overtime on the keyboard.

"Now, you need to go to bed and get some sleep. Tomorrow will need all of your attention," she said.

"You're right, but I need to send Guzman an update on the current situation and my recommendation. Then I promise I'll be off to bed," Noah said.

"Aren't you nervous about tomorrow? I mean, you haven't seen your mother or sister in twenty-three years. You've handled all of this with such dignity, considering everything that's happened."

He waved off her compliment, which was totally Noah. "I think the better description is numb. But, yes, my nerves are rioting. So many things could go wrong, but I can't allow that to happen. My mother and sister deserve a chance to be happy."

"What do you deserve?" she asked, unable to stop the question from popping out of her mouth.

"I don't know. I'll have to get back to you on that one."

His answer didn't surprise her. "You need to figure that one out, Noah. And for what it's worth, your strength and compassion do impress me. Don't sell yourself short."

She gave him her happiest smile and suppressed the crushing blow he'd dealt her. They were both adults and would move forward with their lives one way or another. There wasn't a moment she regretted with him.

NOAH AWOKE WITH A start, despising any mornings that started at 4:00 AM. He wiped the grit from his eyes and stretched to relieve the pinpricks of fire that worked up and down his legs. Exhaustion and nervous energy were going to be a part of his day. A by-product of staying up too late and knowing that he'd only get one chance to get his mother and sister out of Mexico.

Once he tossed back the covers, he stood staring at the empty side of the bed. He missed having Jasmine curled up in his bed. A natural fit, but he couldn't lie to her. A part of him contemplated sending her home so she'd be safe instead of coming to Mexico with him. He resisted only because he thought his mother and sister would feel more comfortable with her there. After all, his sister had a connection to Jazy.

He closed his eyes and sucked down a deep breath. What he needed was a cold shower and to put his game face on. Success today was the only acceptable outcome. On the way to the shower, he stopped at the dresser and closet to grab the clothing he needed. After his shower, he dressed and went to his office to grab supplies.

The duffel he wanted was on the top shelf. He unlocked his weapons locker, selected which guns he'd take, and stuffed extra clips into the bag. To err on the side of caution, he stuffed his bulletproof vest into the bag. The loud rip from the zipper muffled the sound of Jasmine's voice.

"Can you believe another week has passed?" he asked, then hefted the sack over his shoulder and turned to face her.

"Wow," she said, looking him up and down. "You look like a warrior in your tan cargo pants and black T-shirt."

"Dress for success, right?" he said. A thought crossed his mind.

"Uh-oh, why the serious face?" she asked.

"Do you know how to use a gun?"

"I do. My dad taught all of us. He said if there's a gun in the house, everyone should know how to use it safely."

"Why am I not shocked?" he asked, returning to his locker. When he turned around, he showed her a pistol. "I'm bringing this one for you. I'll leave it with you when Clarke and I deplane, so you have a way to protect yourself."

After she accepted, he motioned for her to lead the way out. Trent was on his way to pick them up and take them to the helicopter that was inbound. So far, everything was on track. As they waited, Guzman called.

"Hey, boss," Noah said.

"Got your update, and I've already forwarded it on. I liked the tracking option, and there's a team already working on the best way to accomplish it. As for your father, that's been handed off to a different group within our department. It's out of our hands, which is best. I do need you to send me that log when you get it."

"Will do. I've gotta to run. I'll call you once we have my family secured and are in the air coming back."

"Keep your head down and be safe," Guzman said right as Trent pulled into the driveway.

Ending the call, Noah pocketed his phone and opened the back door for Jasmine, stowed his bag in the back and hopped into the passenger's seat.

"Morning," Trent said, sliding the gearshift into reverse. "Aimee insisted on taking Clarke, so he'll meet us there."

The rest of the drive was quiet, which Noah appreciated. He wasn't in the mood for chitchat. Instead, he used the time to go over the day ahead of them.

When Trent arrived and parked, he turned in his seat and handed Noah a small device. "It's a personal locator beacon. The sheriff's office uses them when we have to look for lost or injured hikers. That way, if a first responder gets lost or turned around, we can find them."

Noah couldn't help but grin at his friend. "Thanks, and I look forward to returning it to you when we get back."

He grabbed his gear and nodded at Clark, who was currently hugging his soon-to-be wife. The whirl of the rotors became louder as the helicopter approached. Once it landed, Noah ushered Jasmine on board. He stowed his bag and took his seat. Clarke followed behind him.

"Hey, man," Clarke said. "We're all set on my end."

"We're good to go on mine. Mr. Worry gave me a tracker beacon, so I guess he wants us back."

Clarke laughed. "Well, that's good, because I'm pretty sure Aimee would be pissed if that didn't happen."

Noah gave the pilot a thumbs-up as he lifted off and started his ascent. Once they arrived at Boise Airport, a golf cart shuttled them to the FBI hangar where their planes were stored. Twenty-five minutes later, they were loaded into the Gulfstream and ready to taxi to the runway.

He sent a quick text to Waltzer with just the numbers reflecting their estimated time of arrival. The flight would take about four and a half hours, so he planned to catch up on some sleep. The flight attendant woke all three of them up thirty minutes before landing.

Once they were on the ground, he went to the cockpit and instructed the pilot that if any trouble showed up, he should take off immediately and return to Boise. If he and Clarke had to, they could develop a plan B.

When Noah returned to the main cabin, Clarke was chatting with Jasmine, and whatever he had said made her laugh. She had the best laugh. Noah shook off his wayward thoughts and removed the pistol and an extra clip from his bag for her to use. She took the proffered gun and clip and put them onto the table next to her.

"I'll be outside," Clarke said, patting her shoulder as he exited. At least Noah would have a few seconds alone with her before he had to go.

She launched herself into his arms and held him tight. "You be careful and bring your family home. I've got this handled."

He hugged her back and pressed a kiss to her crown. So many unspoken words sat on the tip of his tongue. He hated the look of despair he saw in her eyes. It was the same one he'd seen the other night when he told her he would never be able to marry.

God, he wanted her so much, but if he failed her, it would destroy him. No, he'd do the honorable thing even if it would kill him. "See you in a couple of hours."

She released her hold and smiled at him. No other words were spoken as he turned and exited the aircraft. He walked up to Clarke, who was talking to the marshal who'd be helping them out today.

"Dan, this is Noah. We're the hired help, and this guy is the brains," Clarke said.

"Nice to meet you. Clarke sent me the coordinates, so I've got the route mapped and an alternate planned if necessary. We're picking up your packages at a local restaurant."

Noah knew all that, but was pleased that their driver was thorough. He stowed both bags in the back seat with him and let Clarke have the front seat. The roads weren't paved for a bit, but once they were closer to the city, the ride smoothed out, and the pressure on Noah's bladder lessened. He should have used the lavatory in the plane. Clarke rambled on with Dan while Noah watched the scenery zip past.

The drive wasn't too long, and about forty-five minutes later, Dan drove into a parking lot across the street from the restaurant. "I'll stay in the car and read the paper."

Noah unzipped his bag and tucked a gun into his ankle holster.

"You ready, or do I need to hand you something from the duffel?" he asked Clarke.

Clarke opened his door and spoke over his left shoulder. "I loaded up while I waited for you to play kissy face. I'm ready."

Noah rolled his eyes at his friend, not wanting to encourage his behavior. He grabbed the handle and popped his car door, exited, and looked both ways before he crossed the street. Clarke kept walking down the sidewalk in a stroll while Noah entered the restaurant. The aroma of refried beans, spices, and flour tortillas had his mouth watering.

He scanned the restaurant and saw Waltzer sitting in the corner with his back against the wall. He had perfect line of sight to the street as well as the front and back of the restaurant. A sharp pain hit Noah's stomach and morphed into a tightness in his chest. This was the first time he'd seen Waltzer since the night he'd shot Noah.

Now he was staring at his half brother's face, and in a moment, he'd be reunited with his mother and sister. His heart thrummed so hard and fast against his chest he thought it might just explode. He wondered if Waltzer was experiencing the same type of feelings.

Noah approached the table and shook Waltzer's hand. They'd eaten while they waited for Noah, making this look like a normal lunch. "Good to see you, man. All right, you two ready to go?"

When his mother turned around and saw him, her eyes widened, and her lip quivered. She fought for composure just like he had. His hand itched to hug her so he could feel the loving embrace of his mom—a luxury he'd lost so long ago.

His sister's smile tugged on his heart along with the sheen of tears in her eyes. Sucking down a deep breath, he forced steel into his spine to lock down the emotions popping to life like popcorn in a microwave bag. He had to prioritize their safety above all else.

His mom and sister stood and gathered their bags. He saw two men enter the restaurant from the corner of his eye. Waltzer casually moved his hand to his hip. Noah would bet his life savings his brother had a gun holster settled on his lower back. The men approached the table, blocking his mother and sister's retreat.

The bigger one of the two rushed to speak. "*Alto, porque estas con esta mujer?*"

Waltzer was the first to speak. His smile didn't reach his eyes, but his reaction was smooth and causal. His brother shrugged and cocked his head to the right. "Sorry, I don't understand, do you speak English?"

The smaller of the two men snorted and hooked his thumb toward himself. "Him no, but I do. Are you okay, Mrs. Reyes? Who are these men?"

His mom surprised him when she extended her hand to the man. "*Hola*, these are my sister's boys. They're here on business from Mexico City but carved out a little time to have lunch with their aunt and niece. Isn't that sweet?"

The smaller man translated her answer to his sidekick, who nodded and smiled. Noah wasn't sure, but he'd bet that Waltzer spoke Spanish, so he'd follow his reaction. The men studied them from head to toe before the same guy asked. "Where is Mr. Reyes?"

His mom laughed and waved her hand around her head. "Working. That man works way too much. He sent us here to relax before all the holiday celebrations begin. He'll be so sad that he missed seeing his nephews."

The two men conversed for a few seconds before the big guy took a step backward. His mom grabbed Lisa's hand and tugged her past the men. Waltzer dug out his wallet and tossed a few bills onto the table.

His mother stopped and turned back to face the two men. "*Buenas tardes.*" She waved, then turned back Noah and Waltzer. "Come on, boys, it's time you take us home so you can head back to the city."

Noah moved ahead of his mom and held the door open for them to pass. They stopped on the sidewalk, waiting for his brother who came out moments later. Noah scrutinized the nearby areas and didn't see anything that stood out, but his neck was tingling.

Waltzer surprised him when he tugged Noah's mom in for a hug first then his sister, but his brother was probably sticking to the story. His shock and danger meter exploded when he hugged Noah in that manly embrace. This man was lethal, not emotional.

Waltzer whispered against his ear in a low voice he almost missed. "Those two could be trouble. I'll assess and clean up if needed. Go now."

Noah slapped his back, then grabbed his mom's hand. The car wasn't across the street, but he'd noticed Clarke talking on a phone at the end of the road. Noah casually headed in that direction, and they crossed the street and got into the car's back seat. Dan had already stowed their bags in the truck, so there was room.

"Noah, we've picked up a bit of activity," Dan said.

Noah scanned the perimeter. Dan had parked in a perfect spot. Due to the buildings surrounding the lot, there was no line of sight from the street.

The sensation at Noah's neck surged along with his trepidation. His bark of instruction was a little harsher than he intended, but speed was important. "Lisa, get down in the floor well. Mom, lie across the seat. Keep your heads down. Hurry, and no matter what, stay down."

Clarke turned the corner in a casual stroll, then jogged to the car and jumped into the front seat. "Let's move. Two jeeps loaded with men just arrived. I'm unsure if it's just bad timing or something else, and I don't plan to find out."

A twinge of worry stabbed Noah's chest as his mind snapped to Jazy. If anything happened to her, it would gut him. He wasn't ready for a world that didn't have her in it. She could handle herself, but this environment was different, and she wasn't a trained agent.

They rode in silence as Dan navigated the roads just above the speed limit. At this moment, the only job that mattered was monitoring the streets and air to ensure they weren't pursued or tailgated.

"What happened with those two men?" Clarke asked, keeping his focus on monitoring the situation.

"They wanted to know why Diana and Lisa were with us in the restaurant. My mother handled the situation beautifully."

"Thanks, son," she said. Her voice was full of emotion and quivered.

Noah patted her shoulder. "Waltzer's handling the remaining details."

Clarke didn't respond, just bobbed his head with understanding. The rest of the drive back to the airstrip was silent and uneventful. Two words that made Noah happy. The tension in the car was heavy, but it diminished some when they arrived at the airstrip and parked alongside the plane.

Noah blew out a deep breath. "Okay, stay low just a little longer. Let Clarke and I check everything out. Dan, if a surprise party breaks out, haul ass to your office."

Clarke surveyed the metal structure and the area outside. Noah headed to the plane and stopped as the pilot and Jasmine stood in the doorway.

"Right as rain," the pilot said, which was the right phrase to let Noah know all was clear and good. And Jazy, who didn't miss anything, added her own phrase. "Potato chip sandwiches are ready."

He smiled and turned to give Clarke the all-clear. His friend pointed to the steps and herded his mom and sister toward them.

"Lisa, you know Jasmine. She'll get you two settled while we wrap things up," Clarke said.

Once they started up the steps, Clarke walked toward Dan, giving him his thanks before grabbing their equipment from the trunk. Once he had everything, he closed the trunk and dashed for the plane. Moments later, the aircraft door was secured, and the pilot had them taxiing toward the runway headed to Mill Creek.

The first thing Noah did was hug his mother and sister. He couldn't believe they were with him in flesh and blood. He tugged them both into the circle of his arms, not wanting to let go. "Mom, you look great. Lisa, I can't believe how big you've gotten."

She gave him a crooked look. "Uh, I was like three, so yeah, I'm bigger. I have so many years of pestering my big brother to make up for."

Noah smiled at his sister. "Don't forget that goes two ways."

He extended his hand to Jazy, and the moment she made contact, he crushed her to his chest. The heat and power from her hug soaked into his bones. His heart expanded deep in his chest, and a warmth he couldn't describe filled his body. He bent his head and claimed her lips, kissing her deep and hard. Life was pretty damn perfect at this moment.

He introduced his mom and sister to Jasmine and Clarke. Then he took his mother's outstretched hand and sat beside her. Tears and laughter followed as they shared stories and reminisced. The deeper emotional discussions were coming, but it was about reconnecting right now.

Jasmine brought out a plate of sandwiches, water, and soda and placed everything on the table. They discussed where his mom and sister would stay and that Jasmine would get them the supplies and clothing they needed the following day.

Noah smacked his forehead, almost forgetting that he had to call Guzman. He excused himself and headed toward the back of the plane. As soon as his boss answered, he replied, "Success with no major issues."

"That's great. I won't keep you. Send your report when you get a chance. Real quick, I wanted to let you know that the rest of the weapons are moving Friday morning. The trackers are being placed now. Senator Dubin has been alerted, and he's following his normal communication protocols with Reyes, so everything appears normal."

Scenarios of everything that could go wrong churned in his mind. He ended the call and pressed the phone to his head. That whole operation could go sideways in so many ways, but he had to remain calm. There was no reason to worry because nothing good ever came from it. It wasted valuable brainpower and wreaked havoc on the body. That was a fact, yet he stood there irritated that he was doing just that.

Fifteen

THE FOLLOWING MORNING, JASMINE came to a decision. That kiss Noah had given her yesterday had betrayed all the excuses he'd muttered. The possession and passion behind that touch had shredded the last of her sanity. She couldn't be with him anymore, or she'd find herself begging for a chance, and she refused to do that.

He had to realize that he didn't need to fear the unknown. He could just trust his instincts, know he would be compassionate, and conduct himself using his moral compass. But, the more time she spent with him, the blurrier her lines would become. Her chest constricted with the knowledge of what she had to do.

The time had come for her to leave.

Noah tossed her his truck keys and credit card so she could purchase everything on his mother and sister's list. Once again, they had to leave their belongings behind to start over. Never in her life had she met a stronger woman.

Watching the three of them swap stories and talk about all the time and events they'd missed had been both sweet and sad. The power of love had no boundaries and was eternal. All of this made Jasmine miss her family.

She climbed into the driver's seat, and Noah stood outside the door.

"Thanks for all your help yesterday," he said through the open car window. "It's a bizarre feeling to know I can visit my mom and sister. I'm going to tell my father today that they're alive. This whole thing is such a disaster and a blessing. Does that even make sense?"

"Yes, it does. The important part is you're all going to get through this together," she said, turning the key in the ignition.

"And thanks for helping with the shopping," he said, backing away from the truck.

Jasmine shifted the gear into reverse. "I'm happy to help. I like your mom and sister. Don't forget I'm heading to the library to see Irene afterward to talk to the children about photography and journalism. Maggie told me today and Friday are early release days before winter break."

"That's great, and you'll be safe there. Call me on your way back. I have to make a call and have about an hour's work to wrap up."

She nodded, then slid the gearshift into reverse to pull out of Clarke's driveway. The tasks she had to complete didn't take that long because Rayna Outpost, whose name didn't do the store justice, was incredible. The store had all the typical mountain apparel and supplies, but the rest of the store should be called a boutique.

If Jasmine had more time, she would have gone on a little shopping spree. She purchased a suitcase to replace the one taken from her in Mexico City.

She found the local drug store and picked up the remaining items on her list before heading toward the library. It was earlier than she'd expected to be there, but Irene was gracious and gathered the children for Jasmine's presentation. She'd taken one of Noah's laptops so she could access her website for a little show and tell.

An hour later, she wrapped up by answering the last question. Irene had been right—the children loved to see new ideas, and speaking with them today had made Jasmine happy. Their eyes were as wide as saucers. At least ten children told her that they wanted to be photographers when they were grown.

On the way to Clarke's house, she called Noah, who said he'd meet her at the gate. When she arrived, he jumped into the passenger's seat.

"I've never ridden on this side of my truck," he said with a big smile. "How'd everything go?"

"Great. Irene thinks I need to teach a summer photography class for her youth program. She doesn't stop, but I love that about her," she said as she drove them toward the house.

"That's not a bad idea. It would be something different for the kids to learn. Irene's always looking for new things for the kids of this community. Speaking of photography, didn't you order a camera?" he asked.

"Yes, but it got delayed. It's supposed to be here next week. How's your family doing today?"

He closed the garage door with the opener Clarke had given him. "Really good, considering everything. Today, they're helping Aimee finish up a shit-ton of cookies for the town's annual Christmas Festival. I promised we'd cross our fingers for snow."

Jasmine would have enjoyed going to the festival. She could only imagine all the baked goods. The town already looked festive, with the giant decorated tree in the park. Lights were on in every store and office, and all the window fronts were beautifully decorated.

She loved the poinsettias and spruce adorning the town's light poles and flower pots. The magic of the season flowed through every corner. Chicago would also be decorated for the holiday season, but the people she adored wouldn't be there.

"Yeah, I would have thought you'd have colder weather up in the mountain," she said as she put the truck into park at Noah's home, then handed him the keys.

"The weather's been warmer and dryer than usual up here, according to Trent. This is my first winter in Mill Creek, so I have no context," he answered, taking the keys. "You bought a suitcase."

She heard the question in his tone but ignored it. "I have to get my stuff back to Chicago somehow."

He didn't reply to her statement, so she followed him into the house. He left her luggage in the kitchen and hollered over his shoulder, "I need to call my father," he said. "Come join me."

She sighed because she was delaying the inevitable, and she knew it. What she should be doing was packing because there was flight from Boise to Chicago leaving tonight.

"HELLO, SON, WHAT'S ON your mind?" Senator Dubin asked when he picked up the phone.

"We need to talk. I'm sorry it's over the phone, but it's important. I have Jasmine with me."

"Give me a minute," the senator said. Noah heard him excusing himself, then a door closing. "Okay, I'm alone, what's happened?"

Noah tried to put himself in his father's shoes but couldn't, so he went with the ripping-off-the-Band-Aid method. "Mom and Lisa are alive. They're at a safe house. Reyes lied to you the entire time. He staged their deaths and has been deceiving you ever since."

A loud thud came across the line, along with deafening silence. Concern knotted Noah's stomach. "Dad! Dad, are you okay?"

It took a minute, but finally, a low moan threaded across the line. His father cleared his throat, but his voice was heavy and raw with emotion when he spoke. "I'm okay, just lost my balance. Did he hurt them?"

"No, I think he cares about them in a twisted way."

"I'm sorry, I need to lie down for a bit." The senator's voice wobbled. "I'll call you later. Thanks for trusting me with this information."

The silence that followed weighed on Noah's shoulders and stabbed his heart. The pain caused by all these actions had taken its toll on every member of his family. His anger toward the Garcia cartel had reached the maximum level and was threatening to explode. He vowed that from this moment forward, he'd spend the rest of his career working to bring them down.

When his phone rang from an unknown number, he answered immediately, thinking it might be his brother. "Hello."

"We have a problem," Waltzer said, his tone sharp and clipped.

"What's happening?"

"I've been directed to have my men scout a route and be prepared to intercept the other half of the weapons. Once secured, the weapons will be transported to a location that Marcelino will provide so they can be handed over to Buranda soldiers. How the hell does that country have that type of cash?"

Noah shook his head as he remembered what his father had told him. "I think Ambassador Cruz is working with the dictator, and they are using the aid money they received from the US to pay for those weapons. I've got an idea on how to finish this, but the approval for this plan is above my pay grade."

"Since you've embedded yourself into my operation, bring in the brass, and let's get a plan set up. I can meet in forty-five minutes after I take care of a few things here. Shit's going to happen fast," Waltzer said.

Noah's other line beeped, prompting him to end his call with Waltzer to accept the incoming call.

"Son, you have a problem. Miguel just called to thank me for my continued support and said we'll meet next year to review some new projects. Since his business concluded earlier than planned, he's heading back home tonight on the last flight out of Washington," his dad sputtered.

Noah pinched his nose to stop a headache from forming. "Jeepers, that seems to be today's theme. Okay, I'm working on it."

"I know I have no right to ask, but please keep me posted. That asshole has made my life miserable. The fault belongs to me for allowing him the opportunity, but I still hate that man."

"I will, Dad," Noah said, pausing at his use of that word, which had been gutted from his vocabulary until now. It was strange yet fitting to use the word. "I've got to go. Everything is escalating." He terminated the call and sighed.

He punched in the digits to his boss's number. The moment Guzman answered, Noah rattled off the latest, which included the update from his brother. Just over an hour later, he was on a joint conference call with Guzman, Waltzer, Lieutenant General Banks, and several analysts who had been updated on the most recent intel. The objective was clear, so there was no need for a preamble.

"I understand from Waltzer that Noah has been an asset during this operation, which has become an urgent and fluid situation. Let's hear the plan of attack," Banks barked.

Noah cleared his throat and presented the strategy he'd been revising for the last forty-five minutes. "Since we know the players and risks involved, I suggest we plant several small remote explosives on the weapons. We won't need many due to the obvious fact that the ammunition will trigger a larger blast, destroying the weapons. The ability to track and monitor the truck transporting the stolen contraband via satellite gives us the upper hand. If anything happens along the way, we can assess and either destroy the cargo or follow it to see where it lands. This dictator could be selling his new toys to another buyer."

Waltzer interjected, "Best-case scenario, the package arrives at the compound in Buranda, the dictator rushes to inspect his weapons, and boom."

"Yes, ammo can be unstable. That gives all parties a layer of protection and distance in the event the wrong people survive the blast. This will eliminate fingers being pointed toward anyone," Guzman added.

Another voice chimed, one of the analysts. "Sir, we have the perfect devices for this job. They're both powerful and reliable."

Noah tapped his pen on his notes. "Waltzer would have to sell Marcelino on not transferring the weapons until he verifies the wire has been sent before he hands over the package to the buyer."

"Why does that matter?" the general snapped.

"Because it will keep Marcelino close to Waltzer, and he can eliminate Marcelino after the money has been deposited. It'll also motivate the dictator to inspect his new toys since he had to pay in advance, and that will give us the best opportunity to take him out. Lastly, in relation to the evidence being presented by Senator Dubin, we need to get the president to revoke Miguel Reyes's diplomatic immunity in order to detain him before he leaves for Mexico City tonight. That way, we'll eliminate two known enemies of the United States," Noah said.

"Anyone in disagreement or have logistical issues with this strategy?" Lieutenant General Banks asked. When no one opposed, he continued. "I'm behind this plan, but I need to run it past the president. I'll get back to you in short order."

When the call finished, Noah stood and then left his office. He needed some fresh air. This part of his job both excited and exhausted him. One could be so close to eliminating another risk to the nation's security and yet so far in the exact moment.

He scanned his space. His backyard was basic and needed landscaping. A built-in outdoor kitchen and a mix of grass and pavers would be amazing additions. He could picture it and would put that on his to-do list for this coming summer.

Taking a seat on one of his deck chairs, he lifted his gaze. The majority of the blue sky had been masked behind thick gray clouds. The chilly wind lashed out at his skin, promising a storm.

He welcomed the cold because it sharpened his mind. The next twenty-four hours would be stressful if they got the green light. He double-checked his phone to ensure he hadn't accidentally muted the ringer. The snick of the door had him turning his head to see Jasmine approaching.

"Oh, it looks like a storm's brewing. Maybe Aimee will get her snow. How'd the call go?" she asked and took the open seat next to him.

He liked being able to share things with her and getting her opinion. He spent the next several minutes updated her on the latest. Her face contorted with different expressions as she processed the information he shared. Then, without missing a beat she asked the million-dollar question, "When is the general going to know if this is happening?"

"That's the magical question, and it depends on the chief of staff getting us in front of the president."

Her nose scrunched. "Wow, that's another obstacle that sounds tricky. I don't know how you handle all that anxious energy. It'd drive me nuts."

"It has its moments, that's for sure. But when you get a big win, it erases most of the negative aspects. It's a high like no other."

"It's been an intense couple of weeks, but getting to know all of you has been worth it. Hell, I've even gotten to know myself better. I've finished a very rough draft of the senator's story for you to review. Obviously, I'll need to finish the last part once we learn how this all plays out officially and if his crimes will or won't be made public. You'll have to call me with the outcome because it's time for me to go home," she murmured the last sentence.

A lump formed in his throat. "Are you sure? You could stay to see how it plays out. I wouldn't mind."

"Goodbyes are difficult, but it's time. I need to get home and see my family. I have so much to tell them. And I have one grumpy dad who needs some love from his wayward daughter. I'm going to have that conversation with him like you suggested."

"I––just stay one more night, Jazy." His voice was strained by emotion.

She huffed out a breath and stood. "What will staying another night give us, Noah? We can't pretend. Just like we can't control the future. I believe in us, and I hope you analyze this six ways to Sunday because you're discarding the possibility of a brilliant future together."

No truer words had been spoken, but fear gripped his heart and nailed his feet to the ground. Two words came to his mind, unreasonable and selfish, and that grounded him. Jazy was correct; it was time for her to go. He had to put his job first and concentrate on this operation—too much was at stake.

She pivoted and entered the house, and he thought he might crumble into a thousand pieces right there on his deck. His checked the time on his watch. It was nearing two in the afternoon, which was 4:00 PM in Washington. Could this fucking day crawl forward any slower?

When his phone rang, he did a small fist pump. "Hey, boss, what's the word?" he asked, ready to cross his fingers if it'd help him hear the right decision from the president.

"We didn't get a green light for the entire operation. The only part that's authorized is to destroy the weapons once they arrive in Buranda or if it appears they are breaking up the shipment," Guzman said, no emotions lacing his words. This was just a factual update. "I know this isn't what you wanted to hear. Are we good?"

Noah threw his head back and exhaled. He wanted to scream at his boss, but what good would that do? It wasn't Guzman's fault the higher-ups hadn't approved his entire plan or that Jazy was leaving. "I'm disappointed, but there's not much I can do about it. Has Waltzer been updated?"

"Yes. The president also wants the whole exchange on record, so Waltzer is wearing a camera. We've been invited to watch the operation tomorrow morning at eight sharp."

"I'll be there," Noah said.

"I'll forward the authentication information for the portal and conferences feed," his boss said, then he ended the call.

Noah pressed the edge of the phone against the bridge of his nose. He'd called his father so many times recently his number had been committed to memory as he tapped the digits.

Dad answered. "Son, do we have good news?"

"Not really," he said, then reviewed the team's plan. "The president shot it all down except for blowing up the weapons. He wants to retain Waltzer's cover and monitor the situation."

"There's always a bigger picture at work we don't always have line of sight to. We have to trust the president's judgment. He's purview is much larger than ours."

"I know, it's just frustrating," Noah said.

"I have faith this will work out. Obviously in a different way than we anticipated, but at some point, Marcelino and Miguel will pay for their crimes," his father said. "You're a good man, son, and I'm proud of you."

Noah ended the call and slid his phone into his back pocket when Jasmine approached him with her suitcase rolling behind her. "You got everything?" he asked, dangerously close to spinning out of control.

"I think so. I fly out tonight," she said, handing him a sheet of paper.

"What's this?"

"It's my address so you can forward my camera, and you'll know where I live. Not that you couldn't find that out using your superspy skills," she said with a sheepish grin.

"Come here," he said, tugging her into a fierce hug.

Her phone beeped. "My ride is here. Give me a call when you can. I want to know how all of this unfolds."

His entire being shut down. She grabbed the handle of her bag, turned, and then walked out the front door. The moment the door closed, his world darkened.

What the fuck am I supposed to do now?

Friday morning, Noah sat on a call that annoyed him. As a grown adult, he had to listen to a roll call on a secure video conference that took him twenty minutes of time to log into using a ton of authentication codes.

He'd woken up on the wrong side of the bed and was pissed at world. It hadn't even taken him a month to ruin the best damn thing that had ever walked into his life. The other fact that sat heavy on his chest was if this operation wasn't a success, it would leave his family vulnerable.

"Noah Parker, present," he said when they got to his name.

Next came the instructions that this was a listen-only conference. The camera feed they were seeing was attached to a deep-cover asset. Finally, the screen came to life, and he saw Marcelino and Miguel sitting on opposite ends of an elegant sofa in a massive living room. A hallway ran to the right and left, with the big double glass doors in the middle. The audio started broadcasting next, making it an eerie scene because it seemed like they were watching a movie, but it was real.

They could hear Marcelino and Miguel talking about plans for Christmas. After this meeting, Miguel would head to the coast to pick up Lisa and Diane. That boiled Noah's blood. Little did Miguel know they weren't going to be there. Noah noticed several armed men coming and going while two stood guard at the edge of the room.

Waltzer approached the sofa. "Marcelino, will you confirm that you've received the funds? My man's reporting that the money was wired."

Miguel stood and then ambled toward a table on the opposite side of the room to retrieve an iPad. When he returned, he handed it to his father. Finally, the man nodded after studying the screen for an extended period of time.

"The money had been transferred," Marcelino said in a joyous voice.

"God bless the United States," Marcelino said, raising a flute of champagne to his son.

Miguel tipped his glass until it clinked with his father's, then took a celebratory sip and returned it to the table. "Now, before I leave, I have a surprise for you. He should arrive anytime now."

Marcelino's face brightened even more. The two started talking about trivial items while they waited. No business was discussed, which didn't surprise Noah since they were too careful. After a few minutes, Waltzer approached the two and waited to be given permission to speak. Noah had no clue how he managed that nicety. Marcelino looked at Waltzer, then gave him a brief nod.

"Are you good with my men letting the truck leave?" Waltzer asked.

They both laughed for a moment. "By all means," Marcelino said. "They bought them fair and square."

A melodious ringing sound filtered through the speakers, and a maid in a traditional uniform trotted past everyone toward the front door. Waltzer snapped his head in that direction, and at the same time, a familiar voice teased Noah's memory banks. Once the maid stepped aside, he saw his dad standing in the entryway of Garcia's home. *What the hell?*

Miguel greeted the senator with a firm handshake. "Senator, it's nice to see you. Let me introduce you officially to Marcelino Garcia."

Noah's father set down a case he carried next to an open chair that faced the sofa. Then he moved forward to shake the patriarch's hand. "It's a pleasure to meet you."

Waltzer stood to the side, allowing the camera to see everyone in the room. Once everyone was seated, Marcelino motioned for one of his servers to bring refreshments. In a matter of minutes, a tray of fruit and cheese was placed on the coffee table, and the senator was given a flute with champagne.

"What are we celebrating?" the senator asked.

"We sold the weapons this morning. To friendship and partnerships," Miguel said, tipping his glass toward the senator.

Noah's father sipped his drink and placed the glass on the table. Then, he popped a chunk of cheddar cheese into his mouth and chewed.

"So, Marcelino, the senator is bringing us an early Christmas present. It seems it pays to have friends in the right places. Please tell him what you shared with me."

Noah's father cleared his throat. "There's a new prototype weapon in the late stages of production that will revolutionize warfare. The United States has been funding a secret program to perfect laser weaponry. I'm pleased to announce we have finally done it. This is the future in warfare, men. These babies will be in high demand. No one in the world will have them except for the United States, and perhaps you."

Marcelino's and Miguel's eyes almost bugged out of their heads. The two whispered between them before Miguel leaned toward the senator. "This is a unique opportunity."

"Imagine the carnage. The price you could get for the weapon would make you and your family wealthy beyond your wildest dreams for generations to come."

Miguel pointed toward Noah's father. "The senator explained that this is happening soon, which is why the senator pressed for a meeting. As you can imagine, the secrecy and security around this information is guarded at the highest levels. If we waited until after Christmas, it would be too late."

The senator interjected with, "The defense subcommittee was just debriefed yesterday afternoon. The weapons are being produced in a high-security facility in New Mexico. They are being shipped to Washington over the holidays and are due to the Department of Defense on New Year's Day."

"Is that one of them?" Marcelino asked, looking at the case the senator had brought, his hands rubbing together.

Noah's father took a sip of his beverage before answering. "Indeed. I wanted you to get a sense of what it'll look like and how it's designed to work. This is one of the prototype models."

"How will you communicate the coordinates for an intercept?" Miguel asked.

"As you know, I'm one of the leads on the subcommittee that gets the specifics. When I receive the route coordinates, I'll pass them along as usual. The problem is the tight window, so your men must mobilize fast. Gentlemen, are you ready to see the future?"

Noah's stomach slammed to the floor. He couldn't believe what he had heard. What the hell was his dad doing? The senator moved his drink to the side, making room for his black case. He lifted the lid, took out the weapon, and placed it on his lap.

"A man should protect his own. It's up to him to right the wrongs of the past," he said, abruptly standing.

In one fluid motion, he aimed and fired his automatic rifle, killing the two men sitting in front of him.

Marcelino and Miguel slumped over. It took about three seconds for the shock of what had just happened to pass. Next, the two security guards behind the sofa fired, hitting Noah's father. His brother rushed forward from his position to kick the gun away from their father. Waltzer checked his pulse and announced him dead before repeating the same process for Marcelino and Miguel.

The next voice heard was Lieutenant General Banks speaking into the earbud Waltzer wore as they watched live via their conference feed. "Disinfect, bug out, and RTB, confirm."

In a low voice that was barely audible, Waltzer responded with, "Roger that."

The video conference ended, and Noah sat staring at a blank screen. His chest tightened, and unshed tears filled his eyes. The words his dad had uttered before he killed those two were for Noah's benefit.

A rush of nausea had him reaching for the trash can. His mind raced with all the things he'd left unsaid. He'd never told his father that he forgave him or that he loved him. His father had made many mistakes, but he'd sacrificed his life so his family would be safe. Noah wished Jasmine were there standing by his side. Instead, he stood alone, trying to pick up the shattered pieces of his life.

The ringtone of his phone startled him. He snatched it up and saw on the display that it was Guzman.

"Don't speak, just listen. I just finished a call with the general, the chief of staff, and the president. The good news is your father made up that weapon. The president is not happy with this situation, but he's made a deal with Mexico to label his death an assassination. He died in service to our country, and his wife and daughter were found alive after being held captive for years. No more details regarding this event will be released. Your father's body will be returned to your family once everything has been cleared with Mexico. I'll keep you updated on that front."

"Before you ask, I didn't know about any of this. It shocked me as much as it shocked all of you," Noah sputtered.

"I know, and I'm sorry. Take as much time as you need to process all this and get your family settled. Let's talk in the new year or before if you need me."

Sixteen

J ASMINE LEFT FOR CHICAGO with dignity and a shattered heart. She already missed Mill Creek's uniqueness —there was no place quite like it. Her decision to leave made sense because she needed to focus on the future.

On the other hand, Noah still had one foot planted in the past, and he needed to reconcile those issues and emotions to find himself. It was not a small task because events that shaped his life and person were based on lies and heartache.

Now, her apartment seemed too empty and small since she was used to sharing her space with a certain man. Not liking the silence, she turned on her television, flipping through channels until she found one that slammed her right back into Noah's world. The headline inching across the bottom of the screen was shocking.

Breaking news: Senator Dubin assassinated. His wife and daughter were found alive after twenty-three years. Story developing.

She recoiled and covered her mouth with her hands. *Oh, Noah, this is so unfair. Just when you were reconnecting with your father and reunited with your mother and sister.*

There was no question about what she had to do next. With her phone in hand, she dialed his number, which she knew by heart, and then pressed end. God, she was nervous about speaking to him. She wasn't sure what to say.

Maybe she was afraid to find out if he'd even take her call. Why, she couldn't answer, but she also hadn't heard from him since she'd left. Frustration burned through her blood, and she threw her phone against a pillow. She rationalized that he was busy handling his work, so she'd try later.

Her sisters were coming over in forty-five minutes, and she couldn't wait to see them. She dashed off to get in the shower and then got dressed. Ready for their arrival, she decided to stop being silly and call Noah.

She sat on the sofa, and after curling her legs underneath her body, she dialed his number. Her stomach twisted into a horrible knot when she got Noah's voicemail. A sliver of doubt licked down her neck. What if he'd just ignored her call?

Pushing the doubt aside, she left him a message. "Noah, I heard about your father, and I'm so sorry. If you want to talk, I'm here, no matter the time."

The doorbell had her ditching the phone and racing toward the door. When she pulled it open, her older sister, Olivia, launched into her arms. Then the youngest, Marion, hugged her. The tears in their eyes hurt because her absence had caused them pain and worry. Jasmine sucked down a gulp of air, trying to compose herself. After she closed the door, she followed her sisters into the kitchen. They'd already taken a seat at her table.

Olivia latched on to Jasmine's hand and tugged her into a chair. "I'm so happy you're home. Now, spill the beans. We want to know what the heck you meant when you said you were kidnapped."

Marion watched her intently with her eyebrows knitted together. Jasmine recounted her story, or as much as she could without breaching her NDA. The part that seemed to pour out of her mouth like a flood was her time with Noah. When she finished, she looked at her sisters, waiting for their reaction. When they showered her with more love and hugs, she sobbed.

She wasn't sure how long she sat like that, purging every ounce of anger, frustration, devastation, guilt, and love out of her system. Now, she sat at the table with a mottled face and snotty nose. "I'm sorry I worried you all, but I'm not sorry for following my gut and uncovering the truth for my source. Then, when I found out Noah was involved, there was no other option than to see it through."

"We love you no matter what. Dad also loves you, but he doesn't like to be challenged," Marion said, patting her hand. "He will always be our dad, good or bad."

"I can't believe all you went through. It's mind-blowing. Noah sounds like a wonderful man. Not too bright since he made a mistake by letting you leave, but I want to hear more about him," Olivia said.

Jasmine felt her cheeks heat not only at her sister's directness but also for what she was about to confess. "He's the one. I love him, but he's been through so much and can't open his heart to the possibility of marriage or children."

Then to her horror, she bawled right in front of her sisters again. It was therapeutic and exhausting. She hadn't meant to cry, but he mattered to her, and she wouldn't hide it. Getting over him would take a long time, and she feared no other man would match up to him.

Marion handed her a tissue. "If it's meant to be, he'll figure it out and find his way to you. He's trying to process so many different things at this moment, including grief. That's a heavy burden."

Her younger sister was so wise for her age. Deep down, Jasmine knew she was right, but when your heart was involved, you wanted a faster timeline.

"If he doesn't, he's an idiot," her older sister quipped.

The three of them laughed. Gosh, she had missed her sisters. "I love you both. So what have I missed while I've been gone?" Jasmine asked.

Marion wore a big smile, and her eyes sparkled with wonder. "I was saving this just for your return. I'm pregnant."

"Oh, Marion, that's wonderful. I'm so happy for you both," Jasmine said.

Her youngest had wanted to be a mother her entire life. When someone talked about innate skills, her sister was the nurturer of the family.

Olivia winked at her little sister. "Seriously, you've always liked Jasmine better than me."

Marion grabbed her hand. "That's because she isn't as bossy."

They burst into laughter like they always did together. The next hour was spent talking and passing the time like sisters do. Jasmine made them sandwiches. Then they moved to the couch to watch a movie together, just like when they were kids. It was the perfect day and what she had needed.

Her mind drifted to Annika, Aimee, and Maggie. She'd love to introduce them to her sisters, but she was sure that day would never come. The six of them would have so much fun together. Right before her sisters left to return home to care for their families, Jasmine decided to tell them what she'd decided to do about Christmas.

"I want to come for Christmas, but when I called Dad to have a heart-to-heart, he was still mad. He said he's not sure I should come over, so we'll have to see. I know this will make things awkward, but he has to agree to accept me for who I am, not who he wants me to be. He doesn't have to approve of my every decision, but I expect him to support me. If he can't, that's on him."

"You know that was his anger talking, right?" Olivia asked.

Jasmine rolled her eyes. "Yes, but he needs to learn that his words hurt."

"You're right, Jasmine, but you hurt him too. You're not doing anything wrong with your life, but you need to give dad a break. Mom has been working on him to see reason, but an olive branch from you would help," Marion said.

"I know, and I hate that she's in the middle. Mom's the best, but you're right. I need to sit down and talk to Dad," Jasmine said, then hugged her sister.

Olivia stood and started toward the door. "That's our mom, playing interference between Dad and whichever one of us is in trouble. You know we support you."

"I love you, too, and thanks for always having my back," Jasmine said.

She walked her sisters to the door and waved as they disappeared into the elevator. Her body hummed with happiness, even though her eyes still stung and were a little swollen from all her tears. Somehow, those two women had the power to cure all the wrongs in Jasmine's life but one.

When she checked her phone, there were zero missed calls and no new messages. Noah had to be busy with all things FBI and helping his family grieve. She had decided to believe he'd call her back when he had a chance.

She ordered a deep-dish pizza for dinner, which she'd missed while she was gone, then tugged her laptop out of her bag and set it up on the kitchen table. She was determined to finish the draft of her story. The senator's untimely death had given her the closing portion. The other details to incorporate would be a follow-up action or authorized by Noah's boss when appropriate. There was zero chance that she'd let this story go cold. The time to strike was now.

Once she finished, she'd forward the draft to Noah and his boss for review. She checked her phone again. Should she try him again? *No. The ball was in his court.*

N OAH OPENED THE FRONT door of his childhood home and stood in the entryway. His mom and sister were right on his heels. An emptiness he couldn't describe hit him squarely in the chest. The slightest tingle of cold air crawled up his spine, making his hair stand up on its ends.

He couldn't remember the last time he'd been in this house. Every spot he touched held a memory. The resounding silence had been replaced with the erratic beat of his heart.

Exhaustion had him moving farther inside the structure that used to be his home. They had spent half the day traveling to Virginia. His boss authorized him to use one of the FBI's planes, which allowed them to travel faster and without having to face public scrutiny. When one returned from the dead, a lot of work had to be completed. At least his mom and sister had the government assisting them from the inside, which would make it that much easier.

After they landed at the airport, Noah had a car waiting to take them to his father's private attorney. The lawyer had informed his mom that her late husband had just updated his trust and will and had left everything to her and the children.

His father had taken the time to put his legal affairs to protect his family before he went on his suicide mission. Noah's head spun with so many questions. All this time, he'd misunderstood his father's actions. He'd despised a man who hadn't deserved all that animosity. He'd made huge mistakes, but they had cost him literally everything.

His mom glanced around and shivered. "God, it's been twenty-three years. It seems odd to be here without Thomas."

His sister moved right in between them and headed up the stairs. "I don't remember this place at all."

Noah took his mom's bag and hollered back at his sister, "That's because you were a baby." Then, he turned back to face his mom. "Do you want to sleep in a guest or master bedroom?"

Her eyes widened, and then she pointed toward the master bedroom. After a few seconds, she answered in a hushed tone, "Master, but would you help me change the sheets?"

He nodded, then climbed the stairs. When they entered the room, she gasped from behind him. "Good grief, the room is exactly the same. He didn't remove any of my personal belongings, not even our wedding picture."

She wobbled on her feet. Noah let the bag fall and clutched her arm to steady her. "Careful, Mom. Would you prefer a hotel?" Once she was steady, he let go of her arm.

"No," she said, turning to walk down the hallway toward Noah's room. "I feel like all of this is a dream, and I'm going to wake up."

His room seemed the same to him. He dropped off his duffel and followed his mom down the hallway to Lisa's bedroom. Wow, all her dolls and toys were still scattered about the room. The room was decorated with pink walls and rainbows, perfect for a three-year-old girl.

Lisa sat on the floor cross-legged, going through her collection of dolls. He couldn't imagine why their dad hadn't cleaned out any of their belongings. He lived at home the first year before attending boarding school, then he stopped coming home, when his father had made it clear he had no time for Noah. He hadn't returned home since because there was no reason.

Who wanted to return to a broken home, especially when no one in it cared about him? A pang of regret pulsed deep, like he'd entered a time machine and was seven years old again.

Lisa now sat on her bed. "Mom, this is weird. It's like I'm visiting a museum with children's bedrooms on display, but it's mine."

His mom buried her head in her hand and teared up. "I don't know why your father did what he did, but I guess he left everything untouched because he missed us. It's like he created a time capsule. Tomorrow, we'll go through the house and make decisions on what stays or goes. We'll start fresh for this new chapter of our lives."

Noah stood in silence and watched his mom help Lisa change the sheets on her bed. Such a mundane task he couldn't stop watching. Maybe it was because he thought he'd never see this image again in his life when his mother and sister were ripped out of his life. When she finished helping his sister, he followed her to the master and helped her change the linens on the bed.

A clatter caught his attention. His mom had flipped their wedding picture over on the dresser. He sat on the bed and stared out the window while she disappeared into the closet and returned with a blanket. Her face was as white as a ghost.

"What is it?" Noah asked, standing to rush toward her.

"Your father kept all my clothes. Why?" she asked on a sob. "I'm mad at him, but a part of me feels guilty for being mad at him after all I've learned. I mean, who keeps a house the same way for all these years?"

Noah held her while she cried. "I know, Mom. I'm still struggling with all of this too. It'll take time, but we'll get through it together. That I promise."

They stood silently for quite some time until she pushed herself away. She wiped a few tears from her cheeks, sat on the bed, and patted the space next to her. This was the same thing she had done with him when he was a little boy.

When he sat, she cupped his cheek with her hand. "I love you. I'm so fortunate to do this with my boy again. I know all of this is surreal, but what's wrong, honey? You're different, and I can't put my finger on it. Please don't lie and tell me it's all this crap we've been through. You're distant and distracted, so talk to me."

He leaned his head against her shoulder, loving the familiar touch and comfort that flooded his system. "I love you, Mom. It's just that everything I believed was false. I took actions based on lies, and now I'm stuck. All these mistakes, and the one I regret the most is pushing Jasmine out of my life."

"Why did you do that if you like her so much? I thought she was lovely, and the chemistry between you when you kissed her that day on the plane—" She waved her hand like a fan in front of her face.

He lifted his head and felt the heat on his cheeks from her comment. "Geez, Mom, that's embarrassing. We are so not going there."

"Oh, hush. I may be your mom, but I'm a woman, too. Why did you do that, then?" his mom said, waggling her eyes.

Noah scrubbed his hand down his face and stared at the floor. "I don't know who I am. I don't know that I wouldn't do what Dad did to protect the family, and it destroyed all of us. I mean, my job is a little wild at times. She wants marriage and children, and that scares me the most. I'm not wired that way, and I'd screw it up. No offense, my childhood wasn't the best."

His mom's lips pursed. "I know, and that's my biggest regret for both my children. That's honorable, son. I think letting her go was the right decision then. Besides, with her good looks, she'll find a wonderful man to marry who will give her a happy life. Even her personality–"

"What the hell, mom? Whose side are you on? I love her. I don't want to talk, let alone think, about her being with another man. I should be that man, but I don't want to destroy our future..."

She grabbed his hand and squeezed. "Got ya! I know that, honey. I just needed you to hear it from your mouth. Don't be dense. That woman loves you to the moon and back. You love her, so I'm failing to see the problem. You realize that what your father and I went through and what happened to our family is frightening but unique. There isn't a gene that gets passed from the mother or father that will cause a repeat performance. It's you who holds the power. Life is messy, complicated, wonderful, sweet, and full of surprises."

"That's easier said than done, and I do share both of your DNA. My solution was to push everyone away," Noah countered.

"Where I'm sitting, I don't think you like that decision very much. You, my son, are different because you always put others first. You hold those who do wrong accountable. You did what was necessary to survive. Now that you have all the facts, you'll need to decide how to process all this crap so you can move forward," his mother said.

He listened to her words as he took comfort in her presence. After several long minutes, he turned to face his mother. "So, if I were to fly to Chicago to try and get Jazy back, would you be all right here by yourself?"

His mom folded him into a hug. "We'll be fine. Now, don't forget to grove, because I want to help plan a wedding for my son."

He grinned. "Well, don't get too excited. She may not take me back."

"Love is powerful, but you'll never know unless you try," his mother said. "Now, I'll handle everything here so you can concentrate on your future. Go to bed and get some sleep. You have a plane to catch tomorrow."

He needed some fresh air before he went to bed. He went out the back door and walked over to the firepit. His dad's words flooded his memory as he stared at the circular structure. Tears welled up, and he lowered his head.

God help him because he never expected to have this thought, but he missed his father. He should have told him that he loved him. His father's mistakes would never be forgotten, but Noah would forgive him.

His mom was right. He governed his actions with facts and compassion, and he'd adjust if the facts were wrong. His father hadn't learned that lesson, and it buried him in the end. Noah's thoughts drifted toward his brother. It was time to check on Waltzer to make sure he was okay, and Noah needed to tell him a few things.

"Now what?" Waltzer asked in lieu of a greeting.

"Can you talk?" Noah asked, not sure if he had returned to the States or if that was still in progress.

"Yup, I'm back stateside. We moved fast after that clusterfuck. What about you?"

"Virgina, with my mom and sister. I needed to know that you and the team got out safely. I learned something from our father that you should know. He admitted to the affair and mentioned that he checked in on you from time to time. When you showed an interest in the military, he supported your career and advocated for you as a senator from behind the scenes. I thought you should know that for what it's worth.

Waltzer didn't immediately respond, but he gave his own update when he spoke. "Appreciate the information. You probably know, but the shipment was destroyed, and intel shows that the dictator died alongside it. Your idea worked."

"That's the same update I got, minus the I was right part. Don't be a stranger. I kind of like having a brother, even one who shot me," Noah said, feeling lighter than he had in days. He wanted to let Waltzer know he cared about him and was open to having him in his life however that might look.

Waltzer chuckled. "Those weren't my words, brother. Stay out of trouble, and we'll talk again."

NOAH HURRIED FROM THE airport to pick up his rental car in Chicago. Before reaching his final destination, he needed to stop at the Miracle Mile shops before entering the address for Jasmine's parents' house into his GPS. If he was going to do this, he intended to do it right. Jazy didn't deserve anything less.

His heart thumped against his chest when he pulled up in front of the home. He took a deep breath as he strode to the front door. Even though nervous energy rioted in his stomach, it wasn't because he'd decided he wanted to marry their daughter. It was because he wanted their approval. He tapped his pocket to feel the small blue pouch he'd tucked inside earlier, then he rang the bell and waited.

An older woman answered the door.

"Hi, ma'am, I'm here to meet with Peter and Susan regarding their daughter, Jasmine. I'm Noah Parker."

"Hi, I'm Susan, her mom," the woman said.

Her face betrayed her curiosity. She opened the door wide and ushered him into the family room where a man sat in a recliner. A large Christmas tree decorated with ornaments and lights took center stage and underneath gifts were piled around the base.

"Peter, this is Noah, Jasmine's friend. The one who works for the FBI."

Noah hated the sound of that because he wanted her to be more than a friend. It also made it appear as if he was there on business. The man stood and approached him.

Peter didn't reciprocate when Noah extended his hand.

His brows were pinched, matching the concern etched on his face. "Is everything okay?"

"I'm sorry for the confusion," Noah blurted out, dropping his hand. "She's fine, I think. Well, except that I upset her. I'm here to remedy that, I hope."

A voice Noah didn't recognize spoke from behind him. "Mom, Dad, she's home. This is the man we were telling you about. Olivia and I spent time with Jasmine on Saturday."

Noah turned to see the young woman who approached him and held out her hand. "I'm Marion, her youngest sister. You must be Noah. It's nice to meet you. I've heard a lot about you. I hope you're worthy of her. Mom, Dad, I'm heading home. The toys are wrapped and under your bed for Santa Claus's big night."

"Thanks, honey," Susan said, then turned her attention back to him. "I'm glad you're here. Please sit so we can talk."

Peter took a seat. "So, you're the man who rescued her and kept her from her family?"

Susan closed her eyes and shook her head. "Seriously, Peter, I love you, but she has always been a free spirit. You can be so smothering.

Noah, as I'm sure you know, Peter and Jasmine can sometimes be oil and water."

He sat and debated how to proceed. This whole visit had not happened the way he'd envisioned in his head. "Uh, this may not be the best time, but I'm here to talk about Jasmine. I want to tell you how she turned my world upside down and inside out."

Susan claimed the spot next to Noah on the sofa. He took a deep breath and started from the top. He shared the crucial tidbits and skipped the ones that couldn't be spoken. Her parents listened to everything. When he got to the part during their capture when Jasmine secured paper clips to aid their escape, he even saw her father smile. He kept the harrowing parts light but wanted to ensure her parents knew how brave and resourceful their daughter had been.

When Noah got the end of the story, he explained how he screwed up. "I'm here to make amends with Jazy. She is truly a magical and special woman who knows no boundaries when she loves someone or something. And for what it's worth, she loves you very much, sir."

Susan dabbed her eyes and hugged him. "Oh, my girl is so lucky to have found you."

Peter sat up and locked his gaze with Noah's. "Thank you for protecting my girl and getting her home safe. I happen to love her more."

Noah nodded at her father and continued. "Here's the deal. I'm here to ask you both for her hand in marriage because I will spend the rest of my life making her happy. I love her adventurous spirit, her bravery, and how she loves unconditionally. She is the most transparent person I've ever known, and I wouldn't change anything about her. She makes me want to be a better man. I can't promise that I won't screw up again, but I'll spend my life trying to grow and learn from those mistakes. I need her in my life."

"You have my blessing," Susan said, turning to look at her husband, who stared at Noah.

Peter leaned forward and extended his hand to Noah. "Love her and keep her safe. That's all I ask of you. And for what it's worth, I happen to upset her a lot, too. We'll have that in common."

Noah laughed. "I'll spend my life making her happy, as well as the afterlife, because I'm never letting her go. Her strength and compassion can't be contained. That's something I experienced and saw firsthand."

"Do you know where her apartment is, or do you need directions?" Susan asked, tears streaming down her cheeks. "You're the perfect man for our daughter."

Peter stood, and when Noah did, too, Peter pulled Noah into a backslapping hug. "Welcome to the family, son. When you become a father someday, you'll understand that you will worry about them forever. Then you get a silly idea that they'll always be protected if you control everything around them."

"At least I'll have a great sounding board when we decide to start having little Jasmines running around the house."

Susan clapped and hugged her husband. "You tell my daughter that her mother and father love her. We can't wait to see the ring."

Noah winked, then headed back out the front door to his rental car. Warmth and happiness radiated throughout his body. However, his stomach rioted when he parked his car in the lot of Jasmine's apartment complex. God, he hoped she would forgive him.

This moment would be the most important of his life. He bypassed the elevator to take the stairs so he could surprise her. All in a matter of minutes, he stood outside her front door. His heart hammered against his chest. He sucked down a deep breath and squared his shoulders.

He pressed the ringer and waited until she opened the door. Just like that, her standing opposite him knocked the air from his lungs because this woman meant everything to him. Even without a drop of makeup on her face and with her hair pulled into a ponytail, she was so damn beautiful.

J ASMINE PEEKED THROUGH THE peephole, and her heart lurched to a stop inside her throat. She yanked the door open, then launched herself into familiar arms. The reaction was natural, even if she realized a little too late that maybe she shouldn't have done it. She wasn't going to spend time worrying about it.

Bottom line, she was thrilled to see him. "Noah, why are you here? I've been trying to call you, but I figured you didn't want to talk to me. Are you okay? Where are your mom and sister? I'm so sorry about your father."

"Can I come inside, or do you want to talk here in the hallway?" he asked.

She left his arms and stepped back to open the door wider for him to pass. "Sorry, please come inside. You being here has me off-kilter and forgetting my manners." She took him to her living room and turned off the television. "Would you like something to drink?"

"No, I'm good, but come sit down so we can talk," he said.

"Everything has been hectic since you left. I should have returned your calls, but something else happened every time I thought about calling you. I have no excuse other than I was processing many different emotions."

She couldn't imagine how he'd handled everything and was still functioning, but that was Noah. "I'm so sorry about your father," she said, covering his hand with hers.

The moment she touched him, a rush of energy surged through her body. That was all it took to make everything go haywire in her heart, mind, and body.

"Me too. I watched the entire thing on a video feed. On the day of the operation, Waltzer wore a camera, and we saw it go down. My father went there to protect his family. He was killed doing it, but as far as the public knows, he died in service of his country."

"You didn't answer earlier, but where's your family? How are they doing?"

He blew out a breath. "They're hanging in there and are back in Virginia at his home. He changed his trust and left everything to us. I'm still processing it all. Right now, Guzman is helping me get my mom and sister back into the land of the living."

"Oh gosh, I hadn't even thought of that issue. At least they have good connections to get the process started. I finished my story, and Guzman has approved it," she said.

He nodded. "He forwarded it to me. You did a great job with it. It'll be a huge hit because people like murder mysteries and scandals. Speaking of that, I spoke to Waltzer. He's back in the States. I guess he'll be waiting for a new assignment now that the Garcia cartel is finished and the weapons were tracked and destroyed."

She squeezed his hand, forcing all her strength and support into him. "That's great news. Does that mean you can get some rest? You look so tired, Noah."

"I plan to while I'm on leave, but I'm also here to tell you that I'm glad you left me."

She bristled at his comment, pulling her hand back. The hope blooming in her chest popped like a balloon. "Why are you here? You could have told me all of this on the phone."

He grabbed her hand. "Sorry, that came out wrong. Just give me a minute to get this all out. I'm glad you left because it made me realize a life without you isn't worth living. I still worry that I will do stupid things, but I know you will have my back. Your strength will help guide me. It took an awkward conversation with my mom to make me admit I'm madly in love with you. Now, the obvious next step was to go and ask your parents for your hand in marriage."

She smacked his arm. "That's not funny."

"You're right, it's serious. I told them why I wanted to marry you, and afterward, they gave me their blessings. They also told me to tell you that they love you."

Jasmine couldn't believe what she was hearing. This was her dream, because she loved this man with every fiber of her being.

"Are you sure? Because there will be bad times. I promise you that, but if we stick together and listen to each other, we can solve anything."

He cupped her cheeks. "I want the whole thing, right down to dirty diapers. Not today, but sometime down the road. I'm far from perfect, but together we make one formidable team. Please forgive me for being so slow in getting to this conclusion."

Joy bubbled from deep down in her body and threatened to explode. "I do, I love you, Noah."

He knelt before her." I haven't asked you yet."

"Sorry, I was practicing." She replied, trying to be patient.

He pulled the blue pouch from his pocket and pulled the ring free "Jazy, the best day of my life was being shackled with you in that hut. It brought us together and made me understand that I want to be chained to you for the rest of my life," he said, slipping the flawless two-carat diamond and platinum band on her finger. "Will you be my forever adventurer, best friend, and wife?"

She tackled him, knocking him to the ground and pressing kisses to his face and mouth. Then she pulled back and held his face. "Yes, I will love you and rescue you forever. I do, I do, I do. You—"

He interrupted her next statement with a kiss. When he finally ended the toe-curling kiss, he added, "Good. My mom is super excited to plan a wedding, so I hope your mom will be open to having a partner."

Jasmine sat up and smiled. "Yes, that will be amazing."

Just two days ago, she had wallowed in sadness, trying to figure out how to move forward without the other half of her heart. Now, she was his fiancée. Life had a strange way of giving and taking, and she had learned that one must cherish every moment. She would take that lesson and pay it forward as she and Noah worked together to build their future and a legacy different from his childhood.

Dear Reader:
Thank you for reading Breaking Point.

The saga continues for the residents of Mill Creek.

Kane's Reckoning, the story of Annika and Kane is coming soon.

Have you read the story that started the Mill Creek Mystique series?

Fall in love with Trent and Maggie in Trent's Redemption.

Turn the page for a sneak peek.

XO-Bailey

Enjoy this sneak peek of

TRENT'S REDEMPTION

Book 2 in the Mill Creek Mystique romantic suspense series

One

T HE RAPID KNOCK AT Trent's front door had him hoping that this unexpected interruption would spare him another lonely evening. Hastening his steps, he twisted the knob and sucked in a sharp breath. Nothing would have prepared him for this sight. His partner's sister, and the woman he had dated. Margaret King's haunted green eyes stared back at him. Her blonde hair was thrown into a loose ponytail. Several strands had escaped and fluttered in the evening breeze. Even disheveled, she was still beautiful.

Dread settled in his gut, anchoring a weight to his chest as Dalton's last words filtered through his mind. *Promise me you'll look after her and keep her safe.*

"Maggie, what brings you here?" Trent's mind raced with possibilities, and none settled the growing dread that rotted in his stomach.

Her eyes widened briefly before she found her voice. "Can I come inside?"

"Of course, sorry," he stammered, moving aside and making a sweeping motion with his arm.

She hesitated for a second, then looked over her shoulder toward the driveway. Turning back, she met his gaze and released a deep breath. Remorse slapped him in the face as she entered his home. The last time he'd seen her was about ten months ago at Dalton's funeral. Not once had Trent reached out to see how she had adjusted to life without her brother. Now, the weight of his mistake stood in his entryway. Guilt riddled his body and his gaze shifted toward the floor because he'd let her down.

The subtle scent of oranges and vanilla floated by him as she passed. The moonlight shining through the open window cast a silvery glow across her pinched face. He clicked the deadbolt then flipped on the light before he sat on the sofa, waiting for her to join him. Her feet didn't budge, but her gaze circled the room.

Maggie raised an eyebrow, her eyes blank. "I'm sorry I didn't call first. I thought this discussion would be best in person. I can't believe I had to search the internet for your address."

"I'm glad you're here, and I should have given you my address. There's no excuse for that..."

The tension in the room increased with every second of silence that followed.

"I-I don't know what to think anymore. You might think I'm crazy or worse, have overreacted to drive all the way here." Her voice sounded like sandpaper on wood.

Trent grabbed her hand and swiped his thumb softly across her knuckles. A rush of emotions flooded his system with that simple touch. He hated the strain emanating from her body. "Are you okay, Maggie?"

He released her hand and patted the spot next to him. The cushions dipped as she sat, her gaze lingering on the room and surroundings. "Why do you have scaffolding outside? Did something happen to your home?"

Trent smiled and shook his head. "No, I just finished renovating the interior and have decided to upgrade my roof. What's going on, Maggie?"

She turned to him, flashing a brief smile. "Good. I'm glad nothing bad happened to you. Could I have a glass of water?"

"You can have anything you'd like." He meant those words and vowed to himself to prove it to her. "But you need to tell me what's upset you. What made you drive all this way to find me?"

The single tear traveling down her cheek gutted him. Her resolve and strength may have had her sitting beside him, holding herself together, but her vulnerability undid him. He tugged her body against his, to feel her warmth and the pulse of her heart as he held her tight. To remind her she wasn't alone in dealing with whatever worried her. Even if his actions these last ten months told a different story.

A niggle of hope bloomed in his chest when she hugged him back just as fiercely. This wouldn't erase his absence from her life since the death of her brother, but maybe she'd see it as an olive branch to reconnect them to days long past. To the days when they were friends and all three of them spent time together.

When she sat back against the cushion, dark circles marred the delicate skin beneath her eyes. Trent's mind whirled with a million questions. Had someone hurt her? Had Maggie been with a man who threatened her? Why was she here? All of them remained unspoken because shame swamped his system. Not only was he a shitty person, but he'd broken a promise to his friend.

Dalton would still be here if I'd taken out the shooter in the rafters. Suffocated by the memories of that horrible day, Trent shot up off the sofa, desperately needing air and space. "I'll get you that water. When I return, how about you start from the beginning and explain why you're here? We'll figure this out together."

"Thanks. You're the one person I knew would understand," she said in a mere whisper.

Jesus, what had she been through that would make her run? The woman he'd known was full of mirth and energy. He hated the mixture of defeat and uncertainty radiating from the depths of her green eyes.

"Here you go, Miss Margaret King." Trent handed her a glass of water.

"Ugh, call me Maggie, you know better. My parents called me Margaret, and that was when I was in trouble." She stared into the distance for a moment. "Maggie Moo was the nickname my brother preferred," she added with a slight wobble.

"Sorry, I miss him so much. I just never thought I'd lose him after my parents died. I figured we'd grow old together. It's been difficult knowing I'm all alone in the world."

Trent's heart was clogged with condemnation. "Never apologize for missing him. Dalton loved you. He would've done anything for you. You were his little sister. Hell, I'd known him since training at Quantico, and I knew then, he'd be the biggest pain in my ass and best friend. His death left a hole in our lives." The words he left unspoken were that he'd abandoned her, too.

A soft giggle escaped her lips. "Yes, he could be a pain. He also tried controlling my life down to who I dated."

Trent nodded in agreement. "Yes, he had firm opinions on who should date you and why."

"If I recall, you did, too, since you cited your job as a complication of our relationship. Anyway, blood or not, you've always been a part of my family, which is why I'm here." She forced a slow steady stream of air into her lungs. "You were both logical and rational men who worked from facts to solve life's problems. I've lost count of how often I've endured a lecture about being observant and always aware of my surroundings."

He interjected, "A smart person assessed their situation and acted accordingly. That coincidences rarely, if ever, exist. Yes, I speak that same dialect."

"You are cut from the same cloth as Dalton, which is why I'm in Mill Creek. I've analyzed my situation, and my findings have shocked me." She gulped the cool liquid. Straightening her spine, she continued, "Dalton made me promise—almost to the point of ritualistic chanting—that if I were ever in trouble and couldn't reach him, I should call you. I always thought he'd meant while he was alive..." Tears streamed down her face. "Someone has been following me because I'm Dalton's sister."

Trent's eyes narrowed. She'd piqued his curiosity with that assessment. He then schooled his features so they'd remain neutral. "Why would you think that?"

"I first noticed a white van parked on the street facing my apartment. It appeared after Dalton's death. The days and times were random, but it was the same van. It disappeared for a while, then returned a few weeks ago. I can't explain it, but I got a strange feeling about it."

Maggie fidgeted, cracking her fingers one by one. He sat quietly while she fidgeted with nervous energy. He didn't want to add to her stress, so he gave her the time to process her thoughts.

"How? What made it seem unusual?"

She lifted her gaze to meet his eyes and shrugged. "I only saw the driver and passenger twice, but I'm pretty sure they were the same men from the first time. This sounds bizarre, and I know it does, which is why I didn't report the van to the police. Those men could have lived in the complex or in the area. What happened the other night changed my mind, but instead of calling the police, I headed straight to you. This is personal, Trent, and it scared me."

"I'm glad you came to me." He gently urged her to continue by nodding and keeping his expression neutral. Deep down, his stomach knotted with apprehension over what came next.

A tiny smile crossed her lips. "God, you remind me of him, fierce and protective. I appreciate that you're not judging me—at least until I'm done."

"You're doing just fine, now, keep going."

"Early Saturday morning, I was working at my computer when the fire alarms went off. When I went outside to check, the adjacent unit had smoke billowing from inside. My neighbor appeared outside with her child, panicked, and talking into the phone about a grease fire and firemen coming. I ducked back inside my place to retrieve my messenger bag, which held everything that mattered to me and waited outside with my neighbor. After the firemen arrived and controlled the scene, I was informed that the fire was out, but it would be a couple of hours before I could return. I decided to head to our local coffee shop to hang out while the chaos passed. When I returned..."

The color drained from her cheeks. She lowered her head to stare at the carpet between her feet. "My front door was ajar, again, which I figured was so the firemen could finish their investigation. I caught a glimpse of that white van pulling away. When I entered, everything seemed fine...until I reached my office. Drawers were opened, and papers and folders were scattered across my desk and floor. Then, I noticed a knife stabbed into my desk holding a note that read, 'What did he know?'"

Trent snapped his brows together, his mouth drawn tight. He couldn't quell his reaction to what he'd just heard. The hairs on his neck bristled. He didn't know how, but he'd find a way to slay every one of her demons...or die trying. He owed Dalton that much.

"Why didn't you call the police? Do you know if anything was taken? Were other rooms searched?" Trent squeezed her hand a few times, bringing her gaze upward.

With her other hand, she reached for the glass and gulped the last few sips before she answered, "In my gut, I know this reaches beyond the police. The only 'he' in my life was my brother. My brain went into survival mode. I had to get out of my apartment and get to you. You'd know what to do. I-I didn't look any further. All I kept thinking was, this can't be good to have a knife stabbed into your desk, especially with how he died. I took my bag, hit the bank, and withdrew as much money as allowed. I left my car at the office and called a car rental company. I decided leaving my car behind was best. I stopped at one truck stop to rest, used only cash, then drove until I pulled into your driveway."

She sat still as if she had waited for him to say something. Processing what he had just heard shredded his insides. The last time they had spoken was at the funeral, and that encounter was strained, not ugly or mean, just distant because of him. This was opposite to how he and Maggie usually interacted. Instead, he struggled with his anger and self-condemnation while nursing the injuries he'd sustained that day alongside Dalton. As a result, Trent's job and assignment changed, which deprived him of retribution. He hated the exhaustion etched across her face. Starting now, he would atone for his wrongs.

"Brave and resilient is what you are." A surge of pride and respect flood his system. "You did damn good with disappearing off the grid and adapting in the face of adversity. You're far from an agent but acted cautiously and logically."

Fatigue, stress, and fear radiated from her, but he also saw a brief glimmer of relief. That was something he would build upon.

"Your brother would be proud. Hell, I'm proud of you. I'm also so damn sorry I haven't reached out before now. I own that. My apology doesn't change anything, but I hope my actions will. *If* you give me that chance. I'd say you read the situation right—a clusterfuck for sure."

Her eyes closed for a moment, and her shoulders dipped as tension seemed to fade from her body. Something deep inside Trent's stomach twisted painfully. Had she thought he might deny her his support and protection? Of course, why wouldn't she? It wasn't his intent, but he'd removed her from his life. Another epic screw-up to add to his list that he needed to fix.

He cupped her chin. "I understand why you weren't sure about coming to me for help, so I'll clarify that misconception now. I will always protect you, Maggie. You have my word."

She shifted her head from his grasp and stabbed him in the chest with a finger. "You hurt my feelings, but I'm not blameless either. You have to promise you won't put yourself in jeopardy in any way. I can't stand the thought of losing another person."

The painful truth behind those words constricted his chest. The vibrant woman he had known seemed to have retreated somewhat. Trent snatched her hand, loving how buttery soft her skin was under his fingertips. "Give me your keys. I think it's best to put your rental in the garage for now."

She stood and dug into her front pocket to retrieve the key ring. "Thanks for allowing me into your home, especially with my trouble in tow."

Trent extended his palm and caught the keys. "You always were trouble. I'll give you the grand tour first and point out the highlights from my renovation."

"I thought you liked living out of boxes. You know, afraid of commitment."

"Smart ass," he lamented. "I'm working on unpacking everything."

He couldn't imagine her thoughts when she arrived but was glad she'd come. He started in his kitchen, explaining how his friend Kane had updated everything to stainless steel and gas.

"This is amazing. I love the gas stovetop. That refrigerator must keep you fed for months. It's huge."

"I've heard that bigger is always better," he deadpanned.

She rolled her eyes and protested, "Seriously? You haven't changed one bit."

He flashed her an exaggerated wink and guided her through the rest of the house. When they reached the master bathroom, he showed her his second favorite feature from the renovation: his walk-in shower with multiple adjusting heads that also produced steam. He owed Kane for this gem, too. Her small whimper when she spied the shower didn't go unnoticed. Trent also hadn't missed how closely she followed him the entire time. He'd do anything to diminish the worry radiating from her body. He ended his tour with the room she'd be using and the bathroom.

At the door to the bathroom, he paused and met her eyes. "Why don't you shower in my bathroom while I move the vehicle? You can give me a woman's perspective on my shower."

She leaned her head against the doorway and sighed. "A shower sounds heavenly, but I'll use the guest bath. Will you grab my bag from the front room and put it on the bed?

"Sure, do you have anything in the car you need?"

Her mouth twisted into a frown. "No, I didn't pack any clothing or even think about bringing my bathroom supplies. In my haste, I went with the less-is-more theory. Do you have a toothbrush and paste? And if I could borrow a few things to wear, that would be super. Walking around naked might be awkward."

He groaned internally as his mind conjured several inappropriate scenarios involving her sans clothing. Built like a goddess, with her curves and creamy skin, he'd love nothing more than to see her naked. He caught her staring at his reflection in the bathroom mirror and knew he'd been nailed. His traitorous cock stirred behind the confines of his pants. This woman still caused his mind and body to want more from her. His cue to leave.

"I'll put a T-shirt and a pair of sweatpants on your bed. Leave your clothes outside the door, I'll wash them for you. We'll go shopping tomorrow to fill in whatever you left behind."

She opened her mouth as if to speak, then clamped her lips together as she moved into the bathroom.

"What's on your mind?" he asked.

"Do you have any cereal or yogurt? Something easy to fix."

He put both hands on his waist and cocked one eyebrow. "You can have whatever you want. When did you eat last?"

Her eyes narrowed, and her mouth gaped. "I-ah, a granola at the truck stop."

He shook his head. "You're my priority. That includes food, sleep, protection, and whatever else I've forgotten to mention. Get that through your thick, stubborn, and beautiful head." Trent punctuated his point by wrapping her in a crushing hug. He wasn't sure what else to do, a move so familiar from all the previous times he and Dalton had visited between assignments or while on break.

He sighed as her curves melded perfectly against his frame and in all the right places. A surge of possessiveness roared to life within him, and not only did it startle him, but it also made him back away, breaking their connection.

"Shower, then kitchen," he said in a tone that encouraged no debate.

He headed down the hall and heard the snick of the door as it closed behind him. Needing to put space between them, he'd take care of her car. This woman in his home was Dalton's sister. The same baby sister his partner proclaimed off limits to any man who worked in a risky profession. Dalton was adamant that Maggie should marry a man with a stable job, allowing him to come home every night. A man whose existence wasn't nestled in danger, with the potential to cause her harm because his job encompassed every aspect of his life. Trent had squashed his attraction to her because he hadn't wanted to ruffle Dalton's feathers. Even though he hadn't been exempt from Dalton's censure, he had to agree with the man. She deserved better. She deserved a marriage where her husband would be around every night, a man whose job wouldn't risk her safety or threaten their lives. A fact of his employment he couldn't offer.

RELIEF WASHED OVER MAGGIE's body when Trent agreed with her assessment–she hadn't overreacted. She should never have doubted that he'd support her, but hearing it from his lips alleviated her apprehension. The warmth from his embrace grounded her. If she could press the rewind button, she'd rather go back to when Trent held her in his arms. There was a familiarity to it, and she'd missed the simplicity of knowing someone had her back.

She'd gotten to know him when she went to college in Washington, D.C. and had chosen to live in Dalton's place instead of on campus.

Her brother brought Trent home during break when they were both at Quantico. Not only had they become partners but friends. It wasn't like he was home often with his career, but it gave her an excuse to be close to her brother. She and Trent had dated a few times, but he had ended saying he didn't have time for a relationship due to his career. Her brother would never answer her question, but she would put money down on the fact he interfered.

When Trent smiled and flashed the bluest eyes she'd ever seen, it could melt the panties right off a girl. Never in her life had she experienced such a strong reaction to another person. It also didn't hurt that he was devastatingly gorgeous at six feet tall with his athletic build and all those well-defined muscles. His touch still made her girly parts tingle.

She'd cranked the shower tap to the left. When the bathroom mirror fogged over from the steam, she tugged back the curtain, adjusted the heat, then stepped inside. The hot spray pulsed against her tired muscles and sluiced down her body. She visualized removing Trent's shirt off his body to reveal raised pectorals and a ripped abdomen that flowed into a trim waist with sculpted hips. She bit her bottom lip and moaned. Well, that was what happened when one was sex deprived and surrounded by male hotness.

She adjusted the dial until a cold blast of water jolted her system. That daydream would be her little secret. She needed to stop this line of thinking. He probably had a bevy of beautiful women on speed dial. The type who looked perfect even after a torrential rainstorm. The same type her brother had circling him at all times. A girl could dream, couldn't she?

After stepping from the shower, she dried off and slathered on some lotion she found in the cabinet. She finger-combed her hair and mentally added an actual one to her list of things to buy. There was nothing like a shower to make a person feel human again. Towel wrapped around her body, she padded to the bedroom he assigned. As promised, the clothes and items from her car were sitting on her bed. She removed a stuffed animal from her tote and kissed the cow on its nose before putting it back inside. She'd give anything to hear Dalton call her by her nickname again.

She took in his home as she made her way to the kitchen. It had the perfect blend of cabin and modern.

The center of the room had a wooden dining table with four chairs, and in front of one chair sat a grilled cheese sandwich, her absolute favorite. Especially when she was having a crappy day.

Trent looked over his shoulder, holding a spoon. "You look more relaxed. The tomato soup will be ready in a minute. These are my go-to choices when I need comfort food."

Her insides melted like the cheese in the sandwich.

"Mine too," she said. The part she kept to herself, watching a hot man cook for her, did wicked things to her body. Good grief, she needed to get a grip. He was being nice, not offering her a night of decadent sex. Or a life of love, marriage, and children. The fantasy train needed to stop so she could disembark because that destination did not exist.

The last few months had changed her. She had to find a way to survive before her grief and despair consumed her entirely. Being around Trent has created a few sparks in the recesses of her mind, reminding her of the woman she had been and what they had shared.

"Are you for real? A good-looking man who can cook and isn't afraid to admit that grilled cheese and tomato soup have the power to cure most things in life. I think I've died and gone to heaven," she tossed out and took a seat at the table.

He rolled his eyes and huffed dramatically. "I hate to burst your bubble, but men can do many things these days. I can even load the dishwasher and do laundry, but I draw the line at ironing."

Maggie burst out laughing. "Ah, I needed that. It's been a while."

Trent ladled soup into a bowl. "Feel free to laugh anytime. It suits you very nicely. I also happen to appreciate the eye candy comment."

Did he just flirt with her? She took a bite of her sandwich and moaned. "This is delicious."

"The secret is mayonnaise instead of butter. It's how my mom makes them. Tonight, I want you to promise me you'll rest. I don't like seeing those dark circles under your eyes."

"I'll try, but it's hard to get my brain to stop churning over everything." She blew on a spoonful of soup.

"Well, I promise to keep the boogie men away. Hey, one question, though. Something you said earlier confused me. You said you left your car at the office. Do schoolteachers refer to their classrooms as offices now? Are you still teaching?"

She put down her spoon. "No. I quit teaching."

His eyebrows knit together as he processed what she said, but to her relief, he didn't question her any further. She didn't want to get into it tonight. Her love of teaching had died after she buried Dalton. The burden of life's truths wore her down, and she couldn't handle deceiving those precious faces daily.

Trent filled in the prolonged silence. "We can talk about all of this tomorrow after you rest."

"Okay," she said between a spoonful of soup.

"Oh, one more thing. I'm meeting some friends for breakfast tomorrow. I want you to come. Afterward, we'll head to the store to pick up whatever else you need."

Maggie took a big gulp of water. "I don't want to impose."

"I see your listening skills haven't improved," he muttered sardonically. "We're meeting them tomorrow at eight. I'll have your clothes folded and waiting for you outside your door. You'll love the Knotty Pine Tree. The food is delicious, and I want you to meet my friends, Kane and Annika. They're good people; you can trust them. Besides, your smart actions put distance between what happened in Dallas and here. It'll give us some time to figure it all out."

There was a time when meeting new people and being a social butterfly came naturally, but that part of her died when she put Dalton in the ground. She should label her life accordingly now. BD—before Dalton—and AD—after Dalton.

The scaffolding outside the kitchen window reminded her of a skeleton in the moonlight. She hated the nights the most. All her fears and problems grew into large, creepy monsters that caused her constant worry that whoever left the note would find her.

Trent's Redemption, Book 1 in the Mill Creek Mystique romantic suspense series is out now.

Enjoy this sneak peek of

HIDDEN IDENTITIES

Book 2 in the Mill Creek Mystique romantic suspense series

One

THE PULSE FROM THE beat of the music vibrated down Aimee Lang's spine as endorphins flooded her body. Memories of dancing with her father filled her head while lyrics from a popular western song echoed through her ears. She shimmied against the vinyl seat of the booth, longing to join her friends who were on the dance floor.

Friday Fresh was her favorite event at Two Stepping Bar and Grill because they showcased local bands the second Friday of every month. Listening to up-and-coming performers of all types ranked high on her list of favorites, a cathartic experience allowing her to support artists who took risks to share their love of music.

She loved music almost as much as she enjoyed making up stupid little moves and dances. Her father had shared his eclectic love of music with her, and together they'd danced their way through life. To most, their moves had been pathetic, perhaps even silly, but to them, choreographed masterpieces.

A giggle escaped her lips until the warmth encircled Aimee's heart from those memories began fading. When would she stop torturing herself by remembering the past? That life had ended; now she had to focus on the present.

A prickle of awareness washed over her body. Aimee inhaled, moving her neck from side to side. Her gaze scanned the crowd until she saw the hulking man with all his muscles who appeared to be casually leaning against the wall, listening to the band. Clarke Dragoon was anything but casual and pushed all her buttons, from his overbearing personality to his rugged good looks. He'd won over the residents of Mill Creek when he'd helped her friend, Margaret "Maggie" King, out of a perilous situation not long ago, but Aimee had to keep her distance, even if it grew harder every day. Since she couldn't trust her decision-making skills toward men, it was easier to avoid romantic entanglements altogether. She would not make the same mistake twice.

What she wanted more than anything else was to break a damn sweat on the dance floor. To stop observing from the sidelines while everyone else got to enjoy their life—but that was the point. Now, her job was to embrace a new existence and not fall into any norms of the past.

Warm air circled around her body from all the activity surrounding her. Maybe she could allow herself an hour, an amalgam of her old and new self. How much trouble could that cause? That thought rolled around in her head while her heart beat against her chest in excitement. Who would even know?

"You okay, Aimee?" Maggie asked, a frown marring her face, but concern radiated from the depths of her big green eyes.

Aimee hated all the secrets, but that burden would squarely sit on her shoulders until she died. "I'm fine, just tired from a long week."

"I don't know about you ladies, but I'm parched from shaking my derrière," Irene quipped as she approached the table.

Laughter erupted around Aimee at Irene's comment. That woman had a heart of gold, but that didn't mean this petite woman in her late fifties with those beautiful blue eyes and long white hair was a pushover. Neither was Maggie. She fought for the people she loved, but her charm came from her subtlety. There was no doubt Aimee had been lucky in the friendship department since moving to Mill Creek. Both women were fun, loyal, and loving. The burden of not being able to tell them the whole truth weighed on her, but she'd made an agreement that which couldn't be altered. Her lungs constricted with that knowledge.

Maggie headed toward the dance floor. "Oh, I love this song."

Her declaration interrupted Aimee's maudlin thoughts.

"It's time to throw caution to the wind. Dance on wood instead of the vinyl on your seat. You're not fooling anyone," Irene added, extending her hand to Aimee.

Holy smokes. There were times like this when she really thought Irene possessed the ability to read minds. Yes, Aimee wanted to dance, and again, what harm would come from it? It's not like she had a signature move that would give away her identity. She made a snap decision after scanning the surrounding area. Her body vibrated with excitement.

Aimee slapped her hand into Irene's and smiled. "You're right, but only one dance."

Irene's grip closed around her hand, pulling her closer to Maggie. "And at least two encores."

Maggie's pleasure lit up her face when she saw Aimee. "Crap, now I owe Irene twenty dollars."

"What?" Aimee stopped moving, her gaze going back and forth between her friends. "You bet on this?"

"Of course we did. You practically forced our hands with your stubbornness," Irene said, shaking her shoulders to the beat.

"You're both incorrigible," Aimee replied with a laugh. She threw her hands in the air and twirled to the beat.

Before long, her cheeks strained from the size of her smile. She felt alive. The three laughed and danced through another song before the band slowed it down to a familiar love ballad. A slight twinge of longing pinched Aimee's heart as she watched Trent Jacobs, the town's sheriff and her boss, navigate his way through the couples gathered on the dance floor toward his fiancée, Maggie. Those two were a perfect pairing, and Aimee didn't begrudge their merriment. They made each other insanely happy. It was the fact that her dream of love, family, and a picket fence would never happen.

Trent slid Maggie against his body and gave his assistant his best puppy-dog face. "I know it's ladies' night, Aimee, but I need this dance, then she's all yours."

"If it keeps you smiling at work, dance twice," Aimee replied.

He winked at her before twirling Maggie farther into the mass of dancers.

A hand snagged Aimee's arm, halting her exit from the dance floor. "Don't leave now, hot stuff. I need a close-up after watching your sweet performance," a man she hadn't seen before said while he tugged her closer. His breath smelled like stale beer, and his brown eyes were dilated. His fingers dug into the tender flesh of her upper arm, making her wince. "Curvy and plump."

She jerked her arm back to try to break free of his grasp. "Take your hand off me right now. I'm not interested."

"Don't play hard to get." He tugged her against his body.

Aimee's ire erupted at this man's barbaric behavior. She'd never been a pushover, but a sense of *déjà vu* assaulted her. There was no way she'd allow herself to be trapped or powerless again. Straightening her spine, she placed her hands on his stomach and shoved herself backward and out of his embrace. "I said—"

"You nitwitted Neanderthal, no means no!" Irene barked from behind her.

Aimee turned away from the man and looped her arm through Irene's. "Thanks for having my back. What a jerk."

"Anytime, dear," Irene said before she turned to give that man one last glare. "He needs a serious attitude adjustment and lessons on how to be a gentleman."

Once they reached the booth, Irene ordered three water bottles from their waitress. Aimee took a seat and fanned herself with her hand. She'd forgotten how much energy she burned when dancing.

A familiar deep voice caused her to look up. "Do you want me to remove the trash you bagged?" Clarke motioned toward the jerk who watched her from across the room.

"No, it's handled. Besides, I think Irene scared the crap out of him." She appreciated that he'd asked her instead of making a scene.

Clarke nodded and headed back toward the group of men he'd just left.

When the band finished the ballad, they announced a fifteen-minute break.

"I love slow songs," Maggie purred as she approached the table, her cheeks rosy and her eyes bright.

"That's because you and lover boy engaged in dancing foreplay," Irene announced like a host of a wildlife show on television.

Aimee burst out laughing at Irene's reply, especially when Maggie's mouth popped open and her eyes went huge.

She slid into the booth next to Irene. "Oh my God, at least Trent didn't hear you. You'd embarrass the poor man."

"What? I'm old, not dead," Irene said, before twisting off the cap to her water the waitress had delivered.

"Ladies, I'd like to introduce my friend, Noah. Noah, this is Irene, and you should remember Aimee," Trent said as the two stood in front of their table.

Noah extended his hand to each woman. "Irene, Aimee."

"Noah, it's so good to see you again. When did you get into town?" Maggie asked before hopping out of the booth to give him a hug.

"A little while ago. I sent Trent a text to let him know I'd arrived, and he told me to meet him here."

"Let me get you a beer, buddy," Trent said, getting the server's attention.

"Well, at least you're willing to come to the table, unlike our friend who prefers the shadows." Irene pointed to Clarke—who lingered in the background chatting with Lance Charles, Trent's deputy sheriff—and waved them both over.

"Irene, he's a good man. Maybe he's just overwhelmed by your constant critique of him," Maggie admonished.

Irene raised an eyebrow. "Oh hush, it builds character."

"Sorry, we only allow her out every so often," Aimee said as her cheeks tightened into a slight smile.

Irene turned her attention toward Noah. "You, honey, are easy on the eyes. Are you single? Visiting for a little R and R?" she asked, waggling her eyebrows.

Noah's cheeks reddened, but he recovered, rolling with the punches as he said, "Wow, that's quite a welcome. It seems I made the right choice in moving to Mill Creek. All this lovely female attention will be good for my soul."

Everyone laughed except Trent, who grumbled at Irene. "Be nice, or you're going to chase away all the eligible bachelors."

Maggie's eyes widened briefly before her eyebrows drew together, concern written all over her face. "Don't get me wrong, having you here permanently is awesome, but are you okay? Did you retire from the FBI?"

Lance and Clarke joined the group in time to hear Maggie's question. Everyone turned their heads back to Noah, as the group waited on his answer.

Noah shook his head. "Nope, too young for retirement, but my boss, Special Agent in Charge Tim Guzman, offered me a new assignment. I start in a few weeks. The best part is I can live wherever I want, provided there's an FBI office close, which means Boise fits that requirement."

Trent slapped his friend on the back. "Hot damn, that's great news. Welcome to Mill Creek, man. I'll give you the official tour of the area tomorrow."

"Perfect, and a real estate agent," Noah added.

"I guess it's up to me to get the conversation back on track before we all smack backs and celebrate. Right or left? And do you even know how to throw a ball?" Clarke asked.

The waitress delivered a new round of beer and drinks to the table. Trent handed one to Noah and snagged one for himself. "To friends and new beginnings," he declared, raising his beer and clanking each glass and bottle. "Don't worry, Clarke, Noah will pick up your shortcomings."

The guitarist started to play a riff, signaling they were back and interrupting the banter between the men.

"That's our cue to leave. Enjoy the dancing, ladies," Trent said to the group. He pressed a kiss to Maggie's lips before guiding Noah, Lance, and Clarke toward the bar.

"Let's dance," Maggie sang out, grabbing Irene's hand and holding one out to Aimee.

Aimee declined with a wave. "I'm going to head home early. I've got a terrible headache starting, and I'm exhausted."

Maggie grasped Aimee's hand. "Do you need anything? I can have Trent take you home."

"No, I'm good, and I'm not leaving this second. Go dance," Aimee replied, shooing her friends to the dance floor. "Besides, it's Mill Creek, not some big city," she tacked on, not wanting to have an escort as her friends headed toward the crowd.

Aimee sat and listened to a few more songs before making her exit. When she reached the big front doors, she turned to say goodnight to the bouncer and exited. The cool, damp air from fall wrapped around her heated body, carrying with it a subtle scent of pine and rain. Mountain living appealed to her, especially the gorgeous views of the stars at night. Tonight was darker than normal since the stars were hidden behind a thick blanket of clouds.

Droplets of water dotted the sidewalk, which caused Aimee to alter her route by taking the shortcut through the alleyway between the bar and Knotty Pine Tree. She paused briefly at the opening of the narrow passage to look and listen because being drenched, cold, and taking the long route held zero appeal. Bright lights illuminated each end but left the middle section darker. No noises or movement caught her eye, so she squelched her concerns and strode down the pathway.

Around the halfway mark, she heard male voices and laughter in front of her, but the big metal trash bin blocked her view. She slowed as she approached the square object. Beyond the metal structure were three men, and the one in the center was the jerk from the bar. The beat of her heart quickened and caused a rush of blood to pound in her ears. Like a slot machine landing all sevens, her brain registered the mistake she'd made. Now, being cold and wet a little longer didn't seem like the worst choice. Decision made, she propelled her feet to move with purpose and would ignore anything they said.

"My luck has improved tonight," Jerk-o announced to his friends. He stepped directly in front of her, blocking her path.

Refusing to show this idiot any fear, she forced steel into her words and gave him a piece of her mind. "Get out of my way. I already told you no, and nothing has changed—" The words abruptly stopped as her breath whooshed out of her mouth when he yanked her against his chest and into his arms.

"She's that girl I told you guys about earlier. All I want from you is to finish our dance."

Aimee struggled against his grasp. "You're upsetting me. Just let me go. I don't want to dance."

He pressed his face next to her ear and whispered, "Come on, don't embarrass me in front of my friends. Besides, who wants to go home alone?"

Aimee's eyes widened at this creep's gall. She jerked her knee up, disheartened when she narrowly missed his groin. He'd sidestepped her attack and shoved her backward. In a flash, she twisted her body to miss the wooden pallets stacked off to the side but landed hard on her hands and knees. Her skin burned from the asphalt and rocks that tore her flesh.

"Stupid bitch," Jerk Face spat out as he moved toward her. "I told you, I only want a fucking dance. What's your problem?"

To her surprise, instead of being attacked, all she heard were the pounding of footsteps as the three men retreated. Aimee grimaced as she lifted her body from the ground, her knees raw and bleeding. Her white tropical knit skirt and long-sleeved T-shirt did little to protect her skin from the ground or the elements. Her legs trembled, threatening to give out, so instead of ending up back on the ground, she sat down on the stacked skids. When she looked up, a hulking form headed in her direction. *Clarke.* Taking a moment to catch her breath, she flashed back to the night she loathed.

She'd escaped. Had pushed her body as hard as she could toward the big gate that separated the house from the road. The sound of a single gunshot echoed through the air. Aimee's breath caught in her throat while fear crawled up her neck. Her footsteps lumbered as she struggled to stay upright. Seconds later, her face slammed into the newly laid turf; a mixture of grass and dirt infused her senses while her knees dug into the soft ground. In the distance, a flicker of red, blue, and white lights caught her attention, a beacon of hope encouraging her to keep fighting—to keep moving forward.

A deep voice bellowed out her name a second before strong arms hefted her body off the ground. Her memory faded as warmth infused her body. Clarke cradled her to his chest. Tears streamed down Aimee's face and bit into her cheeks from the cold air that funneled through the corridor. The adrenaline that had coursed through her body moments ago retreated, leaving her limbs heavy and her eyes drooping from exhaustion.

"I've got you, you're safe now," he crooned, sitting on the same spot she'd just occupied.

He supported her in his arms as if she were precious to him. This strong, virile man with his bald head, numerous tattoos, and blunt attitude could be so soft and caring. So many people misunderstood him. They lumped him into different categories due to his appearance or his motorcycle. Human nature seemed to gravitate toward making judgments without seeking facts or details in many situations. Something she, too, was guilty of doing when she'd first met him.

"I know," she replied, content to stay in his arms for a little longer while she soaked up his body heat and tightened her resolve.

"Can I see the damage?" he asked, his dark brown eyes angled down to assess her.

When she nodded her consent, he kept her anchored against his body with one hand while he used the other to lift each leg and inspect her knees. After he finished, he tilted her head up with his index finger so he could see her face. His movements were gentle. His brows were drawn together while he studied her. The clenching of his jaw was his only sign of anger. A deep, sudden intake of breath shifted her in his arms.

"I'm sorry, I should've insisted on taking out that trash earlier. That man, he was the one from the bar earlier, right? I'm guessing the other two were his friends?" He exhaled a deep breath and the sincerity of his gesture caught her off guard. The warmth of his breath feathered across her skin.

She nodded. "He wanted to finish his dance, and when I tried to knee him where it counts, he shoved me to dodge my attempt."

Clarke's smile transformed his face. "I like a fighter. I'm just sorry he avoided your knee. He deserved that and much more."

"I don't want to excuse his behavior because it sucked, but I don't think he meant for me to get hurt. I think he's just an obstinate pig."

"So, I guess that leaves me with the 'what the hell were you thinking?' when you broke what I'd call rule number three."

"What are you babbling about? What's rule three?"

"You know, rule one: stranger danger. Rule two: don't jump in front of moving vehicles, and rule three: avoid dark alleyways when alone. No, scratch that, every damn time."

Aimee pushed out of his arms and stood. "Your timing was perfect. Now I need to get home. I appreciate your concern, but I don't need a lecture."

"I'd beg to argue; however, I'll give you a pass tonight if you promise I can walk you home to clean and bandage those knees. That'll satisfy the protective side of me. I'll call Trent on the way so you can file an assault and battery report on that dickwad."

Aimee panicked. A police report would be the exact opposite of what she was supposed to be doing—lying low. That certainly did not live up to blending into her newly crafted identity. She could practically hear the US Marshal in charge of her protective detail reinforcing, ad nauseam, the importance of staying in the background and embracing her new identity. She hadn't seen that loser before, so he had to be a tourist, which meant the odds of seeing him again would be slim. The thought of letting him go stung, but she had other concerns.

She thrust her hand against the impenetrable wall of Clarke's body and stopped him from standing. "You can walk me home and help me with my knees. I'm not filing a report because of a stupid decision."

Clarke's brow lifted. "Run that past me again? What he did was wrong on so many levels."

"Yes, he overstepped. I'm not going to ruin his life because he made an ass out of himself. I know you don't understand, but it's my decision." She turned and took one step down the alley and winced. Her knees hurt from the movement.

"You're right, and for the record, I don't agree with your decision. Let me give you a boost to your place."

Did this man miss anything? She winced shaking out her hand. Her world went sideways for a second time tonight. In a flash, his strong arms slid around her body, hoisting up against his chest. Damn him, she liked how she felt in his arms.

She directed him toward her place on Main Street above one of the stores. It wasn't much, but it was all she needed now. After he ascended the stairs in the back of the hardware and feed store, she removed her keys from her pocket and laid them in his outstretched palm. She expected him to put her down, instead he easily held her and unlocked the door in one fluid motion.

Once inside, she flipped the light switch on the wall by the door and pointed to the sofa. He hesitated momentarily before depositing her on the center cushion.

"Where's your first aid kit?" he asked. His gaze roamed the small living area.

"Bathroom under the sink, and the washcloth on the towel rack is clean."

She took the opportunity to study his powerful, muscular frame as he moved to get her supplies. He had to be at least six feet five inches tall and weigh over two hundred pounds.

Even at his size, his motions were efficient and graceful. He was comfortable in his own skin. His presence took up most of the free space in this tiny studio.

When he returned, he squatted in front of her and examined her wounded knees. Carefully, he wiped away the dried blood, added antibiotic ointment, and applied several bandages.

When he finished, he looked up and watched her for a few seconds. "Do you have any frozen vegetables in the freezer? That'll help with the bruising."

"Uh, no, I have a tray of ice, though."

He nodded and made his way toward the kitchen. When he returned with ice wrapped in a towel, he instructed her to alternate icing each knee. "I know a thing or two about icing injuries. This'll help keep the swelling and bruising down."

She wondered what type of injuries he'd sustained, but the words stuck on her tongue. "Thanks, Clarke."

He took a seat on sofa and ran his gaze over her body. Her skin tingled under his intense scrutiny. "I've got be honest, I'm pissed at myself for not taking care of that douche earlier. I also wish your knee would've had him singing soprano. Are you okay?"

"I'm fine, really," Aimee replied, then shifted the bag of ice to her other knee.

"How long have you lived here? Are you still unpacking?"

That question threw her off balance and wasn't what she'd expected him to say next. "No, I decided to purge a lot of things from my life when I moved here. When this space became available, I jumped at the opportunity. The location is prefect. It's easy to clean, and Daniel and Lana have placed me in charge of security for their Hardware and Feed Store."

His eyebrows scrunched together. "What does that mean?"

"I'm kidding, it's our joke," Aimee replied on a stifled yawn. "I'm sorry, it's not the company. I'm exhausted."

"Understood. I'll head out so you can rest." He pulled out his cellphone. "Give me your number so I can call you. Then, you'll have mine. If you need anything, don't hesitate to use it."

She hedged for a moment, then relented. Having friends helped her blend in and build her new life, but she still controlled what she shared and how close she allowed anyone to get. She called out her numbers while he diligently typed the information into his phone. Seconds later, her phone vibrated, so she answered his call before adding his data to her contact list.

"Good night, Aimee." Clarke said. "Lock the door after me," he added after he crossed the threshold and closed the door behind him.

His concern and thoughtfulness about her safety caused a spot deep inside her chest to expand. Knowing she had support mattered to her.

It was nice to have a few people you could count on from time to time. Loneliness sucked and could overwhelm a person.

That thought made her stomach flutter with hope, until her mind caught up and stomped on that bubble until it burst. She didn't deserve a do-over with her life. She was alone for a reason.

Two

CLARKE DRAGOON HOVERED HIS mouse over the camera icon on his monitor's display before clicking it. A ritual that was ingrained in him, not that he'd expected to find anything amiss on his footage. When you had more enemies than friends, you learned to put in safeguards. His thoughts turned to the day his mother's sister, Elizabeth Pickle, had informed him she was giving him her house. That had been right before she'd been diagnosed with Alzheimer's, well before she'd moved into a long-term care facility.

His aunt enjoyed life to its fullest, and being a flight attendant had allowed her to travel the world. His mother had always teased her sister since she had these wild thoughts zipping through her head that typically ended with a streak of paranoia. Now, Elizabeth lived in Boise at a memory care facility. This past June, he'd decided it was time to move into her home, but he'd kept her name on the deed. He liked the mountain setting and the small town of Mill Creek.

Getting used to nosy residents took patience, but the bomb shelter his aunt had built into the basement during the original construction trumped any negative. Those layers of protection provided a buffer between his personal and work life.

Over the last four months, he'd been occupied with renovating his new home. He was proud of his accomplishments, from the updated kitchen, bathrooms, new roof and windows, to the fresh coats of paint inside and out. The bomb shelter, which he now called his command center, had been perfectly constructed from the beginning. It had its own ventilation system, air filtration, reinforced walls, and an emergency exit, which saved him a good deal of cash. *God, I love my aunt.*

All he had to do was transform the shelter's interior into a wonderland. He'd worked with an electrician to rig the space for all his high-tech gadgets, which included a secured area with a biometric lock that housed his weapons locker, medical supplies, bug-out gear, food, and other gadgets he'd acquired.

Frustration still pulsed through his system, even after his two-mile run earlier. He could blame it on a sleepless night, but his culprit had bright hazel eyes with curves and a killer smile. Aimee's adamance about not pressing charges and reporting last night's incident bothered him. That asshole deserved to be prosecuted to the fullest extent of the law. It made him itch to run into the bastard so he could educate him on the proper way to treat women.

He finished reviewing his surveillance footage and started to cycle through each individual camera feed. He rubbed his eyes with the heels of his hands and let out a deep breath. Why hadn't he taken care of that bastard when he'd seen him being handsy with Aimee on the dance floor? The world didn't need men who acted like that, and Clarke had a real problem with anyone who victimized women, children, and animals. Had that douchebag threatened Aimee, making her afraid to defy him? No, she wouldn't allow that, she had too much pride.

There was also the disturbing fact that her home had zero personal items—no mementos, photographs, or magazines. Hell, she didn't even have food in the freezer. Not that it was wrong either way, but most people at least had a frozen meal or something. If he hadn't known better, it looked like a hotel instead of her home. The place she'd lived for the last ten months was barren.

He clicked on the next camera and did a double take at the screen. *What the hell is my neighbor doing?* He shot out of his chair, ascended the stairs, and exited his house, rushing toward Irene, who clung to the top rung of a ladder. "What the hell, Irene? Are you trying to kill yourself?" Clarke asked in a stern tone, shielding his eyes from the sun as he looked up at her.

"Good grief! Didn't your father teach you that you shouldn't startle a person while they're on a ladder? What does it look like I'm doing, my hair?" she shot right back at him as he looked up at her.

He had to give it to her, she was determined. She redefined "busy-body," but her mind worked like a race car. He'd never admit to this out loud, but she had a heart of gold. Her cantankerous spirit was another matter altogether. A Mill Creek lifer, she protected everyone and everything she cared about, right down to the books at the library where she worked.

He grabbed a hold of the ladder to steady it. "Get down, right this minute. I don't want you to kill yourself. I'd be the number-one suspect."

"If the brooding shoe fits, Mr. Dragoon. Besides, you'd be lonely without all my attention. Oh, and who would complain to the sheriff regarding your insane need to walk and inspect your property? What's the rock count this week?" she asked, while she worked her way down each rung.

Clarke smiled and rubbed his head. He stepped back to make room for her when she got to the bottom step. Once she was clear, he climbed up to inspect the section of gutter that had held her attention. After several minutes, he identified the problem. "These gutters need to be cleaned out," he said, then moved closer to the sagging section.

She folded her arms over her breasts and huffed. "Thanks, Captain Obvious, I had that much figured out."

"Stubborn woman," he muttered under his breath. "Okay, this section separated from the weight of all these wet leaves and debris. One clamp from the hardware store should solve the problem. This fix and a clean out should take about three hours, more or less."

Irene held Clarke's gaze. "You're offering to help? That could ruin your bad boy reputation."

He cocked his head at the small woman. "That's a risk I'm willing to take. Stay away from that ladder. I'll be back in a bit."

Irene called out to his retreating form, "Keep the receipt. I'll pay you back."

C LARKE GUIDED HIS MOTORCYCLE into a parking space outside the diner to catch an early lunch. He planned to call Aimee after he ate to see if he could bring her food.

Mill Creek might be a quaint, small town, but it had some amazing restaurants. The town's architecture appealed to him with the mix of wood, brick, and siding. He loved the long wood-planked sidewalks on Main Street, complete with horse hitching posts. Pretty much each building had its own look and style, which made it unique but showed personality. The residents were good-hearted and loyal, even if the gossip mill worked overtime.

He glanced at his phone when he received the text message alert and grimaced. The psychologist he'd been dodging for the last two weeks had now resorted to messaging him. He knew it was procedure, but it irked him to have a shrink digging into his personal space. Clarke was confident he could discern if he were having a mental breakdown or losing his shit. He didn't need a therapist to sugarcoat it and ask repeatedly, "Tell me how that makes you feel." His psychological fitness evaluation would have to wait.

He'd return the call after he finished his mandatory leave. That last assignment had been a clusterfuck and would haunt him forever. By his calculation, he had just over a week left to figure out what the hell had him all twisted up. He enjoyed his time off. Now, he poured his energy into home improvement projects. It'd been a nice change of pace to let his guard down some and not sleep with one eye open. His aunt's home had now been converted into his primary residence, and he liked the idea that he'd lain down roots. Not sure why that appealed to him, but it did.

Mentally, he complied his to-do list for after lunch. Since the forecast had called for more rain on Sunday, the gutters became a top priority. Hoping to see Aimee put a smile on his face. He wanted to verify that she was doing all right from last night. Also, he wanted to see if she'd change her mind and press charges.

The chimes above Knotty Pine Tree's door jingled as he moved over the threshold. He'd looked forward to Saturday's special all week long. The owners, Peter and Sally, were masters in the kitchen, but Sally's fried chicken and fixings were legendary. Clarke planned to order two servings—one for now, and the second for dinner later.

When his vision adjusted to the interior lighting, he scanned the restaurant for an open booth. He'd taken no more than three steps before his feet stopped dead in their tracks. *What the hell?* Disbelief slammed into him while his hands curled into fists at his side. His body coiled tight, ready to strike. Clarke was torn momentarily over confronting that very same dickwad from last night who'd just finished speaking to Aimee sitting in a booth in the diner. Or follow him outside and let his fists do the talking. Although he'd love to hunt that man down and make him pay, he chose Aimee over revenge.

AIMEE DIDN'T HAVE TO turn her head to confirm what her body already knew. She'd sensed Clarke's presence the moment he entered the diner. She turned to greet him as he approached the table. His eyes were drawn together, and a scowl stretched across his face.

"What the ever-loving hell is going on? Is that thug harassing you?" Clarke asked in a deep, low voice she hoped didn't carry to other tables.

She motioned for him to sit and waited for him to fold his large frame into the booth. His dark brown orbs scanned and cataloged every minute detail. The man missed nothing and had her at the center of his attention. There was no point in holding anything back. He'd dig until he found out what he wanted to know. The sooner she could put this behind her, the better.

Aimee pinned him with a look. "I'm not entirely sure. He approached my table and uttered an apology then left. I didn't say one word to him. I'm not sure if he saw you and left or if that was all he wanted to do."

"I think you need to tell Trent. I don't buy it."

"As I said last night, it's over. Hopefully, that's the last time I'll see him. I'm pretty sure he's a visitor, since I haven't seen him around before last night."

Clarke put his elbows on the table and exhaled. "I don't agree, but I'll respect your decision. Something is off with that man. Promise me, if he *just appears* again, you'll let me know immediately. If that happens, then you should report all of it to Trent."

Her insides churned with indecision because a part of her agreed with him. That man should be held accountable for his actions. People can't force others to do things against their will. He'd scared her half to death last night. The problem was, she'd made a promise when she'd entered the Witness Security Program to embrace her new identity—to live in the shadows and blend in. A police report and potential court hearing were the opposite of that pledge. A simple fact that she couldn't divulge to Clarke or anyone in her life, which meant keeping secrets. *God, why did I take that damn alley last night?*

"I'll promise to let you know," she said, turning her attention toward the menu on the table.

Those words she meant, but she knew he didn't miss her sidestep about reporting the incident. The glimpse of disappointment that flickered in his gaze bothered her. Hopefully, she'd never see that man again, and this would be a moot point. This whole WITSEC thing sucked, but she couldn't go back and undo the past. A lesson she'd mastered in her life.

A waitress stopped by their table with a pad of paper and pencil at the ready. "You two ready to order?"

Aimee closed the menu. "The special and a slice of apple pie. To go, please."

The waitress jotted down her notes and turned her attention to Clarke.

"I'll have the same, but with two specials."

The waitress smiled and winked at Clarke, who seemed oblivious to her flirting. His entire attention was directed at Aimee. "How are you feeling today?"

Pursing her lips, she took a quick survey of her body. "I'm good."

"Whoa, slow down, all those details are overwhelming me, sweet-heart."

"My knees are a little sore, but nothing I can't handle," she said, ignoring his arrogance.

She glanced past him to look out the window then snapped her head further to the right. Dark plumes of smoke stained the air surrounding the hardware store and her studio. The deep wail of sirens and horns from the firetrucks reached her ears moments before she saw the streaks of red metal pass the diner. People walking down Main Street either stopped to stare or hurriedly moved toward the frenzy. She grabbed her purse and zipped out of the booth. Determination and anxiety fueled her steps as she ran toward her home. *Please don't let the fire destroy that box.*

"Aimee, wait!" Clarke hollered at her retreating form, but she kept running full speed toward the disaster.

Hidden Identities, Book 2 in the Mill Creek Mystique romantic suspense series is out now.

BOOKS BY BAILEY THOMAS

ROMANTIC SUSPENSE

Mill Creek Mystique Series

Watch for the next book in the series
Kane's Reckoning

CONTEMPORARY ROMANCE

Torrent of Hearts us also available in the
Pack Your Bags short story collection

As an only child, Bailey Thomas' active imagination and adventurous nature always kept her busy. Now, she channels those creative powers into storytelling.

Living in the Southwest, Bailey splits her time between crafting heartfelt stories and indulging in her favorite pastimes—whether it's devouring books, marathoning shows, or catching a game.

Life is too short, so Bailey tries to live by her motto of finding adventures that make you smile. She loves to hear from her readers. You can find and connect with her at the links below.

Website/Blog:
baileythomasauthor.com
Instagram
instagram.com/Author_BaileyThomas
BookBub
bookbub.com/authors/bailey-thomas

ACKNOWLEDGEMENTS

I'm so fortunate to have the best readers in the world; none of this would be possible without you. Please leave a review. They are a tremendous help to the author and other readers looking for their next book. Also, don't forget to sign up for my newsletter or follow me on social media to stay updated on book news and events.

Thank you to A Fabulous Productions for creating the stunning print and eBook layouts and outstanding marketing support. You've made everything more manageable and taught me so much.

Lastly, to my Vicki Jean, who has always believed in me, thank you for always wanting me in your life. I love you to the moon and back!

www.ingramcontent.com/pod-product-compliance
Lightning Source LLC
Chambersburg PA
CBHW031553240626
47153CB00002B/493